Lock
AND LOAD

A DEMENTED SONS MC NOVEL

KRISTINE ALLEN

To my grandma.
You were here to see the success of my first book and your pride in me
was humbling. I miss you more than you know.
I hope you're still proud. Love you forever.

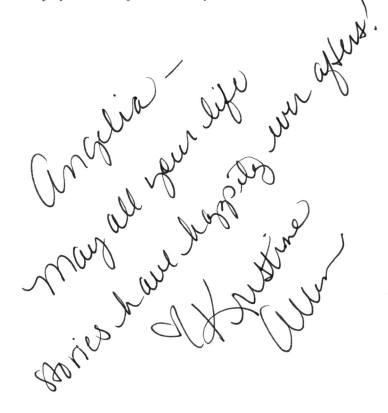

Angelia —
May all your life
stories have happily ever afters!

Kristine
Allen

LOCK AND LOAD

A DEMENTED SONS MC NOVEL

PROLOGUE

Taking the last curve before we hit the straightaway, I leaned the bike heavily to the side. I knew I was going fast, but I'd done this a million times.

Letty had her arms tight around my waist, and her laughter carried on the wind. Every so often, I caught a whiff of her perfume, and it made me want to go faster to get to the clubhouse. It was our first night out in ages.

Feeling on top of the fucking world, I certainly wasn't prepared for the events that unfolded.

As I entered the tightest part of the curve, I started to increase the throttle.

There was no time to react, because I didn't see it coming. What was normally a smooth asphalt road was scattered with fine gravel.

Both tires broke loose, and the air was filled with the screeching of metal on asphalt and Letty's screams. Within seconds, there was silence, broken only by the gasps of my labored breaths.

It took too long to regain my breath and roll over. When I tried to push myself up, I fell flat on my face, whacking my helmet on the ground. The pain hit me in waves that nearly took my breath away again.

The unnatural angle of my arm told me what adrenaline had initially masked.

Fuck.

"Letty? Baby? Where are you?" My voice croaked as I tried to see if anything else was broken. Both legs seemed to be intact, so I used my good arm to get to my knees. "Letty?" When she didn't answer, I shouted for her. "Letty!"

The only answer was the sound of crickets and the hiss of the bike where it rested in a crumpled mess. The headlight lit up the ditch, but beyond that was the deepest black.

"Letty!" Scanning the road, I shakily struggled to my feet. I couldn't see her anywhere, and she wouldn't answer me. My heart was racing, and I was on the verge of hyperventilating.

With my shaking hand, I fumbled for my phone. It was in the inside pocket of the side of my good arm, so it was a feat to get it out. Finally, I was able to free it from the confines of my jacket and I turned the flashlight on.

Shining it up and down the road, I didn't see anything but the trail the bike had left across the asphalt. Checking the ditch next, I searched around the bike. Nothing.

"What the fuck? Letty! Where are you?" Panic was starting to set in, and I didn't normally succumb to shit like that. Realizing I still had my helmet on, I struggled with one working arm until I ripped it off and threw it down the ditch.

Goddammit!

As I lit up the patch in front of me, I stumbled. Luckily, I caught myself before I fell on my fucked-up arm again. Moving cautiously through the tall grass, I finally saw something up in the field and pointed my light in that direction. It reflected off the Harley Davidson on the back of her jacket.

Relief hit me like a sledgehammer.

"Letty!" Jogging toward her in the tilled-up earth was like running through knee-deep snow. Every step was in slow motion. By the time I reached her, I was aching and feeling every jolt and roll I'd had on the road.

She wasn't moving, and I immediately called 9-1-1 as I dropped to my knees beside her. Terrified to turn her over and exacerbate any injuries she'd sustained, I tucked the phone next to my ear and used my functioning hand to press against her throat.

"9-1-1, what's your emergency?"

Panic began to creep in like an insidious fog. Moving further up her neck, I told myself my fingers were in the wrong place.

"Come on. Baby. Help me out!"

"Sir? What's your emergency?"

"My ol' lady and I were in an accident." Rattling off our location, I tried again to find a pulse. "Letty…, please. God, please." I tried everywhere I could reach. Her neck, her wrists after jerking off her gloves, and back to her neck in case I'd fucked up.

The phone dropped to the ground and the light shone out into the field as the unthinkable began to sink in. Sobbing like a baby, I dragged her into my lap with one arm. Unable to remove her helmet, I choked on my tears as her head lolled at a sickening angle.

"Letty. Oh God, Letty…. I'm so sorry. So fucking sorry. Baby. I love you. Please, baby, wake up." Rational thought was gone. I was a fucking mess.

Sitting in the dark field with her lifeless body cradled to my chest, I fell apart.

By the time the sirens sounded in the distance, my tortured screams were echoing into the dark night sky.

ONE

Lock

"BROKEN GLASS"—THREE DAYS GRACE

"Ask me to tear down a Harley motor and I'm all over that shit. Piece by piece, I could put it back together with my fucking eyes closed. But now I'm tryin' to do pigtails and teach a little girl to potty. What the fuck happened to my life? I wasn't supposed to be doing this alone." I ran a hand roughly through my hair.

"I'm sorry, little brother. I don't know what to say." Gunny, my brother in the club and my older brother by blood, dropped to my couch. His expression held helpless sorrow for me, and while I appreciated it, I was sick of it.

The past year had been pure hell. I'd had to fight Letty's no-good, meth-head family for custody of Presley. The shitty thing was, they didn't really want her. They'd only wanted the social security they'd get by having her. They'd drained my bank account.

Money was so tight thanks to them, I'd had to borrow my brother's bar-hopper bike to ride so I didn't get kicked out of the club. I couldn't afford a new one after the accident. My insurance hadn't even paid off my loan. Thank God for GAP insurance.

The whole county knew they were scum, but they'd tried everything from accusing me of being in a violent motorcycle gang, to having PTSD that would put my child's life in jeopardy, to being a trained killer from being in the army. The worst, though, was their accusations that I'd been abusive to Letty. Which was absolute bullshit, and everyone for miles knew it.

That's the curse of being in a small town. Everyone knows your business.

I was tired of people feeling sorry for me, and I was tired of seeing Letty's ghost everywhere I went. Even the couch Gunny was sitting on was one she'd picked out. She'd decorated my house. Painted Presley's room Disney princess pink. Her stamp was literally everywhere and it was smothering me.

So was I running? Maybe. Was it for my own fucking sanity? Absolutely.

What I didn't tell anyone was that I'd started getting anonymous threats about someone taking Presley from me. I assumed it was her shitty grandparents, another reason I couldn't wait to get out of town.

"There's nothing to say. It is what it is, but I can't do this anymore. I can't stay any longer." My elbows rested on my knees, my hands dangling. Shoulders slouched, I'd never experienced such defeat. Not even when I'd been downrange and shit went south.

You'd think that might've prepared me for anything. Instead, I was the proud owner of one helluva vile temper, the wildest case of insomnia known to man, and I was struggling to keep my life in order. But regardless of what Presley's piece-of-shit grandparents said, I loved my daughter and I'd never do anything to hurt her.

"I wish you'd rethink this. Mom and Dad are gonna hate that they'll miss Elvis's birthday."

"I know, but I need out of here. Trust me, I've thought this all to fucking death. The job is waiting, and Styx said my jump to their chapter was a go." Styx had been up visiting for a few months. I'd talked to him and Snow about it after the first threat came through, and when he'd gotten back to Texas, he'd talked to his prez. The chapter had put it to the vote. I probably should have involved the club regarding the threats, but Letty's parents weren't their problem.

He shook his head as he mimicked my position with his forearms on his knees.

"Daddy! Unka Gunny!" The patter of little feet across the wood floors preceded a whirlwind of wild curls that refused to be tamed. All I saw was that mass of blonde hair, pink unicorn pajamas on backwards, and a floppy stuffed dragon before twenty-five pounds of raw energy launched herself into my brother's lap.

"Hey, Elvis. Good morning. What's up with this hair?" He held her in his massive arms as she used both palms to push the crazy curls out of her face. My mom said she looked like a little Shirley Temple doll.

"I gwoh it wike Wuhpunzo. Wight, Daddy?" Despite my earlier melancholy mood, I smiled. She'd been the only thing that had kept me pulling air into my lungs some days.

"Sure, princess." I was a heartless dick, which made me the perfect sergeant at arms for the club. But with her, I was mush. She had me wrapped so tight around her little pinky, I wondered how I functioned at times.

"You haffa bwaid it wike Ewsa, Daddy." Gunny laughed as I groaned.

"Presley, did you go potty when you woke up?" I belatedly thought to ask her. I was utterly failing at this single-dad business.

Her face screwed up in a grouchy little frown as she crossed her arms belligerently. "I no haff to."

Gunny poked at the back of her pajama pants, then gave me a wrinkled-nose look. In other words, it was too late.

"Did you pee in your pull-up?" Exasperation bled through my words.

"No."

"Presley," I drew out in warning.

She jumped off Gunny's lap and hauled ass back down the hall.

"Be right back," I tiredly muttered as I stood to follow the little shit.

Gunny chuckled and stood as well. "I'll start some breakfast."

"Roger that," I confirmed as I stalked down the hall after my little hellion.

The few moments the conversation with Gunny took was all the time Presley needed to strip naked in her room.

Fists propped on my hips, I narrowed my gaze at her. "Where is your pull-up, and where are your pajamas?"

Big, innocent blue eyes blinked up at me. "I fowded my jammies." Sure enough, they were sort of folded, more wadded, and sitting on her rumpled princess toddler bed. The pull-up was nowhere to be seen.

"Where is the pull-up?" I demanded, and she simply shrugged. Sighing, I knew I'd have to look for it before it stunk up the entire house.

I snagged a few wet wipes from the packet on her dresser. "Come here. Let's wipe you off."

Cleaning her so she didn't get sore was something I'd learned the hard way in an incident I never wanted to repeat.

Once that was done, I started to open her drawers and closet to pull out clothes, but she grabbed the little padded-crotch panties from me. "I do it mysewf. I's a big gewl. You go."

Raising my brows, I couldn't believe the little termagant I'd raised. She was hell on wheels. "Fine."

As I returned to the kitchen, Gunny had bacon frying and eggs scrambled in a bowl. Ever since he and his ol' lady had split, he'd started coming to our house nearly every morning. We'd take turns making breakfast.

I wondered what he'd do after I left and experienced a moment of regret for my decision.

"Where's Elvis?" he asked over his shoulder.

Chuckling, I shook my head. "Well, she was naked."

A bark of laughter exploded from him.

"And now she's dressing herself." I grinned.

"Oh Lord." We both were aware of the possibilities she might come out wearing.

The little pixie didn't disappoint.

It wasn't long before she came out in a black T-shirt with the Harley-Davidson bar and shield in hot pink, a pair of denim shorts, an orange tutu, and little pink Chucks with the laces dragging. Oh, and dangling from one hand was a sparkling silver tiara. The other held her purple hairbrush and a hairband.

"Hewe, Daddy." She held out the hair stuff.

I plopped into a kitchen chair and positioned her to stand between my knees. Carefully running the brush through the ringlets spilling around in a wild array, I got all the sleep tangles worked out.

Per our routine, she held out her hand for the brush when I was done. I handed it to her, then turned her to the side. Pulling the soft curls to the side, I struggled to get my thick fingers to separate them in three parts. It was barely long enough to braid into a three-to-four-inch braid but she was happy and that was all that mattered.

Once I finished, she plopped the tiara on her head and turned to me. I grinned at how fitting it was that it was lopsided. Kind of like a crooked little halo.

"Tie my shoes, pwease." She was proper and regal enough that she fit her plastic crown.

As my princess requested, I tied the laces of her shoes and she went to grab her little backpack she took to daycare. "School," as she called it.

She was my perfect little tomboy princess, and I wouldn't have her any other way.

Setting the plates on the table, Gunny grinned at me. "You've gotten pretty good at that. How the hell did you figure that shit out?"

Rolling my eyes, I huffed. "Trust me, you can find anything you might need on YouTube these days. To include 'how to braid.' Want me to forward it to you?" I raised a brow as I smirked at him.

Chuckling, he held up a hand. "I'm good, but thanks."

Tromping up to the table, she dropped her backpack by her chair, climbed into the seat, and began to eat the plate of food Gunny put in front of her. The way she ate, you'd think she was a starved wild animal instead of the princess she was dressed like. Letty was probably rolling in her grave at the job I was doing with Presley. But dammit, I was trying.

Mouth stuffed full, she turned to Gunny. "Unka Gunny! We moobing to Tessas!"

Somber, he stared at her. "I know, little Elvis. I know."

To her it was a grand adventure that I'd played up to the hilt. To me it was an escape. A chance at new beginnings.

We all finished eating, and by then I was running late, so the dishes were all tossed in the sink. I sent up an apology to Letty, because I knew that shit had driven her crazy.

Rushing out the door, Gunny hopped on his bike, and I buckled the princess in as she chattered nonstop. When we reached the end of the road, he took a left as I took a right to swing Presley by daycare.

"Daddy! I wate!" she shouted from the back seat. She wasn't late, since there was no official start time for daycare, but we'd missed curb drop-off. To her, that was late.

"We're fine, baby girl." I whipped into a parking spot and shut off the truck. Jumping down from my seat, I rushed to get her unbuckled or she was gonna trip the fuck out.

As soon as her feet hit the ground, she tried to run off toward the building. Used to being on my toes with her, I quickly snagged her by her backpack. "Whoa there, speedy!"

"I wate! I wate! Wike da wabbit!" Eyes narrowed at my audacity for making her even later, she propped her fists on her little tutu'd hips. Chuckling at her earned me no brownie points.

I crouched down in front of her to have her look me in the eyes. "You hold my hand, Presley. Always. You never run off without me. You hear?" It wasn't the first time she'd heard that, so she nodded, chastised and sullen.

"Otay, Daddy." She pouted.

Heaving a sigh, I stood and held her hand as we crossed the driveway to the entry doors.

"Good morning, Mr. Archer," Shelby called as she leaned forward and pushed her cleavage together. Trying to not to roll my eyes, I waved and gave a grin that probably looked more like a grimace. She'd been trying to hook up with me since I first started bringing Presley.

Not happening.

"Matlock." The airy whisper came up behind me as I helped Presley tie her shoe that had come undone.

Fuck.

"Eve."

And that's why you don't shit where you eat. Eve had been Letty's best friend and was also Presley's daycare provider.

The other thing she'd been was a drunken mistake three months after Letty died. Since then, she'd been trying to convince me how good we'd be together. It pissed me off because she was supposed to be Letty's best friend, next to Steph.

Instead, she'd watched Presley at my house one night we'd had a club party for a visiting chapter at the clubhouse. I hadn't wanted to go, but Snow had insisted I get out of my house and join the living. I'd gotten blitzed that night trying to forget.

When Reaper and Steph dropped me off at my house, I was still three sheets to the wind. Eve had been sleeping on the couch. I'd woken her to thank her and let her know she could go home.

Except she didn't leave like I'd thought she did. When I'd crawled in bed drunk as a skunk and naked, she'd slipped in shortly after. I don't know if in my drunken state, I was delusional or if I had thought she was Letty. Either way, I wasn't thinking clearly, and she'd taken advantage of that.

I'd been sick the next morning and thrown her out.

When she came to me a month later telling me she thought she was pregnant, it was a sock to the gut. Worse was when I found out from Hollywood's ol' lady, Becca, that Eve had lied.

Steph had never liked her, so between her and Becca they were ready to go beat her ass. I'd told them it wasn't worth it and that they'd look awful in orange.

I'd really wanted to pull Presley from her daycare, but there wasn't a huge selection of reputable options in a town our size. So I'd opted for shooting down her advances for the last year, but she wasn't getting the hint. I was on the verge of having to hurt her feelings.

"Give me a kiss, princess." I knelt on one knee so Presley could hug me and give me a big sloppy kiss on my bearded cheek.

"Wub you, Daddy." She ran to her cubby to hang up her little backpack. With a happy wave to me, she was gone to join her friends. She'd never been a clingy child, always independent and strong. An old soul.

I stood and faced Eve with resignation heavy in my expression. "Have good day, Eve. I gotta run."

"Wait. Matlock." Her simpering tone set my teeth on edge.

"I'm late. Does this have to do with Presley?"

"Well, sort of." She bit her lip and gave me an imploring look.

"Either it does or it doesn't."

"Shelby told me you turned in your notice. Is it because of me and what happened?" Her brown eyes took on a soulful expression. One I wasn't buying or falling for.

"No." I didn't owe her an explanation, so I turned to go.

Her hand grasped my arm, and I spun in a fury. "Don't touch me," I harshly whispered.

She had the nerve to step back, looking like she was the victim.

Without another word, I stomped out of the facility, ignoring Shelby's hollered goodbye as I passed by.

Climbing in my truck, I wanted to beat on the steering wheel. I wanted to scream. My anger at myself for my stupidity all those months ago and the weakness I was feeling at that time was overwhelming me.

One more thing to add to the list of things I couldn't wait to leave behind.

"I'm so sorry, Letty." Silence was the only reply I received as I started the truck and headed to work.

I'd been putting an old EVO back together for about an hour when my phone rang on my toolbox. I wiped the grease from my hands before seeing who it was.

Pops's name made me smile.

"Hey, Pops. What's up?"

"Lock, you're still set on going to Texas?" His tone was gruff and abrupt.

"Um, yeah. Why?" I was really hoping he wasn't going to try to talk me out of it. I was getting tired of explaining myself. It made me sound like a pussy.

"Well, I hate to see you go, you already know that. But I need you to make a special delivery to Styx for me when you head down. Do you think you could do that? It's really important to me." Pops knew I'd do anything for him. He'd retired right after I'd been patched, and he'd been my sponsor the entire time I'd prospected. I truly believed I was the brother I was today because of his guidance and mentorship.

"Hell, yeah. Is it at your place?" He'd sold his house but kept a lot on the edge of town with a small shop on it for when they were in the area.

"Uh, no, I have it with me, but we'll be pulling into town early Monday morning. Last I heard, you said you'd be heading out of town then. If so, I can meet you at the gas station on the edge of town. What time are you hitting the road?"

"Yeah, that's still the plan. I'd like to be on the road by six, but if I need to wait that's fine. We'll end up stopping at a hotel in Omaha after the zoo. I'm not in a big hurry, because I don't want to stress Presley. Plus we'll be making lots of potty stops anyway." I rolled my eyes, and though he couldn't see me, he chuckled.

"I can't wait to see her. I bet she's grown a mile since I saw her last."

"Well, in her mouth, yeah." A wry grin slipped out.

"Typical woman. Get used to it." Despite the pang I experienced at his words, I heard Mama Jean in the background getting after him for his comment, and I laughed. He cleared his throat. "Six might be cutting it close, but I think we can be there by seven. Will that work?"

"Sure. It will give me more time to plan for the inevitable delays that come with a two-and-a-half-year-old." I laughed.

"I appreciate that. Well, I know you're busy, so I'll let you go. We'll see you soon."

"Sounds good. You travel safe." Ending the call, I tossed my phone back on the top of the box.

"You ready for your farewell party?" Reaper called out from where he and Hollywood were tearing down an old Hemi Cuda.

"Not really." The thought of leaving the men who'd become my family physically hurt.

"Then don't go." Reaper's ice-blue eyes were unnerving as he stopped with his hands buried deep in the guts of the car.

Hollywood rolled from underneath on the creeper. "Dude. It's only been a year."

It had actually been one year, three months, and four days.

"It wouldn't matter if it had been ten years, brother. I can't stay here. Fuck, I can't drive down that road without having an anxiety attack. I haven't slept in our bed in months. She's everywhere, and she always will be. I need out. I need a fresh start. It's not the club. I fucking love every one of you, and the thought of leaving makes me sick. The problem is, staying is killing me." Folding my arms defensively over my chest, I glanced away from their knowing eyes. That admission was more painful than pulling teeth.

In my peripheral vision, I saw Reaper heave a heavy sigh and drop his head.

Catching movement to my right, I looked over to where my brother was working on a Street Glide. His eyes held mine, and we exchanged an understanding without saying a word. I'd already made my decision, and he knew that better than anyone.

He returned his attention to the bike on the lift.

Both Reaper and Hollywood dropped the subject, and we worked quietly for the rest of the day. The only sounds were the clanking of metal on metal, power tools, and rock music blaring from the sound system.

"I'll see you guys tonight. I need to go pick up Presley." I'd cleaned up my tools and washed up.

"You want me to go get her?" Gunny's voice rumbled from where he was setting his tools in their proper drawers. He knew my shameful indiscretion well. He also knew the trouble it was causing me at Presley's daycare. "I'll take my truck over to grab her."

"Would you mind? Mom's expecting her, and she has pj's there."

"Hell no, I don't mind. I'll take every second with her. You know that." He shrugged like it was no big deal, but I knew it was going to be hard on my family when I took her away. Even if they did understand.

TWO

Lock

"BREAKOUT"—THROUGH FIRE

Walking into the clubhouse that night was bittersweet. On one hand, it was home; on the other, it hurt to know that would be one of the last times I would walk through the door as a member of the Grantsville chapter.

I hadn't drunk since that fucked-up night nearly a year ago. So when I walked through the door and cheers erupted prior to a shot being shoved in my hand, I promised that would be the only drink I had.

I lied.

One drink after the next was put in my hand with a toast to accompany each one.

"Goddamn, we're gonna miss you." Hacker threw his arm around my shoulders and pulled me close. "I'm not gonna lie, I had doubts you'd make it through prospecting but you've turned out to be one hell of a brother and a fucking badass SAA."

"Damn near as good a brother as me," Gunny joked from the barstool he was sitting on backwards.

"Can't believe you brought your little brother in and he's abandoning us," Joker piped in.

"You gonna be able to pick up where Lock leaves off as our new SAA?" Snow narrowed his eyes with a smirk as he stared Gunny down. Gunny simply rolled his eyes.

Truth be told, he'd been born to be SAA. Except he'd fought it for years because of his ol' lady, Trixie, who'd been a fucking cunt. She'd hated every second he spent with the club and had manipulated the shit out of him. She'd told him that if he took on the position, it would interfere too much in their relationship.

"Like I had a fucking choice." He swallowed hard and looked away from me as he took a long pull from his bottle of Dos Equis.

The ironic thing about Trixie putting up such a fuss about Gunny being SAA was that Butch had been our SAA. Gunny had caught her fucking him at a club party one night. Needless to say, they were both history after that night, and Butch was missing not only his patch but several teeth.

He was out bad, and that's something no club member wants to happen. Ever.

They'd appointed me as sergeant at arms at our emergency church the next day. I'd found out later that Gunny had recommended me to everyone behind my back. I was a little pissed, but also honored when Snow announced it.

Gunny's jukebox started playing "Porn Star Dancing" by My Darkest Days, and a couple of the strippers from the Shamrock came out of the back hall.

"Well look what we have here. Looks like a going-away present for you." Soap chuckled as the two girls strutted up and started to dance around where I leaned back on the bar not far from Gunny.

I was shit-faced but not enough that I had lost my inhibitions. I acted like it was all fun and games, but my hands didn't stray when theirs did. I kept my elbows firmly planted to the edge of the bar. When they tried to take my hands and place them on their tits, I chuckled and acted like I was reaching for my beer.

Outwardly, I was enjoying what the guys must've thought was a grand going-away gift. Inwardly, I was cringing because it was like being unfaithful. Even if it was to a ghost.

"Oh. Before I forget, here." I dropped the keys to my brother's bike in his hand. I'd been borrowing it since the accident because I wasn't in a position to get a new one yet.

Gunny swallowed hard.

"You can hang on to them. You know, in case you come back and need it." He took a drink of his beer, avoiding my eyes.

"I've been saving up, and I plan to get one once I get to Texas. Thanks for letting me use her since the…." I ground my teeth, unable to say the rest.

"Anytime, little brother. Anytime," he said, then hugged me. I fought the tears that made me feel like a fucking wuss.

We partied well into the morning, and I managed to pawn the strippers off on DJ and Soap. Thank God.

After everyone was drunk as fuck or had gone home to their ol' ladies, I snuck off to spend the last night in my room at the clubhouse. I rarely used it because of Presley, but she was at Mom's.

That night I dreamed of Letty. She looked so disappointed in me, and I kept asking her what I'd done wrong. She would only shake her head. I cried and clung to her as I knelt at her feet until, like smoke, she started to slip through my fingers.

At the moment she became merely a mist, I heard her whisper, "Let go."

I jolted awake, soaked and shaking.

A quick but bleary peek at my phone told me it was barely six in the morning.

Knowing I wouldn't get back to sleep, I showered and decided to head to my parents'. As I weaved my way through the passed-out bodies in various stages of undress, I shook my head and chuckled.

Not a soul stirred.

Head pounding, I drove to my parents' house a couple of miles out of town.

14

"Matlock! What are you doing here so early?" Mom looked up in surprise from her coffee and the book she was reading. At my wince, she laughed and got up to rummage through a cupboard, then the fridge.

"Here. You look like you could use these. Good Lord, your breath smells like a distillery." With a wry grin, she handed me some Tylenol and two bottles of water.

Rolling my eyes, I quickly guzzled down one bottle, took the pills, then started on the second. "Thanks, Mom. I did brush my teeth and shower, you know."

"Well, you smell like you're sweating straight whiskey." She wrinkled her nose.

Dropping to a vacant chair, I glanced around. "Dad and Presley still sleeping?"

Mom raised a brow at me. "Really? They've been up about an hour and a half. They're out feeding the horses."

"Mm," I grunted. Figured. At home she would never be out of bed before seven. Not there. That girl loved horses. Another reason I hated taking her away.

"So, your father and I were thinking... what if we had an early birthday for Presley Saturday?"

"No."

"But, Matlock," Mom started to plead.

"No, Mom. Her birthday is months away. She'll be spoiled rotten and expect two birthdays every year. No." Talking made my head pound, so I drank the rest of the water and went to grab another.

In the end, Mom agreed to try to come down to celebrate.

"Daddy! You's hewe!" My dad was helping her remove her muck boots inside the back door as she shouted to me.

Wincing only slightly at the decibel level of her voice, I caught her as she barreled to me. Vaulting up into my lap, she wrapped her little arms around my neck and kissed my cheek. As my head throbbed and my stomach churned, I swore to myself I would never drink again.

15

"I miss you so berry much!" Her palms framed my face, her chubby fingers buried in my beard.

"I missed you too, princess. Were you good for Grandma and Grandpa?"

"I hewped Gwampa wiff da foods foh duh hoe-sees. Dey vewy happy." Nodding sagely, she blinked at me.

"I bet the horses were very happy to have you feed them," I agreed, and she grinned.

We mostly hung out at the house until midmorning, then we packed a picnic lunch, saddled up some horses, and rode down to the quarry by the creek bed. It wasn't a long ride, but far enough to make Presley happy where she rode in the saddle in front of my mom.

"We get a hoe-see when we go to Tessas?" Presley asked me as we were riding at a leisurely gait back to the house.

"Probably not, sweetheart, but we'll still visit here to see the horses." My answer didn't appease my daughter. She crossed her arms and frowned at me.

"Tessas has cowboys. Cowboys wide hoe-sees."

Jesus. I snorted out a laugh. "Well, we'll see." Every parent's cop-out when they didn't want to tell their child no.

When we got back to the house, Presley chattered as the adults unsaddled the horses and groomed them before turning them loose in the pasture. When her favorite gelding trotted off, she hollered out and waved.

"Bye, Bwackie! I missooo!"

"Come on, pumpkin, let's go in and go potty." Mom rested a hand on Presley's escaping curls, and my daughter beamed up at her.

"Okay, Gwamma!" There was proof again of my failure as a dad. My mother could get my daughter to go potty without a fuss, but I was failing miserably.

"Son, are you sure you're doing the right thing?" My dad had pushed his cowboy hat back on his head and was leaning over the fence watching the horses graze.

Sighing, I dropped my head to my arms where they rested on the top rung next to my dad. "No. I'm not. But I need to get away from here. At least for a little while. It's killing me here, Dad."

"Well, they say you can never really go home, but you're always welcome here if things don't work out in Texas." His words were soft but sincere and sent a pang through my chest.

"Thanks, Dad. I appreciate it."

The rest of the afternoon was spent relaxing and enjoying each other's company. Mom made Presley's favorite, messiest dinner to spite to me for not allowing an early birthday party. She claimed it was a concession to Presley for not getting two damn parties.

Damn spaghetti.

Don't get me wrong, my mom makes kick-ass spaghetti, but it's not exactly two-year-old friendly. She'd need a bath before bed for sure.

Gunny and I were helping Mom clean up the kitchen while dad read to Presley. Nights like that were what I would miss. Except I knew I couldn't spend every day at my parents' either.

No, I needed a new start.

I heard Presley squeal and her feet pounding across the floor. She darted into the kitchen of the old farmhouse I'd grown up in, where I'd been sitting with my brother and Mom.

Giggling, she hid behind me. "The ticko monsser is comin' Daddy! Sabe me!"

My dad came in bent over like a hunchback with his hands in wiggling claws and a leg dragging. He'd been doing that shit since Gunny and I were kids, and the corner of my lips tipped up at the memory.

Dad "chased" Presley around the table a few times before they made their way back to the living room.

A hand covered mine, and I looked to my mother. "It's okay. Yes, we will miss you both, but we do understand. You need to do what's best for you, and we need to see you move on and find happiness again."

"Thanks, Mom." She gave my hand a squeeze, and I kissed her cheek.

I didn't know about moving on, but I needed to be happy.
I needed to stop seeing Letty everywhere.

"How was your trip, Pops?" I asked as he sauntered over. He'd lumbered down from the huge rig they'd bought after selling the Oasis to Steph.

"Good. Real good. Mama Jean had a blast in New York State. You holding up okay?" Concern mixed with pity crossed his face, and I hated it. I didn't want nor need anyone's fucking pity. It had been over a year but it still sucked, and the pity only made it fresh again.

"Poppas!" Presley shouted from the back seat where she was strapped in her car seat. We glanced in the window, and she was wiggling and struggling to unbuckle herself. I'd finished filling up as I waited for them to arrive and I was still parked at the pump, since it was early and it wasn't like there was a line waiting to use them.

"Where's Mama?" Looking over his shoulder, I tried to see if maybe he dropped her off at the house first. I'd been hoping to at least tell her goodbye before we left.

"Oh, she's getting the things together for me." He scratched his head as his nose wrinkled a little and he looked away from me.

Gaze narrowing, I tried to figure out what was up with him. He was acting nervous as fuck, which was weird.

"Everything okay? You seem… strange."

"Poppas!" Presley made her desire to see her honorary grandpa and club uncle known again, which distracted me from Pops's mumbled answer.

"Presley! Grown-ups are talking. Is that what you do when grown-ups are talking?" I asked her sternly.

"Awww, she missed her poppas." The man who had mentored me and raised me in the club with an iron fist grinned and opened the back door of the truck to free the little monster-princess. All I could do was roll my eyes. He was only one of many she had wrapped around her little finger.

Once she was in his burly arms and practically sitting on his big belly, she pressed both palms to his gray beard. "You dunna miss me? I's moobing to Tessas!"

"Aww, little Elvis, I sure will. What do you say me and Mama Jean drive our big camper down to see you soon?" The big, tough old biker acted all animated for my daughter, and I had to chuckle.

Suddenly, my chatterbox of a daughter went utterly silent, her mouth gaping open as she stared in the direction of the RV. Turning to see what she was staring at, I lost my breath.

"It's a weel pwincess, Daddy!" Presley whispered with awe.

The woman walking toward us could've stepped right out of the 1950s. That was, if *I Love Lucy* or *Leave it to Beaver* had a bit of a badass goth twist.

The woman wore a full, vintage-style halter dress that was red with black polka dots, her midnight-black hair pinned up with a black-and-red handkerchief tied up top that did resemble a crown. She walked in ridiculously high and sexy-as-fuck red heels as if they were an extension of her long, perfect legs.

"Hers gots skin paint wike you, Daddy." More awe poured from my daughter as the woman closed in on us. She did indeed have both arms tatted to nearly full sleeves.

Shaking my head to pull my attention from her, I swallowed hard in embarrassment at how I'd stared. The immediate reaction my body had to her didn't make me feel any better.

Fuck, I hadn't had a response like that to another woman since before Letty and I got together.

Feeling all kinds of wrong, I frowned and looked to Pops. Except I noticed two things simultaneously. The first was that Mama Jean was walking with the woman. How the hell had I missed that before? The second was that Pops was smiling at the woman like he knew her.

Correction. Like he knew her and loved her.

What. The. Fuck?

"Hey, Uncle Carlisle, would you be able to get my suitcase, I couldn't get it down from the cabinet?" Her voice poured out, all husky and dripping sex. At least, it sure seemed like it.

"Uh, Uncle Carlisle?" Confusion heavy in my tone, I glanced back and forth between the two.

"Hi! You must be Matlock!" She gave an overly bright smile as she took a huge breath. "Thank you so much for letting me tag along." White teeth gripped that lush, full red bottom lip, and I was momentarily mesmerized.

What she'd said finally sunk in after a few moments.

"Whoa, wait. Hold up."

"Uh, Raiven, honey. Can you give me and young Matlock here a minute?" I didn't miss the look that Mama and Pops exchanged as Mama reached for Presley's hand when Pops set her down.

"Hey, sweet thing, how about if we go in and get you all some snacks for the road? Raiven, will you help us?" Mama Jean looked hopefully at the woman, who now had a name.

Raiven.

Fitting as hell, considering her hair was as black as a raven's wing.

"I'd actually like to stay." Her jaw cocked as she crossed her arms.

"Raiven, please go on with your aunt while I discuss some business with Matlock." Pops spoke firmly, but his eyes pleaded with her to comply.

That toe of her ruby-red shoe began to tap impatiently as she ground out, "I'm staying."

I couldn't be sure, but I thought I heard Mama whisper, "Shit," as she led Presley into the gas station.

A lone car had pulled up on the other side and begun pumping gas. I didn't pay them any mind, because I was too busy processing what was unfolding.

I'd been duped.

By my own brother.

Okay, so technically he was retired, but once a Demented Son, always a Demented Son. Unless you left the club or got put out, like Butch.

"Pops," I began in warning.

"Matlock, son. She won't be any bother. You'll barely know she's there. In fact, I bet she'll be a big help with Presley," he cajoled.

"You said something. Not some*one*. I don't need her help, and I don't want it. Besides, I didn't plan on rushing. I was going to stop in Omaha to take Presley to the zoo." Fuck, there was no way I was riding all the way to Texas with her.

Casting a side eye her way, I couldn't help but notice her luscious, round tits heave in indignation.

"You know what? Forget it. I'll take a bus. I'm not riding with this asshole. Just take me to the nearest Greyhound station." Huffing, she'd started to turn back to the RV when Pops wrapped a beefy hand around her arm.

"Raiven, wait." He turned his attention to me as he still held her gently. She tried to maintain her badass attitude, but as her eyes rolled, I was pretty sure they shimmered a little.

"Lock, please. She just needs a ride to Texas. Styx has shit lined up for her there. She'll be out of your hair once you arrive. I'm even going to give you enough to help pay for half the gas." One hand covered his mouth as he rasped it across his steel-colored beard.

"No."

"No way!"

She and I both protested at the same time.

"Uncle Carlisle, I'm not your responsibility. I can pay my own way," she insisted, then clarified. "On a bus."

"No, Raiven. You can't use your credit cards. At least let me pay him and you can pay me back later." He was completely ignoring me as he spoke to her.

"Daddy! I pee-peed!" Presley yelled across the parking lot.

"Good girl!" I told her.

"I'm not going," she said through gritted teeth.

"I'm not taking any money from you, because I'm not taking her." The tugging on my jeans didn't register through my frustration at the conniving old fart.

"Daddy." The tugging grew insistent.

"Not now, princess."

"But, Daddy."

"Wait, Presley."

"I'm not going, and that's final," the raven-haired beauty growled.

"Daddy!" Desperation colored my little girl's tone.

Shoulders sagging, I turned to her in mild exasperation. "What, Presley?"

"We haffa take her. Hers a weel pwincess, and we haffa sabe her from da dwagons. Wight, Daddy?"

Not in the mood to pop her bubble of belief in fairytales, I ruffled a hand through my hair. "Jesus," I muttered.

THREE

Raiven

"RAINING"—ART OF DYING

My uncle was delusional. He'd started to go senile. It was the only explanation for the crazy shit he'd tried to pull. He'd obviously known this Matlock guy wasn't going to want to take me along, so he'd neglected to tell him it was a person he needed taken to Texas.

Now his little girl had burst out with some story about me being a princess… and dragons?

I hadn't paid much attention to her before. She was another thing my uncle had neglected to mention.

I didn't do kids.

Not because I didn't like them, but because they terrified me. They were little and messy and unpredictable, and I couldn't understand what they were saying. It made me feel incompetent and like a failure to all womankind.

"Oh honey, I'm not a princess." Trying my best, I bent down to talk to her, resting my hands on my knees over my full dress. I did have a dragon after me though.

Wait. I'd understood her babble?

Wild blonde curls fluttered in the early morning breeze that se chills down my arms and spine. Enormous blue eyes stared up at me like I was indeed the princess she believed me to be.

"You awe! Wass you name, Pwincess?" She bit her lip as her little hand was swallowed by her father's inked one. Staring at them, I completely lost track of her question. I hadn't taken a lot of time to study the designs on his hands or the letters across his fingers.

Hell, I'd been trying to ignore them, along with each and every piercing. Unfortunately, I could tell anyone who asked that he had smaller gauges, an industrial in his left ear, and his nose pierced on both sides. After that, my imagination ran wild with the other places metal might be resting on his massive body.

I could also tell you he had gorgeous light-blue eyes with an unusual brown spot in one.

Another chill skated down my spine that had nothing to do with any breeze.

God, stop, Raiven. You're moving across the fucking country because of a man.

The last thing I needed was to get involved with another one. One with a kid, no less. And an asshole at that.

Shit. There could be a Mrs. Matlock whatever-the-hell-his-last-name-was, too.

Tipping my head back, I closed my eyes and let out a frustrated huff. I might have been imagining someone's husband naked.

What the ever-loving fuck was wrong with me?

"Raiven. Her name's Raiven, Elvis. And she's as stubborn as my brother was." My uncle sounded defeated, which caused my eyes to snap to him. He was the biggest, strongest man I knew, next to my dad. But at that moment he looked tired, old, and worried as hell.

Pulling both lips between my teeth, I gave no thought to the damage I may have been doing to my lipstick. I was trying too hard not to break down. The last week had been one of the most draining of my life. I was barely hanging on.

24

With apology in his eyes, he turned to Matlock and spoke quietly enough the little girl couldn't hear with my aunt talking to her. I knew she was trying to distract her. "Please, Matlock. She had a bad breakup, and the guy is being a schmuck. Trying to be all possessive and not let her leave him. Got rough with her. She had to leave in the middle of the night with only a single suitcase. Thankfully, we were passing through to visit and she was able to get on the RV with us and get out of Dodge. He's harassed her almost all day every day. I spoke to Styx, and his chapter is helping her get a job and get settled down there. She just needs a ride, and I don't want her taking a Greyhound. They aren't safe. We'd take her ourselves, but I've got a couple of doctor's appointments over the next couple of weeks that I can't miss, and she needs to get down there for the job."

Inside, I groaned that he'd told this stranger my business. Then I wanted to laugh because if he only knew, I was probably safer on a Greyhound bus than with Stefano. Digging my phone out of my purse, I searched for the nearest bus station.

Matlock pressed the heel of his hand to the center of his forehead and threaded his long fingers through his dark blond hair. "Goddammit, Pops." He dragged his hand down over his face and shook his head.

"I know, Lock. And she's the only family I have left now. My brother died right before we got there. I didn't even get to see him one last time."

A gasped sob escaped me before I turned my back to them. Shoulders thrown back, I tried to appear strong and hold my shit together.

I'd barely had time to grieve my father. It was still so raw, but I was doing my best to keep the pain covered until I could deal with it later.

My phone vibrated in my hand. Without giving it much thought, I opened the waiting message. I should've paid more attention.

Stefano: Did you really think you could get away from me that easily? I know where you are and I'm coming for you.

The message froze my lungs. No matter how hard I tried, I couldn't get a breath in. My body quaked head to toe. Finally, I was able to draw a shaky, shallow inhale.

"Okay. Fine," he muttered, and I wasn't sure what he was talking about. Until my mind began to reconstitute from the shock of Stefano's message.

I whipped back around, my eyes flashing as I gasped for breath. "No. Dammit, Uncle Carlisle, I'm not going with him. I'm no one's burden. I can take care of myself. I appreciate everything you've done so far, but I'll be okay. I'll find my own way to Texas."

Fighting anger and terror, I tried to think of a way to get there that wouldn't leave any more of a trail than I had. I should've known he'd find me, but how could he really? I'd told him about my aunt and uncle, but only that they traveled the country in an RV with my uncle's bike as their constant companion. I'd never told him where they were from. At least not that I remembered. Maybe he was bluffing. But did I really want to risk that?

"Well, I can't make her go with me. If she doesn't want to go, I'm not pushing it." There was a flicker of relief in his eyes as he shrugged and scooped his small daughter up.

"Raiven," my uncle pleaded, worry creasing his forehead. More than it already was.

"Pwease, Daddy? Pwease bwing da pwincess wiff. What if hers in danger?" The little girl stretched the word danger out in a low, ridiculously dramatic way that nearly had me smiling despite my current life situation.

"Raiven, I think you should strike while the iron's hot and get yourself on the road. Why delay when you don't need to? I'll feel so much better about you traveling across country if you're with Lock." My aunt reached over and gently caressed my cheek.

When he gave me his full attention, it sent my stomach into flutters. His full attention on a woman was damn near lethal, even as he held his daughter protectively in his muscular arms.

Finally, he sighed. "If she's willing to ride with us, she can go."

My lip curled, and I really wanted to tell him to fuck off and not do me any favors. Because there was a pint-sized princess in his arms, I curbed my tongue.

The phone in my hand vibrated again. Tremors started at who it likely was. Even though I hated to go with him, I did need to get my ass to Texas. My gaze flickered to my phone.

Fear snaked through me, biting me with its venomous mouth, pouring terror through my veins.

Stefano: When I catch up with you, maybe your dear aunt and uncle will go first. And I think you'll watch.

Not wanting to see further messages from him, I shut my phone off and dropped it in my purse.

Decision made, I sucked it up and pulled up my metaphoric big-girl pants.

"If you're willing to have the extra passenger, I'd actually love to take the trip with you." My voice was saccharin-sweet and as steady as I could make it as I batted my eyes and gave the gorgeous asshole a tight smile.

The pretty little hot mess clapped her hands rapidly. "Oh my gosh! We dunna haff a weel pwincess wiff on ow-uh advenchuh!"

"Yeah. It would appear so." His tone didn't convey the same thrill his daughter's had.

A wide grin spread over my uncle's face, and relief filled his eyes. "Thank you, Lock. I appreciate this more than you'll ever know."

Matlock's nostrils flared as his eyes narrowed at my uncle. "You owe me so fucking big."

"Daddy! You saids a bad wood! You gunna gets you mouf wassed out wiff soap!" The little girl crossed her arms and frowned at her dad. In that moment, I loved that kid.

"I'll be right back so you all can get on the road." My uncle quickly took off toward the RV, and I could hear him chuckling the entire way.

"Well, Raiven, sweetie, I'm gonna miss you. It was so nice having you along from Chicago to here." My aunt Jean gave me a huge hug as she tried to covertly wipe off a tear.

"I'll miss you too, Aunty Jean. But you all need to come visit soon. Okay?" I squeezed her small frame. I hadn't seen her a lot as I was growing up, but every memory with her was a fond one.

The sound of my rolling suitcase had me glancing over to see my uncle returning. Matlock placed his daughter in the back seat, and I could hear the clanking of buckles and softly spoken words before he stepped back. He closed the door as my uncle reached the truck.

Before my uncle could lift the suitcase, Matlock rushed forward. "I've got it, Pops."

I wrapped my arms around my uncle's tall frame. My breath quavered. "Please don't stay here long. Stefano…." My brow wrinkled in worry.

"Don't worry about me, sweetheart. I can handle myself just fine." The whole time I hugged my uncle and told him goodbye, I watched the blond god of a man.

Watching that sexy-as-hell man lift my suitcase like it was damn near featherlight had me drooling. I stared as every muscle rippled and bunched when he lifted it over the edge of the blacked-out Ford Raptor, then secured it under a net. It was a beautiful truck for a beautiful man.

Surprising me, he opened my door for me and held out a hand. Blinking in shock, I placed one hand in his as I reached for the oh-shit bar in the truck. The jolt that shot through me as my fingers curled around his warm, callused hand took my breath away for a second.

Shaking it off, I swallowed and took a deep breath. One high-heeled foot lifted to the step, then I launched myself up to the seat.

As soon as I sat, my crinoline poofed up into my face. "Shi—Crap!" Remembering the young ears in the back seat, I bit my tongue. Damn, I was going to have to do a lot of that as we traveled. I had a helluva potty mouth.

"Who the fuck travels dressed like that?" he muttered.

Ugh! An asshole of a beautiful man.

"I do," I said through gritted teeth. Lifting my ass, I slid the underskirt off, pulling one foot at a time out of it after I got it down to my ankles. Once I was done, I tossed it over into the back seat, making sure it didn't land on the spunky little girl back there.

Smoothing my skirt back down, I glanced over where he stood, jaw gaping. With a snarky smirk, I sneered, "See something you liked?"

God, I was being a bitch, but this guy brought out something feisty in me. More so than usual.

Jaw snapping shut, he narrowed his gaze at me and slammed the door. Though I tried to act like I wasn't, I watched him stalk over to my aunt and uncle. He hugged my aunt, swinging her in a circle before he pressed a kiss to her cheek.

She laughed and rested a hand to his cheek. My uncle shook his hand, then pulled him into one of those bro-hugs. I could see his mouth moving as he spoke to the man I'd be traveling cross-country with.

For once, the little girl was quiet. I didn't want to look at her and get her going.

Matlock nodded, and they broke apart. My aunt and uncle came to my open window for one last goodbye.

"Love you, blackbird. You fly high and fast. We'll see you soon." I smiled sadly at his childhood nickname for me.

"Love you, Raiven. Be safe." My aunt was tearing up as she stretched up into the tall truck and squeezed my hand where it rested on the window ledge.

"Love you guys too. But I'll see you soon. Hint, hint." I winked and grinned at the only two family members I had left.

As we were saying our last goodbyes, Matlock climbed into the driver seat. The man set every single one of my nerve endings tingling, as if I was aware of him on a visceral level.

"You take care of my girl," my uncle said to Matlock, then looked in the back seat. "Correction, my girls."

He'd added the plural with a wink. Matlock gave him a wry grin as he shook his head and started the truck.

"You got it." Without a bunch of fanfare, we pulled out of the gas station and into the early morning.

"Daddy! Pway dat song I wike. Pwease?" The last was said as an afterthought.

Within about five minutes, Presley was out, her little head resting on the part of her car seat that sort of curled around her. Music continued to play quietly in the background. Other than that, there wasn't a sound.

"She's quite a character." It was a hopeless attempt to break the awkward silence hovering in the cab.

"Mm," he grunted.

"How old is she?"

"Two. Almost three."

"You don't talk much, do you?" Exasperated at the man's lack of manners, I half turned in my seat to face him.

"Nothin' to say."

"Well, this will be a fun trip." My eyes rolled as I turned to face front.

"Never promised to keep you entertained," he grumbled.

"What's your problem? I told you that you didn't have to take me with you. You can let me out at the next place that has a Greyhound. I don't know why you told my uncle you'd take me when you didn't really want to. I mean, I get that you were pissed that he obviously misled you about what you were taking with you, but I swear I had no idea you didn't know. You should've stuck to your guns. Matter of fact, fuck the Greyhound, just let me out at the next town." My arms crossed, I huffed as I turned to watch the passing landscape. It was a whole lot of nothing. Fields for miles. That's it.

"Fuck, no. I made a promise to Pops. I'll get you safely to Texas, then we part ways. End of story." His hands gripped the steering wheel tightly as he ground out his reply.

"I don't care what the fuck you promised my uncle. I'm not riding like this for days. Fuck that shit." Snarky as hell, I curled my lip at him.

I didn't think he was going to say any more, so I prepared to try to sleep. It was better than being ignored.

30

"What he said. Was it true?" He said it so quiet, I wasn't sure he was even talking to me. When he didn't say anything else, curiosity got the better of me and I sat up.

"Was what true?"

"Did your boyfriend hurt you?"

FOUR

Lock

"WORLD WAR ME"—THEORY OF A DEADMAN

Pops knew he'd get to me when he told me Raiven's ex was abusive, because my only cousin was beaten to death by her boyfriend. Part of me wondered if it was exaggerated to get me to agree to take her. The blanching of her already ivory skin told me there was more than a semblance of truth to the story.

"Um." She turned toward the window but I saw her swallow hard in my periphery as I tried to watch her and the road. "He wasn't very nice. Well, initially he was. Except I fail to see how that's your business."

She shrugged like it wasn't that big of a deal. For some reason, the thought of someone hurting the bundle of badass next to me really pissed me off. I told myself it was because of my cousin, Jennifer. That was an easier explanation than whatever else it might be.

I hadn't intended on talking to her. I was pissed about being duped. I also didn't like the way she stirred shit up in me, making me feel all scratchy and messy inside. It left me on edge and, well, pissy.

Except the words had been spinning in my head since we'd pulled out, and I had some kind of crazy need to know. "Was that the first time he'd done that?"

My words were tight and I barely got them past my lips. Anger was coming on strong, washing over me in waves.

All exasperated and snarly, she turned on me and repeated, "That's none of your business."

The attitude and snark were an obvious defense mechanism, be-cause when I glanced her way, I caught her lower jaw trembling as she turned away. "Look, I'm sorry. I didn't mean to be such a dick back there when we all met up. I was taken by surprise, and let's say it's been a shitty year."

Grinding my teeth, I hated that I'd given that info up to her. I didn't talk about my issues with people I didn't know, and I sure as shit didn't know her.

"Well, you were—so there's that," she huffed. Her face remained turned away as she stared out of the window.

Deciding to drop the subject, I left her alone. I'd get it out of her later, even though I didn't know why it really mattered to me.

Glancing in the rearview mirror to check on Presley, I noted that she was still zonked. Nothing new. That girl fell asleep in the vehicle ev-ery time. Had since she was a baby. At times, it had been a saving grace.

A small grin curled my lips. That little bundle of fire was my world. My everything good.

Sneaking a peek at the other bundle of fire in my truck, I saw her head nodding as her thick eyelashes lay feathered across her cheeks. It wasn't long before she lay her head back on the seat and her lips softly parted.

Swallowing hard, I focused on the road. As I drove, my mind wan-dered. Memories of Letty flashed through my head.

The first time we met, I'd been home from the Army two days. Gunny had arranged a homecoming party for me at the clubhouse. It was my first real interaction with the club my brother had joined after getting out of the Marine Corps.

Letty was a friend of one of the old ladies in high school and had been visiting from down by Omaha where she'd moved after graduation to get away from her loser family. She'd been a couple of years older than me, but it hadn't mattered.

She'd been a one-night stand and then she'd gone back to Omaha. When she'd contacted me a few months later to tell me she was pregnant, it had scared the shit out of me. I'd talked about getting married, but she'd refused. She'd insisted she didn't want to get married because she'd gotten pregnant.

She did at least move up to be near me so I could help with the pregnancy. I'd wanted to experience it with her, and she'd needed the help with the medical bills.

No matter how many times I'd assured her I wasn't wanting to marry her only because of the pregnancy, she wouldn't budge on it. We'd moved in together, and one thing led to another, and before long we were pretty much a couple.

After Presley arrived, I'd continued to ask. She'd continued to say no. Finally, I'd quit asking and accepted that I was a little old-fashioned and she wasn't. The thing was, I'd fallen in love with her, so I'd made the decision to keep her any way I could. We knew who we were faithful to, and that had been all that mattered in the end.

A whimper from the seat next to me pulled me from my reverie.

Pulling my gaze briefly from the road, I saw her brow was furrowed and her hands clenched into fists. I reached to wake her, but then her face smoothed out and her hands relaxed.

The miles slipped away as I listened to music and passed through several small towns. Not once did I stop and let Miss Sassy-pants out.

The phone rang in my truck and I answered, taking another quick look in her direction to see if it had woken her. She was still out like a light, her head moving slightly with each small bump in the road.

"Hey, Gunny. Miss me already?" My brother's answering chuckle carried over the speakers and I turned the volume down a little.

"Actually, yeah I do. It was weird waking up at your place."

"It's your place now. Get used to it." Gunny had bought my house from me. It made sense, since he'd been living in the clubhouse since he and Trixie had split. I didn't need it, he wanted his space. Win-win.

"Yeah, but I've been used to you and Elvis being here." His voice was quieter, and it wasn't because I'd turned the volume down.

"Yeah." I didn't know what to say. It hurt, but I knew with every mile I drove that it was the right decision.

I'd questioned my decision as we'd left the small town behind. I'd wondered if I was going on the run from a ghost. Questioned whether I needed therapy but afraid of the shit that would dredge up.

"Look, I got some information, and fuck, I wish you were here. I don't want to tell you this over the phone." His tone was pensive.

"Mom and Dad okay?" My heart rate spiked.

"What? Oh, yeah, they're fine. That's not it." His hesitation wasn't helping.

"Spit it out."

"Am I on speaker?"

"Yeah, but they're both asleep."

"Both?" I could tell by the tone of his voice, I'd thrown him for a loop on that one.

"Long story. Go on." I waited for him to continue.

"It's about Letty."

"Okay?" It was drawn out in question.

He huffed, and I could picture him running a frustrated hand through his hair. "The accident wasn't an accident."

My heart paused before it started to gallop. "Excuse me?"

"That's not all." He sighed. "It was the Demon Runners. They sent us an explicit message. They said we hadn't listened to any of the subtle ones they'd sent. It said you shouldn't have stolen her and maybe she wouldn't have been stolen from you. They said things were about to get worse."

"What the fuck does that mean? Stole who?" He wasn't making sense.

"I don't know, bro. We're trying to find out. Maybe Letty? We just don't know how. We know her family is shady as fuck but she was a good person. Just in case, Hacker's looking into her and her family to see what he turns up, but I wanted to let you know so you can stay sharp. Watch your six, little brother. Fuck, I wish I was there to do it for you." I hated the worry that echoed through the cab of the vehicle. I could handle myself, and he shouldn't feel responsible for me, but I understood. I'd be the same way with him.

"Roger that. I don't think they'll be after me now. It's been over a year, and they haven't done anything in all that time. I doubt they will now." Regardless, I instinctively checked all my mirrors, but we were the only ones on the two-lane road at that moment.

"Yeah, well there's got to be a reason they sent that message now. Maybe they've done things we don't know about and that's what they meant by subtle messages. Or maybe things that just didn't work out right. Like Becca having the blow-out with brand-new tires. Sera's Jeep getting vandalized. Your accident." When he mentioned the accident, his voice cracked. "Things we'd chalked up to teenage hoodlums." He was right. Over the past year there had been a lot of little things that had happened. Each incident had seemed minor and explainable with no sign of the Demon Runners.

It shouldn't surprise me though, because it was exactly the way they worked. Like cowardly pussies, striking in silence and staying in hiding.

"Maybe. Either way, I'll be careful." I had to. I had precious cargo to watch out for. My eyes flickered to the rearview mirror to take in my sleeping angel. Then inexplicably, they flashed to the spunky woman in my passenger seat.

I shook my head. Sure, she was Pops and Mama's niece, but I didn't know her.

"Maybe you should skip the zoo. It's right in their backyard."

"Hell, no. I promised Presley. Not only that, but I'm not letting them run my life."

"I'm not asking you to."

"Besides, they won't even know we're there."

"I hope you're right, little brother. You still planning on staying in Omaha overnight?" I heard him digging around with something, then a zipping sound.

"Yeah, why?"

"Because I'm heading down. I'll be there ASAP with Soap." There was some shuffling, then he huffed an exhale.

"What the fuck? No. You don't need to come down to Omaha to babysit me," I growled.

"I don't have a choice. Snow's orders and voted on by the rest of the club. It's a done deal. I'm swinging by the clubhouse to meet up with Soap and we'll be on the road. He's packing now."

"Goddammit, Gunny. I'm not even a member of that chapter any-more." Fuck, saying that hurt more than I thought it would.

"Hey. For one, you're a brother regardless of which chapter you're in—you know that. For two, you're my baby brother and the only fuck-ing sibling I have. I'm on my way. See you soon. Text me your hotel info, and keep your head on swivel." He didn't even wait for my response be-fore he hung up on me.

"Fucker." Not that I really meant it. I loved my brother.

The silence had me thinking about what Pops had said about Raiven.

Fuck, I couldn't think her name without it causing a chain reaction in my body.

It was the strangest experience. Not one single woman had had that effect on me since Letty.

By the time either of the females in the truck began to stir, we were hitting the outskirts of Omaha. I'd chosen a hotel near the Henry Doorly Zoo, but it was too early to check in, so I'd figured we'd get some lunch, then hit the zoo.

My plan was to spend the afternoon at the zoo, because that was probably all Presley would be able to handle. She'd probably wear out before we saw half of it. Then I wanted to check out of the hotel in the morning and get back on the road. Now with the brothers heading down, I wasn't sure how that would affect my plans.

My eyes strayed to Raiven as she scooted up in the seat, wrinkled her nose, pursed her lips, and finally blinked a few times. Then she stretched, and I had to focus on the road because her tits were damn near popping out of the top of her dress as she arched her back and yawned.

It was fucking with my head.

Bad.

Everything she did had fucked with my head, from the second she'd strutted across that gas station parking lot. Gritting my teeth, I gripped the steering wheel tighter.

Voice raspy from sleep and her natural husky tone, she asked, "Where are we?"

"Omaha. Figured we'd get some lunch, then I'm taking Presley to the zoo. If I can check in early, I'll get you settled at the hotel first, but you're welcome to go with us. If you want." The last bit I tacked on as if it was no big deal and she could do what she pleased. The truth was, for some crazy-ass reason I was hoping she'd go with us.

Stupid, Lock. Stupid.

I didn't know what the hell was wrong with me.

"Umm, I...."

"Daddy! We ohmost there?" Sleepy excitement poured up from the back seat. The sound of her little voice had me smiling. All it took to make a bad day great was to hear her call me "Daddy."

"Yeah, baby girl. We're gonna get us some lunch first, then we'll go to the zoo." Her little legs bounced as she stared out the windows.

As I pulled into the restaurant parking lot, I belatedly thought to ask my unexpected passenger if she had a preference. "Uh, is Mexican okay with you? We can go somewhere else if you want."

In the truck, it was impossible have a private conversation. "Messican, Messican! I haffa kaysadeeeeeeuh!" the peanut gallery in the backseat piped in.

Luscious red lips I'd tried my damnedest not to stare at tipped up in the corner. Her murmured, "Mexican it is" had chills skating over my skin.

Shaking off the strange feeling, I jumped out of the truck to free the wee beast in the back seat. The door opening sent her into a fit of squealing happiness as she clapped her hands.

"Daddy!"

With a grin, I lifted her into the air after unbuckling her. Then I hugged her tight. "I love you."

Chubby little fingers framed my face. "I wub you too, Daddy!"

That smile. That laughter. Worth everything in the world.

Turning toward the restaurant, I caught Raiven standing at the back corner of the truck. Her expression was hard to read, but the ruby-red lip held captive by her white teeth had my chest rattling and shaking with each beat of my heart.

My eyes raked her head to toe, and I realized she'd put that fluffy thing under her dress again. The thought of someone seeing those long legs as she put it back on had me clenching my jaw.

I felt possessive of someone I had no right to be, and that scared the shit out of me.

"Will all of this stuff be okay back here?" She motioned to her suitcase and the things in the bed of the truck. I'd covered it all in a cargo net. It wasn't much, all things considered. Mostly Presley's things and our clothes.

I'd wanted to start over with everything else.

"Yeah. No one will mess with it. Besides, parked here, we should be able to see it from inside." Motioning, I said, "Ladies first."

A dark eyebrow quirked before she preceded me into the restaurant. Every step had my jeans getting uncomfortable. It also gave me a perfect view of the smooth slope of her shoulder.

I had the insane urge to press my lips where her shoulder met the slender column of her throat.

Jesus fucking H. Christ. Why is my brain going haywire?

39

FIVE

Raiven

"HELP IS ON THE WAY"—RISE AGAINST

I hadn't given much thought to having kids. They weren't on my radar. The fear thing was a big reason.

But watching this big, bad, tatted-up sex god interact with his little girl had my ovaries screaming. My twenty-six-year-old body acted like its biological clock was on the verge of expiring. It was so crazy, I didn't know how to process it.

For years, I'd been happily building my clientele. I'd dated here and there, but nothing serious. Then Stefano had come into the shop, and I'd done a massive piece on his back of a wicked-looking Neptune.

It had taken several sittings. By the last one, he'd convinced me to go out with him. Thinking back to how I thought I'd won the lottery with him had my stomach churning.

"Pwincess Waiven?" The inquisitive little girl had asked me a million questions during the meal, so one more didn't faze me.

"Yes, Princess Presley?" After telling her about twenty times that I wasn't a princess, I gave up on that too. I was in the game now.

"You gonna go to dub zoo wiff me?" She'd finished her meal

as best as I guessed she was going to and was climbing back in the chair.

I'd really thought Matlock was an asshole earlier, but he'd been growing on me throughout lunch, and it wasn't only because of his ruggedly sexy looks. He'd eaten what had to be a cold lunch because he'd spent half of the time putting her back into her chair when she would get down to try to wander. Or she had to potty. Or she wanted to come see me. Or she wanted to look out the window. Or she had to potty again.

He was way more patient with her than I would've imagined.

Not that I didn't catch agitation sneaking through every so often when she would do the exact opposite of what he told her. I'd had to fight giggling, because it was funny watching him try to wrangler her.

"I, uh, well…." Matlock was looking at me like he was bored and couldn't care less what my answer was. Part of me wanted him to ask me again. Part of me wanted him to beg me.

I didn't understand that part of me at all.

My life was in shambles.

Flattened by a tornado of epic proportions.

The last thing I should be thinking about was a man. No matter that he was easy to appreciate.

In the short period of time we'd been in that restaurant, I'd seen he was not only handsome, he was a good father. Which meant there was a mother somewhere.

I had no idea if she was already in Texas, if we were picking her up on the way, or if she was out of the picture completely. There was no way to ask without making things awkward as fuck. I could text Aunt Jean or Uncle Carlisle, but then they'd wonder why I was asking.

"Well, I'm kind of tired. How about if we see if I can take a nap at the hotel?"

Was that disappointment I saw flash in his unusual blue eyes? It had to have been my imagination.

"Naps awe yucky." Presley scrunched up her nose and stuck out her tongue. While I tried not to laugh, her father rolled his eyes but fought a smile too.

I tried to pay for my food, and he wouldn't let me. His rationale made sense but still made me feel like a mooch.

"Pops said he didn't want you using any credit cards. You're essentially off the grid. Okay?" Those stormy eyes had a mesmerizing hold over me. That was the only explanation I had for the cooperative nod I gave him.

"I was gonna pay cash."

He continued as if I hadn't said a word. "Speaking of, where is your phone? We should probably shut it off and remove the battery and SIM card if you can. If he has any connections, he may be able to track your phone." He was speaking quietly enough that only I could hear as he wiped Presley's hands.

"I already shut it off, but I doubt he'd do that." Lord, I didn't want to think that Stefano may have been tracking me. The beautiful little blonde girl gave me the biggest smile, and it made me sick that I could inadvertently be putting her in danger simply riding with them.

"If you don't think he'd do that, then why shut off your phone?" His head tipped slightly, and he looked at me in question.

"He, um, my boyfriend kept texting me," I finally admitted. "Ex," I insisted. I didn't want to give him any more than that. The less everyone knew, the safer they were from the chaos of my life.

Shrugging, I watched as he tied Presley's shoes, then signed the lunch receipt.

His eyes narrowed, but he didn't say anything as he studied me. It was like I was a bug under a microscope and he could see my every detail and secret.

On the way back out to the truck, the man and his daughter walked hand in hand. Together they were like something off a painting or a greeting card. Her pale ringlets were haloed by the shining sun, and his dark blond hair seemed lighter as he towered over her and she looked up to him.

I wasn't so sure a greeting card would have an ass that nice on it though.

Smacking myself on the forehead, I was ashamed of the direction my thoughts were taking. It was as if my brain was on a total disconnect from my current situation.

It didn't take long to reach the loaded-down black Raptor. I stood back, watching like the intruder I was as he buckled her in to her car seat. Once she was secured, he pressed a kiss to his fingertips and reached in to hold it to her nose.

"Daddy kissed my nose!" she squealed as her contagious laughter pealed.

Shit. Their interactions were doing something to me. Making me rethink my life, my goals, and my desires.

We didn't talk on the way to the hotel.

We didn't talk when he went up to the desk with Presley lying on his shoulder almost sleeping and said it would be him, his wife, and his daughter in the room.

Hearing him say his wife would be in the room with him had my heart plummeting to my stomach, and I hated myself for feeling that way. Not that I expected to share a room, and not that I thought anything would happen between us.

God, no.

Okay, if I was honest with myself, I was attracted to him. Not at first, but after witnessing another side of him at lunch, I could admit he was an extremely attractive guy.

Discreetly, I counted up the cash I had in my purse. Thankfully, I'd had a cash box where I kept all my cash tips for an emergency fund. Then I'd drawn out the max I could from the ATM before leaving Chicago.

If we were only staying one night here and there, I'd be okay. The problem was, I'd heard him say he wasn't in a rush to get to Texas. So that meant possibly several days of hotels, plus meals. Then I'd have costs when I got to Texas.

Biting my lip, I decided I'd be okay. I'd figure shit out. I always did.

"You ready, babe?" His question caught me off guard as he spun from the desk and handed me a card key. Dumbly, I looked at it like I'd never seen one.

"Um, what's this?" I tried to ask quietly so the people sitting in the lobby didn't hear. It was none of their business what was going on, but I wasn't going to be part of some weird threesome. With his daughter in the room, no less!

Chuckling, he threw an arm around me as he held his daughter with his other arm. "Let's go get our bags."

Too confused to argue, I followed him out the door, biting my tongue until we got outside.

Before I could question him, he instructed me to sit on the bench. "Do you mind holding Presley while I park the truck? I'll bring your suitcase up."

"Uh, okay?" It came out more a question than an affirmative response. Had he gotten me my own room or was it for his room? I knew I didn't hear him ask for two rooms. At least I didn't think so.

By the time he'd parked the truck where the hotel's cameras could see it to watch our shit and come back with the suitcases, Presley was wide awake. She'd been staring at me the entire time, touching my hair with a finger and feeling my dress.

I wasn't sure what to do, so I just sat there. Waiting.

"You a vewy pretty pwincess," she whispered in awe.

Taking a quick glance down at her, I smiled as her golden hair blew in front of her face before she grabbed it and held it back. "Thank you. So are you." She was a beautiful child, and her eyes were the same gorgeous blue as her father's, minus the brown spot.

Swallowing hard, I pulled one of my bobby pins from my hair and twisted her hair off to the side. Securing it with the pin, I looked up to see Matlock striding toward us.

Sweet baby Jesus, he's hot.

Dark golden blond hair, long on top, blew wildly in the wind. With both hands full of our suitcases, he couldn't hold it out of the way, so it swirled and whipped around his stern, beautiful face.

"Daddy gots my soocase," the little girl in my lap announced, pleased as punch.

Not wasting any time, he nodded and brusquely instructed, "Let's go. Can you hold her hand or do you mind pulling her suitcase?"

It was a cute little hot-pink-and-black case. Nothing I'd ever be ashamed of pulling, nor was it too heavy or a problem. Except for some inexplicable reason, I was loathe to give her up.

"I've got her." No slouch, I stood with her in my arms and raised an eyebrow. "Lead the way."

Belatedly, it dawned on me I still hadn't asked him about the room situation. But by that time, we were already walking through the lobby.

The man's long legs covered a lot of ground, so I was striding quickly to keep up.

When he paused at a room on the third floor and inserted the key, I had to know. "Um, which room is mine?"

He looked over his shoulder at me as he pushed the door open. "Uh, this one."

He said it like I was crazy for asking.

"Oh. So how far away are you going to be?" Even though I didn't really know him, I knew my uncle trusted him, and he made me feel safe. Knowing this room was mine, I didn't set the sweet little girl down yet.

"Right here. I'll sleep on the floor." He said it like it was no big deal; an everyday occurrence.

I set Presley down and watched her with one eye while she ran over, looked out the window, and quietly chattered to herself.

"No. We are not sharing a room. Are you insane? What will your wife think about that? It's bad enough that I rode down here with you and she doesn't know me." As I crossed my arms defiantly across my chest, the color drained from his face. At least the part not covered by that glorious beard. Then it flushed with anger as he took two quick steps my direction.

"I don't have a wife. The only wife I had was years ago and a huge mistake of youth and loneliness. Don't ever mention her again," he bit out. His nostrils flared and his jaw flexed as he clenched his fists in front of me.

So close, I could smell the faintest whiff of his cologne. I couldn't put my finger on the scent, but it was wild and deep, like the man who wore it.

"Look, don't get an attitude with me." I poked him in the chest. "I didn't know. Uncle Carlisle said you'd agreed to take me to Texas. He didn't get into your background. He didn't even mention you had a kid. So forgive me if, after seeing you had a child, I assumed there was a Mrs. Matlock somewhere waiting for you or meeting up with you," I lashed out in a fierce whisper.

He dropped his gaze to the finger that was still poking at his chest with each point of emphasis I needed to make.

"First of all, if your asshole boyfriend is still looking for you, he'd be looking for you, not a family. Husband, wife, and child?" His tone was condescending, and that pissed me off further.

My anger making me ballsy, I poked him again. "Ex. Ex-boyfriend. And what gives you the right to make all the decisions anyway? Maybe I wanted my own room. Maybe I don't want to travel with you anymore."

"Are you done?" His droll tone did nothing for my temper.

"No! I'm not! So why did you say you were getting a room for you and your wife if there was no wife? I hope you don't think that I'm going to actually fuck you." The last part had my eyes almost popping out of my head as I fought to keep my voice down.

"Jesus Christ, Raiven. My daughter is in the room. What the fuck do you take me for? I don't even know you. I'm not sure I even like you." Growling, he leaned closer to me.

The effect his nearness had on my senses sent my brainpower into a tailspin. I wasn't thinking clearly, and it showed.

"Something tells me you don't have to know or like someone particularly well to fuck them." It irritated me that he had me acting like a

46

spoiled fourteen-year-old girl. Except the thought of him not liking me hurt. My mouth was running away with me, as it was prone to do when I was uncomfortable or in defense mode.

Again he moved closer, until our noses were nearly touching, I could smell his minty gum, and his unique eyes revealed green and gray flecks scattered in the icy blue. "No, I don't. But if that was a dig at Presley's conception, tread carefully, because you don't have a fucking clue what you're taking about."

I gasped.

"She had nothing to do with this! I didn't mean anything of the sort, and I think you are fully aware of that. I would never malign her like that." Chest heaving, I would've slapped him if his sweet daughter hadn't been there. Then again, I also might have grabbed him by the T-shirt and pulled him closer.

Oh my God! Where did that thought come from?

Maybe I needed to find that Greyhound after all.

SIX

Lock

"LOST AND ALONE"—FROM ASHES TO NEW

Goddammit, the woman was driving me fucking insane.

The thought of her talking shit about Presley or Letty had raised my hackles. Which was in direct conflict with the desire to rip that sexy-as-fuck dress off her and fuck her seven ways from Sunday to take the glare off her face.

She had me so damn tied up and confused. As she'd removed that fluffy fucking thing from under her skirt earlier that day, I'd caught a peek of the large dragon tattoo on her thigh. It had me wanting to explore every inch of her.

I'd had an insane need to find every piece of ink and know everything about it.

After I ran my tongue over each and every line.

"Fuck, woman. You are the most infuriating woman I've ever met." Shaken, I ran a hand through my hair, pushing it back. I hadn't wanted another woman since Letty.

"I told you I wasn't talking shit about your little girl!" she whisper-yelled as her gaze flickered to where Presley still watched cars driving by out of the window.

The problem was, I was pretty sure she wouldn't, but I was protective and fierce when it came to Presley and Letty's memory. "I'm sorry if I got a little shitty. I believe you. Okay? Now are you going to the zoo with us or are you staying here?"

Her white teeth chewed on her lush red bottom lip in indecision, and I was fascinated by the movement. It obviously was her go-to when she was uncertain.

"I'm not sure if that's a good idea."

"Well, for some reason my daughter seems to like you. Also, it would look strange if a 'family' didn't go out together for as long as I'm going to be gone." Not that anyone would question it, but for some crazy-ass fucking reason, I wanted her to go with us.

She sighed.

"Okay." Resignation weighed heavy in her answer, and it bothered me that she was so against us hanging out. It shouldn't. I shouldn't care, and her thoughts or feelings shouldn't matter to me.

"Well, then you better change your shoes, because we're gonna be doing a lot of walking. While they may be sexy as fuck, I'm not sure those shoes will let you keep up all afternoon." I gave a wry grin.

"Seriously? I could walk in these all day." Her face turned a soft shade of pink, I assumed at my comment. "In fact, I could probably run a marathon in them," she huffed, all cocky and sarcastic.

Shaking my head at the chuckle she pulled out of me with her sass, I inhaled deeply before letting it blow heavily out. "Well, make up your mind, because someone needs to see the elephants."

"Ewephants!" Hearing what she wanted, Presley spun around and ran at me, throwing herself at my legs.

Running my fingers through the fine, silky curls on my daughter's head, my heart nearly burst with love. Pushing the maddening woman out of my thoughts, I refocused on her. "Yeah, little Elvis, we're gonna see the elephants."

Out of the corner of my eye, I saw her bend over and toss her suitcase on the stand she'd opened. The girl was no wimp, and the flex of her toned muscles under the ink on her biceps didn't go unnoticed.

I opened my mouth to tell her I would've done that for her, but then snapped it shut because I knew she'd have been stubborn about it. We'd have wasted precious time arguing.

Funny thing was, the thought of arguing with her was stimulating.

Scooping my little girl up, I kissed her. "You want your hair braided?"

"Pwease, Daddy?"

Our motions were practiced. I quickly and deftly brushed, separated, and braided her silky hair. The entire time, I watched as Raiven pulled out a pair of old-school Chucks and slipped them on after putting on a short pair of socks.

She left the dress on. It was hot as hell on her, and I had to shake my head to clear it.

"Okay, let's go." I called up an Uber on my app so we didn't have to drive the truck and have it sitting in the zoo parking lot with our stuff in it. Not that there was anything in the back that couldn't be replaced.

The photo album and baby book Letty had made for us were in the cab.

Raiven stayed quiet as Presley chattered the entire way to our destination.

The zoo wasn't too busy, since it was still early in the season and the middle of the week.

"Have you been here before?" Raiven asked. I knew she didn't mean anything by her question, but it sent a knife to my heart.

"Yeah." I'd brought Presley here in the fall. The last time before that was with Letty. She'd wanted to bring Presley even though she was only a baby. I remembered telling her Presley wouldn't even know what the hell we were doing and that it was more for her. She'd only looked uncomfortable and shrugged before flashing a big smile.

"She seems to love it here," Raiven observed as we watched Presley clap and laugh as the elephants sprayed water with their trunks.

"The elephants are her favorite but she likes the monkeys too. I wouldn't be surprised if she grew up to be a zoologist." I had no idea why I was sharing so much with her, I hadn't even wanted her along, but now I was all mixed-up inside.

"Pwincess Waiben! Wook! Wook at hims twunk!" Stray hairs had escaped her braid and blew haphazardly across her face. She shoved them back.

Raiven crouched down by her, placing a hand on her back as she watched from my daughter's vantage point with her. When she pulled something from her hair and pinned Presley's stray strands back, I knew where the random bobby pin I'd found in her hair earlier had come from.

Seeing that did weird shit to my insides.

It made me wonder if Letty would've done that. Then it hurt my chest again, because I'd never know, and Presley would never know her mom. It also made me wonder if I was enough. She was getting to the point where she needed a female influence in her life. And I'd taken her from my mom and every female she knew.

Scrubbing my hands over my face, I exhaled roughly. "You girls ready to move on?"

"We see duh monkeys now?" Presley's eyes were wide with excitement.

"Sure, kiddo. Let's go see the stinky old monkeys." She clasped my hand and began to tug me forward. Then she suddenly stopped and looked up to Raiven. When she reached for Raiven's hand, my breath caught.

"Dey not stinky, Pwincess Waiven. Dey so vewy cute!"

Bright blue eyes found mine, and I knew she was seeing the connecting link that my daughter was between us. As if we were a family walking hand in hand.

Bizarre as it may seem, the thought didn't make me want to snatch up my daughter and run for the hills. I had no fucking clue what was going on in my head.

The rest of the afternoon lasted longer than I anticipated. I really thought Presley would fade quickly, but it was like the zoo had energized her. By the time we were getting in the Uber to return to the hotel, my phone was ringing.

"Yo," I answered after seeing the caller ID.

"Hey bro, we're at the hotel waiting on you. You guys eat yet?" Gunny asked.

"No, we were thinking about ordering a pizza and having it delivered."

"I'm good with that. We can swing over to the gas station and get drinks. Text me what you want."

"Cool. Thanks. See you there."

Presley fell asleep on the way back to the hotel. No surprise there. I hated that she wasn't in a car seat, but it was a short trip so I kept my fingers crossed.

Raiven was quiet on the way back. She mostly stared out the window while she absently ran her finger back and forth over the little hand that rested on her thigh.

We unloaded at the hotel, and the guys pulled up at the same time.

I waited for them to park. As they reached me, they held the bags they'd pulled from their saddle bags in one hand and gave me one-armed hugs.

Raiven was unusually quiet as she stood back.

"Hey bro, how was the trip?" I asked Soap and my brother.

"Fucking awesome. I could ride the back roads anytime." Soap grinned, and I couldn't help but bristle as his eyes trailed Raiven from head to toe.

"Since this fucker is a rude bastard, I'm his big brother. They call me Gunny." My brother reached out a meaty hand that engulfed Raiven's as she tentatively shook it.

"Hi. Raiven." A bright grin spread over her face. It irked the fuck out of me that she was smiling like that for my brother when I got sass and attitude.

Soap slickly slid in and shook her hand next. "Hey, I'm Soap."

Holding her hand longer than necessary, he stared into her eyes and grinned his pretty-boy smile. Little fucker gave Hollywood a run for his money with his GQ looks.

"Nice to meet you, Soap." She smirked. "Did your mom not like you or were you just a dirty boy?"

"Oh, I'm dirty all right." His grin turned mischievous as he leaned closer to her.

My blood boiled, and I intentionally stepped between them as I walked toward the elevator instead of going around. "Let's go, she's getting heavy."

I was being a rude fucker, and I knew it.

"Getting weak in your old age? I could've carried her up for you if she's too much for you." Soap snickered, and I wanted to punch him between the eyes.

"Fuck off."

The guys dropped their bags off in the room they'd snagged next door to us.

I carried my sleeping daughter into our room and laid her on the bed.

"Umm, I'm gonna grab a quick shower and change, if that's okay." She tried to look aloof as she grabbed some things from her bag.

"Sure," I said as I pulled up a pizza place on my phone. "Anything special you want on your pizza?"

"I'm kind of picky. I only like pepperoni." She bit that lip, and my fucking jeans got tight in the crotch. Things were getting ridiculous. Turning away, I nodded and placed the order. When I heard the bathroom door close and the shower start up, I adjusted my junk.

The thought of her less than twenty feet away, wet and naked, was driving me crazy, and it pissed me the fuck off. Hell, I'd had plenty of opportunities over the past year.

The thing was, until this chick, I hadn't given a single fuck about sex.

After Gunny and Soap got their shit straight, they came next door. Raiven was still in the shower.

"Lock, we need to talk. Shit is getting real, bro. The fucking Demons Runners sent a package to the clubhouse right before we left." Gunny spoke softly as he glanced at the bathroom door and at my sleeping daughter.

"What kind of package?" My eyes narrowed, and I cocked my head slightly.

Soap, who was usually pretty happy-go-lucky, sobered quickly. His jaw clenched, and he gripped the back of his neck.

"It had DJ's dog in it. He was dead. Shot between the eyes. DJ lost his shit." Soap swallowed hard. "But that wasn't the worst part."

"Christ almighty, spit it the fuck out. It's not like we have a lot of time." I tipped my head toward the bathroom, where the water was shutting off.

Gunny stepped closer and placed a firm hand over my shoulder. His blue eyes mirrored mine as he held my gaze. "There was a note in there that said you and Presley were next."

Fury raced through my veins. Not at the threat to myself. I couldn't give a shit less if they threatened me every day all day. But bringing my kid into it was signing their death warrants. Club, brothers, cops be fucking damned.

No one threatened my baby girl.

"They are dead. I will kill every fucking one of them if I have to," I ground out through gritted teeth.

"You need to think clearly, bro. We'll talk more after we eat. Soap will sit in the lobby to keep an eye out. I'll take turns swapping out with him every few hours throughout the night."

"I told you I don't need a fucking babysitter." I was fuming.

"Yeah, well that little girl is pretty fucking special to me too. She may not be my daughter, but she's probably the closest I'll ever get to having one. If you think I'm not going to do everything in my power to keep her safe, you're out of your fucking mind." Gunny spoke low and as forcefully as I had.

"We'll talk after everyone eats." I was done talking about it, and

I wasn't discussing club business and my personal business in front of Raiven.

Raiven stepped out of the bathroom fluffing her hair with a towel right as the pizza was arriving. Both Gunny and Soap were damn near drooling at her tatted legs and perky tits in the little tiny running shorts and tank top she'd put on. Pushing past them, I paid for the pizza and closed the door.

"You better hurry up and eat so you can get downstairs," I barked at Soap.

Gunny's eyes flickered from me to Soap to Raiven before a shit-eating grin spread across his face. "Oh, so it's like that."

"No. It's not fucking like that. Let's eat."

Gunny woke Presley with a little kiss to her cheek. "Hey, little Elvis. Pizza's here."

Sleepily, she blinked as she tried to wake up. When it settled into her sleep-addled brain who was waking her, she shot upright in bed. "Unka Gunny!"

"Hey, little Elvis. How was the zoo?" Gunny lifted my daughter into his arms, and she rubbed her eyes before hugging him tightly around the neck.

"It was 'mazing!" My little girl's smile was infectious, and everyone was smiling at her exuberance.

"Let's eat!" said Soap as he rubbed his hands together.

"Raiven?" I glanced her way, trying not to stare or let my eyes roam where they had no business going. "Food's here."

"Thanks, I kinda figured that." Her eyes followed my brother's, and I realized Soap was loading up a plate.

"Yo, you better get some before I get seconds." Soap took a big bite out of his top piece and grinned at Raiven as he paused in eating.

Gunny had Presley telling him everything about the zoo as she chewed. Rolling my eyes, I chided, "Presley, don't talk with your mouth full."

It didn't take long to polish off the food. Gunny caught my eye and made a motion with his head for us to go next door.

"Let me give Presley a bath and then I'll be able to go." The guys headed to their room.

I stepped closer to Raiven to speak quietly. "Hey, if I bathe her and get her ready for bed, would you mind sitting here with her for about an hour? We have business to discuss."

"Is everything okay?" She seemed really nervous.

"It's all good. Just some club business."

"Club business?" Obviously, even though her uncle had been a member of the Demented Sons from the beginning, it wasn't a life she was familiar with personally.

"Yeah." I didn't elaborate.

"If you're okay with it, I can bathe her so you can go now," she offered.

I hesitated because I really didn't know her and it was my little girl. She was Pops's niece, and she hadn't done anything crazy all day. I would be right next door, just steps away, but when it comes to your kid, you question everyone.

"Umm, I—" Before I could finish my answer, the little munchkin in question piped in.

"Pwincess Waiven giff me a baff!" Clapping and jumping, she squealed with excitement.

Sighing, I told myself I was generally a good judge of character and I hadn't gotten any weird vibes off her all day. "Okay. But I'll only be next door if you need anything."

By the smirk on her face, I knew she also caught my meaning that I wouldn't be far away.

"Yes, sir." She gave me a cocky salute that caused her tits to jiggle, and I had to tear my gaze away. The throaty chuckle that followed me as I got Presley's clean pajamas and shit told me she'd caught me. It also had me wanting to turn around and push her against the wall. Not to hurt her, but to taste her and touch her until I showed her who ran shit.

If my daughter hadn't been there, I think I might have. Except she was a complication I neither needed nor wanted in my life.

"Daddy will be back in a bit. You listen to Princess Raiven." Fuck, there I was referring to her as a goddamn princess.

"Otay, Daddy!" my daughter exclaimed before she hugged me and gave me a big kiss.

I cast one last glance at the woman who was fucking with my head.

This was going to be a long fucking trip.

SEVEN

Raiven

"HIGHWAY TO HELL"—AC/DC

"**D**addy giff me a Mohawk wiff da bubbows. You do it," the little girl instructed me as I shampooed her silky, fine blonde hair. At first, I wasn't sure how to go about bathing a kid. Then I figured it couldn't be much different than bathing myself.

"Oh he does, does he?" The corner of my lips tipped up at the image I had of the tatted-up biker dude making soap Mohawks in his kid's hair.

"Yep." Her sage nod had me full-on grinning. Though her language skills were muddled with her inability to say *R*'s or *L*'s well, she was quite an old soul. I wondered if it was simply who she was or if it was a direct reflection of being raised by a big, burly man like Matlock.

Working up a good lather, I sculpted her hair into a big, soapy mohawk.

"There. How's that?" I helped her stand in the tub so she didn't slip and she could see in the mirror. Her giggle told me I'd done an acceptable job.

I rinsed her hair, conditioned it, then let her play for a little bit. Once I noticed her fingers pruning up, I told her it was time to get out. I expected her to throw a fit. That's what I figured kids did.

Instead, she shocked me by hopping up and raising her arms as I drained the water. I wrapped a bright white towel around her and plucked her out of the tub. I hated to admit I was getting the hang of this kid stuff pretty easily.

"Do you need my help getting dressed or can you do it yourself?" Her dad had all her stuff setting on the bed.

"I do it mysewf." There was a bottle of baby lotion that smelled like lavender, and I wasn't sure if she could do that part.

"How about if I put the lotion on you to make you smell like a pretty princess, then you get yourself dressed?" I tried to make it sound like an exciting idea. Truthfully, I wasn't sure if I was doing any of this right. I should've gotten more instruction from Matlock before he left.

The little girl's eyes narrowed for a moment, then she grinned. "Otay," she conceded.

Slathering the lotion on her arms and legs, I decided that was good enough. People were weird these days. I didn't want Matlock thinking I'd done anything wrong. He'd trusted me to take care of his daughter. I had a feeling that was big.

A glance at the clock in the room told me my aunt and uncle would still be up. I hadn't talked to them all day and I wanted to check on them. Chewing on my lip, I debated whether it would be safe to turn my phone on for a brief period. It would only be a couple of minutes, I rationalized.

Grabbing my phone from my purse, I supervised as the little girl pulled on a pair of underwear that looked kind of like a diaper, then a pair of pink pajamas with unicorns riding motorcycles. Go figure. I snickered then looked at my phone in indecision.

Surely if I kept the phone on for less than a minute, Stefano wouldn't be able to find me? He couldn't have someone watching for it every second. They were probably only checking every hour or something. Powering it up, I sent a quick text to my aunt. Relief filled me when she replied all was well.

"You read to me?" Presley pulled a book out of a little backpack and handed it to me as she barreled into my legs. I almost fell over so I dropped my phone back in my purse and scooped her up.

I settled her under the covers and began to read. About halfway through the book, the lock clicked on the door and Matlock entered.

At his grin, I furrowed my brow in question.

He raised a brow and nodded to my side.

When I glanced down, I noticed my charge was fast asleep and I'd been reading to myself.

"Oh," I whispered.

"She's had a long day. Thanks for taking care of her." He grabbed a few things out of his bag. "You mind if I shower?"

"Of course not."

Without another word, he closed himself in the bathroom. The water turned on, and I heard the shower curtain slide open, then closed.

Images bombarded my brain of him naked in the hot water. In my mind, I saw water trail down over his pecs and down to his....

I shook my head to clear the visual. It stuck there.

Getting up, I wandered around the room, straightening this and that. When there was nothing left to clean up, I sat in the chair by the window and pulled the curtain to the side to peek out into the night. Two more motorcycles pulled up, and I wondered if they were friends of Matlock and his brothers or if they were random guys looking for a place to sleep.

Closing the curtains, I sat staring into space. Again, I saw Matlock's tatted-up body slick with water and begging for my tongue to worship it.

A knock at the door startled me out of my reverie, and I jumped up to see who it was.

Except before I could get there, the bathroom door flew open and I ran smack-dab into a damp, inked-up, perfectly sculpted chest.

"Oh shit!" My hands went out to push myself back, but as soon as they made contact with his warm skin, tingles and shockwaves ran through my fingertips and up to the roots of my hair.

Wide-eyed, I glanced up at him before stepping quickly back. "I'm sorry!"

Truth was, I was anything but. Good Lord, did he feel good. The visualizations in my mind quickly went from the NC-17 that they'd been before to extremely X-rated.

His nostrils flared, and he stepped back as well. Hooded blue eyes watched me like I was a strange, alien being he couldn't figure out. Then he turned to the door I'd been headed toward and looked through the peephole.

Opening it right as Gunny had raised his hand to knock again, he stepped back to let him in, holding a finger to his lips and pointing to the sleeping girl.

I noticed Gunny was on the phone. He turned it on speaker, and I heard Soap talking but I didn't know who he was talking to.

"You make it home okay? How did work go today? I know it's only been three days but I miss you. Yeah, hold on, let me go outside where I have better signal."

When I looked from Matlock to Gunny, they both had furrowed brows. There was a change in background noise as he stepped out of the hotel into the night.

"Two Demon Runners are at the front desk asking for her. Described Raiven to a T, and one said she was his sister. She got a brother?" They both looked to me. I shook my head.

"My guts are sayin' this ain't good. We need to move. Get out. Take the back door. I'll catch up after I see y'all leave. Have her duck down when you go past the front doors. Move quick." Without waiting for confirmation from either of the two men with me, he hung up the phone.

"I'll go grab our things too. Back in two." Gunny left the room in a hurry.

"We need to go. Get your shit. We have five minutes." Matlock spouted the orders, then stepped back in to the bathroom but didn't close the door. I couldn't help but stand there transfixed as he dropped the towel and started to dress. He pulled jeans on commando, and it was impossible to miss him tucking the biggest dick I'd ever seen inside.

"Pick your jaw up off the floor and let's go." His tone was firm, but there was a hint of a smile on his lips.

Spurred into action, I slipped on a pair of slides, tossed the few things I had unpacked back in into my suitcase, and zipped it shut.

While I'd been doing that, he'd done the same. Another knock on the door had Matlock pulling a pistol out of a holster on his belt. I didn't know how I'd missed that before. A quick peek and he opened the door. Gunny had two small bags in his hands.

"Ready?" He looked around the room. "Give me your bag and you grab Elvis."

Matlock nodded, tossed his bag to his brother, tucked the gun in the holster, and gently lifted his daughter to his arms.

"Let's go."

Pulling my suitcase behind me, I grabbed Presley's small backpack and moved quickly between the two men.

Fear and adrenaline raced through my veins as we hurried out of the hotel.

In no time, Presley was buckled in and, with only a minor grumble as he placed her in her car seat, she remained sleeping. He tossed all the bags in the back seat, and he and Gunny exchanged a few quiet words.

Matlock leaped into the truck, and we pulled out. Gunny was right behind us. As instructed, I leaned down as we passed the front doors of the hotel.

Once we were nearing the parking lot entrance, I sat up. A car was turning in. It all seemed to happen in slow motion. The back window rolled down, and my eyes glued to a pair of dark brown ones.

The same dark brown eyes I thought I'd been in love with once upon a time.

Stefano.

"Go! Oh my God, Matlock, go!" My heart was pounding to the point of exploding.

Thankfully, Matlock heeded my urgency, and we peeled out of the lot as if the hounds of hell were on our heels.

He didn't know it, but they were.

"What's going on?" He checked his rearview. "Who's that?"

"Just go." My entire body shook in fear.

"Who. The. Fuck. Is. It?"

I had no idea how he'd possibly known where I was, since I hadn't used a single credit card during the trip.

My phone vibrated in my bag. Panic reared its head when I realized I'd forgotten to shut it off after sending the text to my aunt. Stefano's smiling face and his name flashed on my screen. I hit Ignore.

Staring at my phone where it lay in my trembling hand, I realized I'd fucked up. Bad.

"Raiven. Goddammit. Answer me. Who was that? And who's calling you? I thought you said you shut it off!" Glancing his direction, I saw the muscle in his jaw tick.

"I wanted to check on my aunt and uncle," I whispered. My phone vibrated again. I stared at it like it would bite me.

"Why didn't you just ask to use my phone?" He sounded exasperated.

"I don't know. You were with your friends and I didn't mean to leave it on. I only meant to have it on for a minute." I bit my lip.

"Answer it."

Not hesitating at his demand, I swiped the screen and held it to my ear. My hand shook so hard I was afraid I'd drop it. Words escaped me.

"Raiven. What do you think you're doing?" The sinister sound of his voice over the phone made my stomach churn.

"I don't know what you're talking about. Leave me alone, Stefano. I told you I'm not saying anything." My voice came across stronger than I actually was in that moment.

"It's too late for that. You know that."

A large tatted hand was suddenly in front of my face. "Give me the phone."

Without a complaint, I dropped it in his hand as if it was on fire.

"Listen, you fuck. Leave her alone or you'll be dealing with me. You feel me?" Matlock ground out in a low growl.

"Who the fuck are you?" I heard Stefano yell.

"Someone you don't want to fuck with." Matlock ended the call, and his gaze flickered in my direction. "You bring this phone with you from Chicago?"

I nodded. Tears floated in my lower lids.

He rolled down the window and tossed it out.

"What are you doing?" I shrieked, then looked back to see my phone as it bounced and shattered all over the road. Suddenly afraid my scream had woken Presley, I looked at her as she slept, peacefully oblivious in her seat.

"If your phone's been on the whole time, he's probably been tracking you since Chicago."

"You don't really think he tracked my phone. Do you?" Except deep down, I knew that was the type of power men like him had.

Fear that he had done exactly that had me swallowing hard as the tears that had previously hovered began to fall.

Fuck that phone. I'd get a different phone on the way. There was nothing in that thing I was worried about more than my life or those of my aunt and uncle. And now the two other people in the truck with me.

In less than twenty-four hours, Matlock and Presley had become two of the most important people in my life. A fact I was sure he wouldn't appreciate now that I'd brought this shit to his proverbial doorstep.

EIGHT

"EVERYTHING FALLS APART"—KORN

Gunny was on our tail as the lights of town faded in the background. Within approximately thirty minutes, a second headlight sped up out of the night and joined Gunny behind us. Knowing Soap was safe eased the tension in my chest slightly but my adrenaline was on overdrive.

"I need to know everything. Now," I demanded. I wasn't in the mood to use kid gloves.

"What do you mean?"

"Don't play stupid. That's not just some possessive, abusive boyfriend. Is he with the Demon Runners?"

"Who?" She seemed genuinely confused. "I don't know who that is."

"The Demon Runners were at the front desk asking for you by name and description. Then we pass that car and you freak the fuck out. Which is quickly followed by what I can only assume was your boyfriend calling. Tell me how far off I am."

She sniffled, and I quickly glanced her way. Despite the tears, her head was held high and her mouth was a flat line.

"Tell me who he is or I'll drop your ass off on the side of the road. My daughter is in the truck. If she's in danger because of you, I have a right to know why." I wouldn't really drop her off like that but I needed to fucking know why the crazy bastard had followed her all this way. My gut told me there was way more to her story than I'd been given. I wondered if Pops knew the whole story.

Her eyes dropped closed and her head tipped to the headrest. Defeat filled her tone. "I thought I won the lottery with Stefano at first."

Impatiently, I waited for her to continue, shoulders tense.

"He was attentive, sweet, lavished me with gifts, bought me jewelry, a new phone, took me to fancy dinners, everything a girl would want. I thought I loved him." The last was a tortured whisper. It made my teeth grind.

Taking a deep breath, she started to speak but her voice cracked. Risking a glance her direction, I caught the glint of tears tracking down her cheeks. Without thinking, I reached over and clasped her hand in mine.

The contact was electric. I'd be a fucking liar if I said it didn't scare the fuck out of me. Except I didn't have time to deal with processing those feelings.

"What changed?"

She sniffled and turned her head to stare out into the blackness of the night. "He'd gotten controlling, but at the time I hadn't noticed it. He hated my job, didn't like me touching other men. He didn't like my clothes because they were too revealing. He didn't like my friends. Little things like that. I was out to dinner with some friends from school. We were having girls' night, a reunion sort of. Stefano and I had argued about it. He finally agreed to let me go. While we were having dinner, I saw Stefano enter the restaurant and head toward the back. I was excited to see him and wanted to apologize for our argument, so I told the girls I'd be right back. I saw him enter a door at the end of the back hall. I almost turned around, but figured I'd just say hi then leave him be. Except, as I reached the door, I saw it was mostly closed. He was talking to a man sitting at the desk. I didn't hear what they said but it seemed like they knew each other. Then Stefano pulled out a gun and...." She choked and her entire body shuddered. I squeezed her hand.

"Oh my God, Lock, he shot him. Twice in the chest and once in the head. It was so quiet. I thought gunshots would be loud. The sound of that man's head exploding was louder than the gun. The blood. Oh my God, there was so much blood. I fell backwards and bumped a picture on the wall. Stefano whipped around and saw me before I could think. I thought he was going to kill me next. He smiled. It was so reptilian. He was on me before I could get my shit together. I begged him not to kill me." She gave a sad laugh.

I stayed silent and let her talk.

"He told me he wasn't going to kill me as long as I could be quiet. I promised him I wouldn't say a word. He pulled me into the room and shoved the gun in my hand. I remember staring at it like I'd never seen one. Then he whispered in my ear that if I left, my prints would be on the gun. That's when I realized he'd been wearing gloves. He left and came back quickly with my purse. I can only guess what he told my friends. He took me to his apartment. He... he...." A sob escaped her, and I rubbed her hand with my thumb. The need to kill the bastard with my bare hands was overwhelming.

"I could barely crawl out of bed, but as soon as he left the next morning, I snuck out. Call it divine intervention, but my uncle called and said he was coming through to see my dad and did I want to have lunch while he was there. I raced to my apartment, packed my bag, and left. I literally rode the train and buses all over town, back and forth. I even slept on the train until I got a phone call from the nursing home where my dad lived. He'd died in his sleep, they said." She sobbed and sniffled again. I was afraid I knew where this was all going.

Then she confirmed my suspicions. "Stefano called my phone. He'd been texting me, but I hadn't answered. After getting the news about my dad, I wasn't thinking straight, and I answered. He told me my dad was a warning, if I didn't come back, he would find me and I'd be next. I wasn't dumb enough to believe he wouldn't kill me anyway. I called my uncle to tell him about Dad and that I needed to get out of town. He argued that we needed to deal with my dad first. When I broke down and told him my boyfriend had beat the shit out of me, he wanted to go fuck Stefano up, so I told him I needed out of town ASAP, he met me at the bus station, and we left town. Dad had actually already made all of his arrangements years ago. He wanted to be cremated with no ceremony and placed in the veterans' cemetery, also with no ceremony. It killed me not to be there even though he had set things up that way." She quietly cried, and I let her.

My mind was reeling. I needed to talk to Gunny and Soap, but they were on their bikes. We'd barely crossed into Kansas. My plan had been to hit the turnpike and skip the stops I'd initially planned along the way.

Deciding I'd stop in Topeka to fill up, I looked her way before returning my eyes to the road. "Pops know Stefano killed his brother?"

"No," she whispered. "I was afraid he'd try to go after him. I didn't want him going up against Stefano after what I'd witnessed." Her horrified gaze met mine as I'd looked her way again. "He killed that man in cold blood without a bit of remorse."

I kept the fact that I'd killed without remorse to myself. Even though the situations were different. A combat situation changed the rules on killing someone. Especially when it's self-defense. Them or me.

"What did Stefano do for a living?" I had a sneaking suspicion but I wondered if she'd realized.

"I'm not sure. He always told me he was in the personal security and investment business."

I snorted.

We reached the edge of Topeka, and I pulled into the first well-lit gas station. The guys pulled in behind me.

"Stay in here with Presley." She nodded, fear in her eyes that tore me up inside.

The guys had each pulled in on either side of the pump behind mine. I started the gas, then moved in their direction.

"What the fuck was that back there?" Gunny was the first to ask.

"Fuck. Evidently, she doesn't know anything about the Demon Runners, but the car we passed was her ex. I'm not sure, but I have a feeling he's connected with the mafia from what she said." Frustrated, I ran my hand through my hair.

"Jesus," Gunny huffed.

"Well, that explains why he whipped around and tried to follow you guys," Soap piped in.

"What happened, by the way? I was getting worried when you took so long to catch up."

He grinned. "Well, I pulled out in front of him in a way they couldn't get around me and pretended I couldn't get my bike started. He was pissed and cussed me out. I was ever so apologetic." He snickered. "When I figured you had a good enough head start and before the Demon Fuckers came back out, I miraculously got it to start. I made sure they weren't following me and then caught up to you." He shrugged like it was no big deal.

"We need to be careful. I think he was tracking her phone." I shoved my hands in my pockets. Now I was worried about my daughter, the woman in my care, and my brothers. We were in a shit storm of a situation.

"So that's what went flying out the window. Thanks for that, by the way. You damn near hit me, fucker," Gunny grumbled.

"Sorry about that."

"Yeah, right. So now what? I'm getting tired. There hasn't been anyone following us. How much longer before we stop to get some shut-eye?" Gunny scratched his beard and yawned.

"We might as well see what's here, because soon we'll hit the turnpike and then the places to stop are extremely limited." They both nodded at my suggestion.

"I'll get the rooms, since he may have figured out who you are if he saw your plates." Soap nodded toward my truck.

"Good point." I searched on my phone for the nearest decent hotel. "This okay with you two?" I showed them what I'd found.

"Sounds good. Fuck, as long as there's a bed and a pillow, I'm good. Let's go." Gunny grabbed his helmet and mounted up.

I put the nozzle back and grabbed my receipt. Scared blue eyes met mine when I climbed in.

"Now what? You want me to take a bus from here? I'm okay with that. I'm sorry I involved you in this. I didn't want to, but I also didn't think he'd follow me, let alone find me." Her nose was red and slightly swollen, and her beautiful eyes were red from crying.

"Hell no, I'm not leaving you. I promised to get you safely to Styx, and that hasn't changed." What had changed was me wanting to leave her with him. He was single and a decent-looking guy. The thought of her being with him set my teeth on edge.

I checked to make sure Presley was still sleeping and started the truck. "We're stopping for the night."

"Okay" was all she said. I didn't like that the previously spunky woman was so beaten down and subdued.

It didn't take long for us to find the hotel and get checked in. We only brought the necessities in with us in case we needed to leave quickly again.

By the time we all made it up to our rooms, we were dragging ass. I laid Presley in one of the beds and stepped back into the hall. Raiven went into the bathroom.

"I plan to be back on the road by eight. You guys good with that?" I asked. That gave us about five or six hours of sleep.

Soap looked at his watch. "Sounds good."

Gunny nodded. "See you in the morning, little brother."

He hugged me, and I was grateful Snow had sent them. Soap grasped my hand and gave me a one-arm hug.

"See you in the morning. Well, later." Ever happy, he smiled and entered the room he'd got for himself and Gunny.

"Hey, Gunny." I stopped him as he moved to follow Soap.

"Yeah?"

"I love you, bro."

The corner of his mouth tipped up. "Love you too, man."

He closed his door, and I stepped next door to our room. Stopping in the entryway, I glanced at Presley as I locked the door. Seeing her sleeping soundly sent a familiar pang through my heart. She was my world.

Raiven was coming out of the bathroom as I turned, and she stopped short, staring at me.

She was getting under my skin something fierce. I didn't know what the fuck was passing between us, but my heart sped up and adrenaline hit me as we stood there. It was like being on the precipice of something big. Like when I was deployed. That feeling I'd get right before we'd entered a village to kick down doors.

"Matlock." Her single word spoke volumes. I loved my full name on her lips.

I stepped closer, her magnetism pulling me in. She instinctively stepped back, putting herself in the bathroom.

Without thought, I moved forward, closing the door once we were both inside. She was still in the tiny tank and shorts she'd been wearing when we left the last hotel. Her full breasts rose and fell with each rapid breath she took, making the peaking of her nipples impossible to miss.

My hand was buried in her dark hair before I realized what I was doing. So close, her warm breath feathered across my lips. I wanted, no, I needed to taste her. When she didn't stop me, I slid my lips across hers.

Tentative.

Seeking.

"So fucking sweet." The tip of my tongue teased the curve of her bottom lip.

With a moan, I cupped her neck with my other hand, spanning her throat and cradling her jaw.

Her hands clutched my shirt. I leaned in closer until my body practically wrapped around her. Need drove us.

I sought entrance, and with a gasp, she granted me access.

God, her taste was pure heaven.

We desperately devoured each other. I tightened my fist around her inky locks while the fingers of my other hand flexed slightly around the white column of her throat. Her moan vibrated across my palm.

The need to consume her was stronger than anything I'd ever experienced.

I found myself wanting to own her heart, body, and soul.

Pulling away from her rapidly addictive lips, I rested my cheek on her, closed my eyes, and fought to evenly inhale. Turning my head a fraction of an inch, I muttered against her temple, "Goddamn, this is so wrong."

I was losing my fucking mind.

Her swallow was audible between her panted breaths. I wasn't the only one straining to breathe normally.

My actions didn't follow my words though. No matter what I'd said, my nose trailed her tenderly, scenting her as I struggled for control.

Before I knew it, my mouth was skimming back over her kiss-swollen lips.

"Wrong," she whispered in agreement.

"Wrong, but I still fucking want you." There was no denying it as I pressed my hard shaft into her softness. Seeking relief. Seeking respite. Needing her.

"Fuck, yes," she gasped.

Though I told myself it was a reaction to the stress and adrenaline of our flight, part of me knew it was a lie.

I didn't give her time to change her mind, because I didn't want to examine my own thought processes. Jerking her shorts down, I groaned when she didn't have panties on under them. Fuck, I'd ridden all that way with her having nothing under those skimpy-ass shorts.

Her fingers fumbled with the button on my pants, and I pushed her hands out of the way, jerking everything open. Once my cock was free of my jeans, I let them fall to my hips and lifted her to the bathroom counter.

"Matlock," she whimpered as I stroked my length a few times while staring at her glistening pink pussy. She reached forward and grabbed the sides of my jeans, jerking me forward.

Fisting her hair, I tipped her head back. My mind was a fucked-up jumble as I actually smelled her need. Lining the tip of my cock with her slick center, I circled it in her wetness before grabbing her hip with my free hand and pulling her to the edge of the counter and onto me.

It only took a short thrust of my hips and I sank to the base of my cock in her warm sheath. "Jesus fucking Christ, you feel so goddamn fucking good."

Control was dwindling quickly. I had to hold myself still for a minute because I was ready to come already.

When she began to wiggle, seeking the friction of her clit against me, I was done. No control, no clarity of thought, nothing but how fucking incredible it was to be deep inside her.

After only a few strokes, I was on the edge and she was panting heavily. Not ready for the feeling to end, I pulled out, yanked her off the counter, and turned her around. Our eyes met in the mirror as I gripped both ass cheeks and spread her open to me.

There was no fumbling. I slid right in as if it was where I'd always belonged. Like her pussy was home.

"Fuck." It was the only cognizant word I could form as I started fucking her hard and fast. Seeing my cock sliding in, then come out shining with her creamy, wet excitement held me transfixed. Bold-colored tattoos peeked from under her shirt on each hip that I wanted to study but couldn't focus on. It wasn't long before I needed to see her expression, and I met her gaze in the mirror again.

Her full lips were red and puffy from our kiss and slightly parted. Her hooded eyes held mine. Vaguely, I was aware of her tits shaking with each hard plunge of my cock into her depths. It made me swell with need. I knew I was close.

"Touch your clit. Make yourself come." It was a rasping demand that she immediately obeyed.

Seeing her hand reach down between her legs as I fucked her drove me crazy. Skin slapping with each thrust, I threw my head back as her pussy tightened around me. She was so goddamn tight I couldn't hold back any longer.

Two hard strokes, and I growled as my spine tingled and my balls tightened. The explosion that was my release had me seeing spots, and my knees actually buckled.

"Matlock! Oh my God! Shit! I'm coming. Ohmagod!" Everything came out as a whispered shout, both of us aware of Presley sleeping on the other side of that door.

As we pulsed and clenched together, I stood her upright, slipping my hands under her shirt and raising it to cup her tits. Finding her nipples pierced had my cock throbbing in her tight cunt again.

Using my nose to push her hair out of the way, I suckled and bit her neck, marking her with satisfaction. In that moment of post-orgasmic clarity, I knew I may be fucked, but she'd be mine.

Once I dropped down from my sexual high, I reluctantly slid out of her perfect pussy.

When our combined release slid down her thigh, I realized I'd fucked up. Massively.

"Aw, shit. I'm so sorry." Swallowing hard, I met her wide eyes. It had obviously dawned on her too.

"Please tell me you're clean," she frantically whispered.

"Fuck yeah, I'm clean. Are you? And the better question is if I just got you fucking pregnant." Worry slammed into me, but what surprised me was there was no regret for being with her.

"I've never had unprotected sex in my life. And we should be fine." Brow furrowed, she bit her lip.

"Should be? You're not on the pill? Maybe I should go get a Plan B pill for you."

"No, I'm not on the pill. He always used condoms, so I never...." She trailed off. "Besides, it's not the right time of the month." She closed her eyes, and I grabbed a washcloth and turned on the warm water.

Her eyes remained closed as I cleaned her up and cursed myself for my stupidity and impulsivity. Then I processed the anger that had surged when she'd merely hinted at the fucker she'd been with.

The thought of any other man's hands on her had me seeing red. I had to shake my head to get the image to disperse.

Though in the after-sex euphoria I'd claimed her as mine, I knew better. A woman was the last complication I needed in my life.

My only defense for what I'd done was the absolute craziness of the last twenty-four hours.

Once she was clean, I dried her, wiped myself, then tucked my dick in my pants.

"You take the free bed, I'll sleep on the floor."

She looked at me like I had a dick on my forehead. "We just fucked like rabbits in a hotel bathroom. I think we can share a bed so you don't have to sleep on the floor. Or you could sleep with Presley. She's small enough."

"That's probably not a good idea," I muttered. The reasons behind that weren't something I wanted to discuss with her.

"I'll stay on my side of the bed. That," her hands waved around toward the counter, "won't happen again."

Hesitating, I debated the intelligence of sharing a bed with her. There were things she didn't know or understand about me.

The problem was, I was tired, drained mentally, and now sexually sated, and I needed sleep. While I could sleep on the floor, I wouldn't sleep well.

"Fine. Let's get some sleep." I waited until she was in the bed facing the wall before I dropped my jeans to the floor and tugged my shirt over my head. Then I climbed in bed, keeping my back to her and space between us.

I expected to lie awake for hours like I usually did, but I drifted off almost immediately.

NINE

Raiven

"</CODE>"—MOTIONLESS IN WHITE

I awoke with a start when a heavy arm landed over me and heat pressed against my backside.

Before I could pull away or wake him up, he began to mumble words I couldn't understand and then pulled me tight to him. It was still dark out and I was tired, so I decided to go back to sleep and not speak of this in the morning.

I'm not sure how long I dozed before I woke to a hand cupping my boob and a hard rod nestled between my butt cheeks. "Oh my God," I mouthed.

It took a few a minutes to determine he was sleeping.

Trying to decide how to get out of his hold without waking him, I slowly lifted his arm and wiggled little by little to the edge of the bed. Once I was far enough, I gently set his arm down. Chancing a quick peek, I was relieved to see he was still out.

Taking the chance to study him, I followed the story his tattoos told all over his chest and arms. His tousled, dark-golden hair splayed over the pillow where it was long on top. His normally groomed beard was going every which way. Even in repose, his muscles were defined and drool-worthy. I almost giggled that his nipples were pierced too. "Samesies," I whispered, still feeling sex-drunk from our bathroom escapade.

Speaking of the bathroom, I suddenly was desperate to go. I tiptoed there, pausing to check that Presley was still asleep.

"Oh sweet Jesus." I caught my reflection as I sat on the toilet. There was no denying I'd been well fucked. Which I couldn't seem to find in me to regret.

I finished my business and tried to tame my wayward hair. Finding it hopeless, I decided to take a quick shower.

I'd been in there long enough to wash my hair when the curtain moved, and I jumped and squealed. My hands tried in vain to cover my lady bits and my boobs.

A brilliantly white grin was the response I got. "I've already seen it, you know. Mind if I join you?"

"In here?" I asked, wide-eyed and squeaky-voiced.

"No, in the parking lot. Yeah, in there." He didn't wait for my answer before he climbed in.

"What about Presley?" I grasped at a reason to get him out as I rapidly rinsed the soap from my body.

"She sleeps like the dead until at least seven. It's six-ten. We're safe." Appearing completely without concern, he moved me to the side to get wet. Then swapped us back as he began to soap his body and his hair. Drool pooled in my mouth.

"Umm, I'm done, I can get out," I offered.

"No."

"Excuse me?" I blinked dumbly at him.

He grasped my upper arms and switched places with me but held one arm as he rinsed off. Once he was done, he pulled me flush to his front, and his lips captured mine.

Melting against him, I slid my hands up water-slicked skin to his shoulders. He tasted of mint and I realized he'd brushed his teeth without me realizing it.

Our kiss deepened, and a low moan slipped from my throat. His hands skimmed up my spine and down again until he cupped my ass cheeks and squeezed. The motion pulled me against his erection, and I shamelessly rubbed on him.

He broke away, releasing his hold on my ass. "Turn around."

"We don't have anything!" I whisper-yelled.

"You said the timing was safe, and I won't come in you."

I clenched my thighs at the throbbing between them. I should've said no. I should've gotten out of the shower. Laughed in his face. Anything.

But did I? Hell no, I turned around like he said.

"Hands on the wall."

I complied.

He grabbed my hips, pulling back until my back was arched. His fingertips trailed up to trace the ink on my back that ran to my hips, sending a shiver through me.

A single thick finger slid up and down through my folds before sliding in and rubbing against my G-spot until I whimpered. Before I could process that he'd pulled it out, his thick cock was stretching me and shoving deep inside me.

"Oh God," I sighed. I'd never had a guy as big as he was, and that was the fucking truth. It was the perfect balance of pain and pleasure. Every single movement was sheer ecstasy. It was so good, I was on the verge of coming almost immediately. Three rapid thrusts and I came harder than last night. He continued to fuck me through the first orgasm until it bled right into another one.

My head was spinning.

Heart racing.

Limbs trembling.

His hand fisted my hair, yanking me upright as his lips trailed along my neck. Steam billowed around us as his tongue traced my skin. Teeth scraped along the most sensitive areas. I whined and ground against him.

It didn't matter that a tiny voice in my head was screaming I was crazy. Nor did it matter that I barely knew this man. The thoughts that my crazy ex was after me were mere murmurs against a crashing sea.

Nothing was more important than Matlock's hands clutching me tightly and his mouth torturing me in pleasure. Every thrust was a loud slap of wet skin against skin as my back bowed and the angle improved.

His constantly moving fingertips that traced my ink and teased me were sending me into sensory overload. Every touch was driving me higher until I shattered once more.

Hands splayed on the shower wall, I bit my own bicep to keep from screaming.

With a moan, he jerked out, then reached around to rub my clit as hot jets of his come splattered across my back and ass. The combination of his fingers working me over and knowing he'd painted me in his come had me quickly climaxing again.

"Jesus, woman. What the fuck kind of voodoo pussy do you have?"

"Me?" I gasped. "You with your wonder cock, there. Christ, you can't go in and out more than a handful of times and I'm coming!"

He chuckled as he washed off my back in the warm water and pulled me upright. After turning me around, he caged me against the wall and kissed me, ending with a light flick of his tongue. "So what are we going to do about this?"

"What do you mean? I thought we weren't doing 'this' again after last night. Then 'this' happened." My hand rapidly waved between us.

"Are you complaining?"

"Well, umm, I mean…." I choked. I really wasn't, but that didn't mean I thought it was a good idea.

He rested his forehead against mine briefly before leaning back and looking me in the eye. "Look, I know there is a lot of shit going on in both of our lives and this isn't something either of us planned.

In fact, it was the last thing on my mind. But we're both consenting adults. If we engage in adult activities that we both enjoy, is that a problem?"

"Honestly, I don't know." I took a deep breath. "You have a kid, Lock." I chewed on my lip in my uncertainty.

"So me having a daughter is a problem for something casual?" Worry filled me as I watched his eyes narrow and chill.

"That's not what I mean. She's a cool little girl." A smile ghosted over my lips. "But I don't want her getting hurt or confused about what this is. I also don't want to bring my shit to her." My lip trembled. If I was honest with myself, there was something about Matlock that made me worry my heart wouldn't be able to do casual with him.

"Hey. It's going to be okay." He pressed a kiss to the corner of my eye where tears welled.

"You don't know that. What if he catches up to us? What if he kills me? What if he kills you because you're with me and helped me? I need to go the rest of the way on my own."

"Over my dead body." His tone held something I couldn't decipher.

"That's exactly what I'm afraid of." Pressing my lips together in a flat line, I ducked under his arm and reached for a towel. He didn't stop me, but he did shut the water off and watch me intently as he dried off too.

"Between me, Gunny, and Soap, that piece of shit isn't going to get near you." The towel was secured low on his hips, and he ran his hands through his hair, pushing it back.

"You don't know that. You can't guarantee that. I need to split off from you. It's what's best."

I turned away, but he clasped my upper arm firmly, making me face him. "No."

"Why are you being so ridiculous about this? It was just yesterday that you didn't want me on this trip with you at all." Exasperation colored my words.

"Look, maybe this changed things. I don't know why or how, but it did. I'm not ready to let you go."

Call me irrational, but my hackles rose at his reasoning. It was too close to Stefano's possessive bullshit. "You don't have a say in what I do. You don't own me. I'm not your property. So you don't get to keep me or let me go," I lashed out before jerking my arm free.

Leaving the steamy bathroom and the man who had my head and insides jumbled, I grabbed clothes and began to dress.

He followed me out, but I ignored him.

As he dressed, I braided my hair. Knowing we needed to get on the road, I didn't bother with makeup. Silently, I packed up the few things I'd used.

It was nearly seven, and true to his prediction, Presley began to wake up. I had to bite my tongue when I found myself wanting to offer to get her ready.

The bizarre nature of my thoughts didn't escape me. Twenty-four hours ago, I wouldn't have so much as talked to a child unless I was forced.

Lost in my thoughts, I missed the quiet conversation he had with her as he dressed her still-sleepy form. What I did hear was her request after she saw me and smiled the sweetest, brightest grin.

"Daddy, you braid my haiw like Princess Waiven?" Her blue eyes looked up at him then to me as she waited for him to answer.

"Sure, baby girl." He proceeded to deftly braid her silky curls, which did something to me. I'm talking ovaries-exploding kind of something.

For the eighty-seventh time, I wondered how he ended up as a single dad raising a little girl. I knew Presley's mom was obviously out of the picture, but I couldn't imagine how she could not want to be a part of her little girl's life.

Memories of my dad raising me after my mom hauled ass flooded my mind. I'd been older than Presley at seven, but not by much. The difference being, I'd been old enough to remember her and miss her.

"You ready?" he asked me without looking in my direction.

"Yeah."

He picked up the room phone and called who I assumed were the other guys.

"Hey. You up and ready? Cool. We'll grab the continental breakfast, then pop smoke. See you down there." He hung up and lifted his daughter up to place a kiss on her cheek.

"You beawd tickos, Daddy." Her giggle brought a small smile to my lips that matched his.

He proceeded to rub it into her neck as she roared with laughter.

Then he stopped and kissed her nose. "Let's go eat."

"We hab panacakes?" Excitement lit her eyes and she clasped her hands together hopefully.

"We'll see what they have. It may be waffles. Let's go check it out."

He grabbed the small duffle he'd brought in with their combined belongings and waited at the door for me. I grabbed my big purse that I'd shoved my stuff in.

Gunny and Soap were waiting at the breakfast area for us with plates loaded down.

"Morning, gorgeous," Soap said with a grin on his handsome face and a bite of food poised to enter his mouth.

Turning at the growl I thought I heard come from Lock, I saw him quickly look away. He took Presley over to get food as I set my purse in a chair. Both men were staring at Matlock with raised brows and mouths agape.

"Something wrong?" I glanced from them to Matlock, trying to figure out what was going on.

"Uh, no." Gunny returned his attention to his food and seemed extremely focused on his plate.

"Okaaaay." Shaking my head, I followed Matlock and grabbed myself a plate of fruit, yogurt, and popped a bagel in the provided toaster.

"That's all you're eating?" he grumbled at me after I sat down.

Looking at my plate in confusion, because it was a lot considering

I rarely ate breakfast, I raised a brow. "It's plenty for me. Mind your own plate."

"Yeah, Daddy, mind you own pwate." Presley was so matter-of-fact in her comment before she shoved a huge piece of waffle into her mouth that Soap nearly snorted orange juice out of his nose. I had to pull my lips between my teeth to keep from laughing. Gunny held his napkin over his mouth.

"Hey. You better watch who you're talking to, pipsqueak." Her dad pointed his fork in her direction. In true Presley form, she raised her unfazed eyes to meet his as she put a forkful of food in her mouth. Half the eggs fell off and back onto the plate, but she was completely unconcerned.

His blue eyes looked more of a stormy gray that morning as he glared at his friends after he finished his food in record time. Matter of fact, all three guys had inhaled their food.

"Did any of you even taste your breakfast?" My eyes bugged at them.

In unison, they all said, "Military," as if that explained everything. If it weren't for growing up with my dad and my uncle, I wouldn't have understood. Since they were both veterans, I remembered them saying the army had taught them to eat when they could and quickly, because they never knew how long they'd have.

All I could do was shake my head at them.

"Any sign of trouble out there this morning?" Matlock asked the other two.

"None that I noticed." Soap became uncharacteristically somber.

"We about ready to roll?" Matlock pitched his empty plate in the nearby trash.

"I full." Presley had eaten nearly everything on her plate.

"Would you mind taking her to potty and washing her hands?" Matlock asked. By their expressions, I knew they wanted to talk about something without us being there.

"Sure. Come on, little princess. Let's clean you up so we can get on the road."

She climbed down and placed her sticky hand in mine. Where before I would've cringed at the feeling, that time I smiled and shook my head.

The little spitfire was doing crazy things to my head.

Just like her father.

TEN

Lock

"WHATEVER IT TAKES"—HOLLYWOOD UNDEAD

"**W**hat did you get back from Hacker? Anything useful?" I didn't waste time once Raiven and Presley were out of earshot.

We stepped out the front doors but kept an eye on the door to the bathroom for the girls to come out.

"Seems Stefano is a *soldato*, a made man with the De Luca family," Gunny quietly informed me.

"Jesus Christ. She knows how to pick them." I ran a frustrated hand through my hair.

"Hey, isn't Joker close with one of the De Luca cousins? That band member?" Soap piped in as he lit a cigarette and inhaled deeply.

Gunny and I looked at each other.

"On it." He stepped away and pulled out his burner phone to call Joker.

"You think that asshole is still following?" Soap took another drag.

"Yeah. After what she told me, I'd be surprised if he gave up." I'd filled them in briefly before I'd gone in the room the night before.

What are the fucking odds she was eating at the same restaurant where he goes in for a hit? Christ. That's some shit luck there." Finishing his smoke, he stubbed it out and flicked it out into the parking lot.

Gunny came back. "Joker and Hacker are on this one. Joker is contacting the cousin and Hacker is trying to see who it was that Stefano killed. Maybe that will give us some insight or leverage with this fucker. One of them will have info soon and call you, since Soap and I will be on the bikes."

"Sounds good." Except I had a bad feeling brewing.

Raiven and Presley came out of the bathroom, and I waved so they saw us outside.

"Let's load up and get down the road. We'll get on the turnpike and stop as needed but try to keep moving. Let me know if either of you need to gas up before I do." They nodded at me, and we got everything packed up, Presley buckled in with her headset on and movie playing, and on the road.

I didn't give Raiven the opportunity to bring up going off on her own again.

She was quiet for several miles before she spoke. "Matlock?"

"Yeah?"

"Where is Presley's mom?" A quick peek at her showed her staring out the window as she chewed on her lower lip.

"Presley's mom is…." I swallowed the lump in my throat. "She died over a year ago."

"Oh my God, I feel like a huge piece of shit. I didn't know. I only wondered if she would…. Well, never mind. It doesn't matter." The protective wall she threw up was almost visible.

Silence ensued after that.

We'd been traveling for a couple of hours when Soap rode up next to me and tapped on his tank. Giving him a nod, I watched for the next service area and pulled in.

"Goddamn, what a boring fucking ride," Soap bitched as he filled his tank. Gunny only laughed. He'd been down this road before when he went down to pick up a bike years ago. I remembered him telling me about it.

"Oh, come on, enjoy the ride." I chuckled.

"Hey, I love riding, but damn, it would be nice to look at something besides fields. Flat fields at that. Not even any hills or trees like we have at home." Soap returned the nozzle and cracked his back. "I gotta piss. You want anything?"

"Naw, but I gotta take Presley in to try to get her to go to the bathroom." I finished with my gas as I spoke.

"Too late." Gunny nodded toward the gorgeous raven-haired beauty walking my daughter back out to the truck, hand in hand. I watched as Raiven threw her head back to laugh at something my little girl had said. Her sleeves were brilliant in the sun, and I made a mental note to ask her who'd done her ink.

I cursed myself for being so preoccupied I hadn't noticed them get out.

"Goddamn, she's fine. Maybe I'll stay down in Texas too," Soap said with a grin as he headed to the building.

My hands clenched into fists at the thought of him trying to get with her. I wanted to throat punch him. It was a pivotal moment for me. One day and one incredible night with her, and I was completely and totally fucked.

Back on the road for less than an hour and both my girls were out.

My girls.

Yeah, absolutely fucked.

How did that shit even happen? I'd never laid eyes on her two days ago. Didn't know who she was or anything about her.

Now I was claiming her as mine? What the ever-loving fuck?

Presley still had her headphones on as her movie played, and Raiven had one of my hoodies wadded up as a pillow against the glass. She looked so damn young as she slept, and it made me wonder how fucking old she was.

When Hacker's info flashed on my truck screen, I turned the volume down and picked up the call. "Hey bro, what do you have for me?"

"Nothing you're gonna like. Joker is waiting for Dominic to call him back. He's trying to get in touch with his cousin, but he's out of the country right now." He sighed.

"Okay? Anything else? You said nothing I was going to like."

"Yeah, man. The only murder that fit the description you gave me was a Giacomo Caruso."

"Who the fuck is that?"

"Was, you mean? He was one of Lorenzo De Luca's *caporegimes*," Hacker muttered.

"What the fuck is a *caporegime*?" I'd never been big on mafia movies or shit like that, so it was all Greek to me.

"A *capo*, a pretty important guy. Falls under the underboss who answers to Lorenzo De Luca himself. The current underboss is Dominic's cousin, Gabe. Talk about connections, huh?" As Hacker spoke, I could hear his computer keys clicking away.

"So how exactly does Stefano fit into this? I thought he was one of De Luca's guys?" I was confused as fuck.

"He is. Stefano Leone. Soldier under Giacomo Caruso."

"Holy shit. So you think he killed his own boss?" A nervous glance in Raiven's direction told me she was still zonked.

"Well, technically, the boss is Lorenzo De Luca, so no. However, yeah, Stefano answered directly to Giacomo."

"How the fuck do you know all this?" At Hacker's low chuckle, I shook my head. "Never mind. I doubt I want to know. So do you think the De Lucas were behind this, or you think he went rogue?" Trying to make sense of all that shit was making my head hurt, because in the middle of all of it was Raiven.

"My guess is he was hoping to blame the hit on a rival family or some random, then step up as the *capo*. If Raiven witnessed it, she could bring down his entire plan with a word to the wrong person. You need to be careful, bro. You have little Elvis with you. Maybe you should drop her off somewhere and wash your hands of her." Though he tried to hide it, I could hear the worry in his tone.

"Fuck, she's Pops's only living relative now. I can't do that. I promised him I'd keep her safe and get her to Styx." That was the excuse I gave him and the one I tried to swallow myself. The truth was, I fucking knew damn well I didn't want to give her up. There had to be a way to keep both of my girls safe.

I also needed to convince Raiven that she should stay with me. Permanently.

Hacker had started to say something about getting back to his search on Letty and her family. Except I cut him off because I noticed a dark car coming up fast behind Gunny and Soap. Before any of it could process, the car went to pass them and clipped Soap's back tire.

"Shit! I gotta go. Car just hit Soap! Out!" Stomach churning, I watched as Soap lost control, Gunny swerved to avoid being taken out, and Soap went down.

Trying to keep my eyes on the road and on what was going on behind me, I started to pull over when I saw Gunny wave me on. The car was gaining on me in the passing lane.

I heard the sound of gunfire and saw Gunny shooting at the car. That told me it was no accident.

Fuck. Fuck, fuck, fuck.

My gas pedal mashed to the floor, I risked a glance at Raiven and Presley. How they were sleeping through all of this I had no idea, but I prayed they stayed that way.

The car suddenly hit its brakes and then swerved at Gunny, running him off the road.

There was no time to stop to see if he was okay, and I wanted to fucking vomit. That was not only my club brother, it was my big brother. My best friend. My only sibling. It had been him and me against the world growing up.

Adrenaline was surging through my veins as I tried my best to get some distance between us and the car. My truck was modified, fast, and it was a badass motherfucker but whatever they had under the hood of that fucking car was a beast. It was quickly gaining on us.

Swerving slightly to cut them off, I cursed when Raiven jolted awake.

"What's going on?" Wide-eyed, she looked over her shoulder. I knew she saw the car by her sharp audible inhale, then her gasped, "Oh my God."

The whimper that slipped from her throat had me reaching over to grasp her hand. "It's going to be okay. Just hang on and don't lose your shit on me. Okay?"

I hated to, but I needed to let go of her hand to keep both hands on the wheel.

"It's him, isn't it?" she rasped in fear.

"I'm not sure. I think so."

For a few miles I was able to stay ahead of them. Of course, there wasn't a soul in sight when you needed them.

As I barreled down the center of the highway, the car suddenly shot over onto the shoulder and up next to me. They rode on the passenger side before swerving at me.

"Raiven. I need you to take this and shoot out the window at that fucking car." I handed her my pistol and she stared at it like it was a poisonous snake. "Raiven! I need your help!"

Her helpless gaze told me she wouldn't be able to fire the weapon.

"Fuck!" Taking the pistol back, I pressed her back with my forearm. Rolling down the window while driving with my knee and praying like a saint, I reached over her and fired out the window. She shrieked, and I fired again. The problem was, I couldn't drive, aim, and fire.

Presley started crying.

Fuck.

I flipped the safety on and set it in the console. The car swerved at us again, and I narrowly missed being hit. If they ran us off the road at the speed we were going, it was likely we'd roll. Then we'd be sitting ducks—if we survived.

"I need you to listen carefully."

"O-o-okay," she stuttered.

"When I get out, I'm going to provide cover for you."

"When you get out? What are you talking about?" she shouted in a panic.

"I'm going to stop the truck, and I need you to climb over here as fast as you can. As soon as I'm out, you gun it and go around them. Haul ass and don't look back."

"No!" Panic was seeping from her pores. I needed her calm if she had any hope of getting my baby girl out of there in one piece.

"Raiven, listen… you need to pull your shit together. I need you to get Presley to safety. Gunny and Soap will be here shortly, and I'll have backup. We'll catch up to you. My phone is here. Call Styx, tell him what's going on, he'll fill Smoke in. Then call Snow. The numbers are programmed in." Her head continued to shake as I fired off my instructions to her.

"No. Please no."

"Raiven! Don't argue with me!"

"I'm not leaving you! He'll *kill* you! Don't you understand that?" Tears coursed down her face and she reached over to clutch my sleeve.

"You don't have a choice, goddammit! Do you understand what I'm saying? Presley needs to be safe." A methodical calm washed over me as I realized I likely wouldn't make it out of this. I rationalized it would be worth it if they were safe.

She cast a terrified glance into the back seat, where Presley was crying.

"Presley, it's okay, baby. Can you put your headphones on so you can finish your movie?" She just kept crying and it was breaking my heart. "Raiven? Are you with me?"

Swallowing hard, she nodded as her shaking hands pushed wisps of hair out of her face and her inhale wavered.

"Good girl. Now, hang on!"

Right at the moment they swerved my direction again, I hit my brakes. Not expecting that move, they shot past me before hitting their brakes and spinning sideways. By the time they stopped, they were facing the ditch.

Time seemed to stand still as my chest rose and fell in heaving breaths.

I turned to Raiven, rapidly trying to memorize every detail about her. Knowing what I had to do didn't make my decision any easier.

Heart shattering, I fought for my earlier resolve. Then I gave my beautiful angel in the back seat one last look, kissed my fingertips, and pressed them to her soft cheek.

"Daddy loves you so much." My voice cracked though I tried to stay strong.

Finally, I turned to Raiven, grabbed the back of her head, and kissed her hard. Before I could second-guess my foolhardy decision, I jerked the door open. The car had backed up and was starting to move toward us.

"Go!" I didn't stop to see if she was listening, I simply started walking toward the car, shooting.

Thankfully, she'd listened, and I heard the engine rev before the tires squealed and she shot around me. The blast of heat and exhaust as the truck passed me caused my hair and shirt to wildly whip around.

I don't think they expected such a ballsy move, because she flew past them as I filled their radiator and windshield with the bullets in my clip. As I was swapping out clips, the passenger door to the car flew open. The dark-haired man who staggered out of the vehicle was pointing a gun at me and we both fired.

A burn across the outside of my bicep registered as I dove into the shallow ditch and tried to find a minuscule amount of cover. Much as Soap had earlier, I cursed the flat, deserted roadway.

Seeing a small clump of brush down the road a bit, I attempted to low-crawl to it. The sharp burning pain in my back took my breath away and I couldn't go any further.

Blackness began to seep into the edges of my vision. Goddamn, all I could think was I had survived a brutal deployment only to die from a bullet to the back in the middle of nowheresville, Kansas.

Right before I succumbed to the dark oblivion, my head was jerked back by my hair.

"Don't worry. We won't let you die. Yet. Two birds, one stone. How's that for luck?"

The sinister laughter was the last thing I remembered before I was swallowed into the midnight abyss.

ELEVEN

Raiven

"NIGHTMARE"—AVENGED SEVENFOLD

The nightmare I was stuck in was shredding me from the inside out. My sanity was unraveling as I floored the truck before the door had even shut. I was surprised I didn't hit him with it.

It had been years since I'd actually driven anywhere.

Not looking as I shot past the beautiful avenging angel with his pistol trained on the car in front of us was impossible. One last glance at him left my chest aching as if razor-sharp talons had ripped my beating heart out.

I'd reached enough speed by the time I passed the dark vehicle holding the devil himself that it was a blur.

It took everything I had to force my eyes on the road ahead of me and not to look in the rearview mirror.

Fumbling without looking, I patted around for the phone I vaguely remembered was in the holder in center console. By the time I found it, my hand was shaking so bad I couldn't even think of looking for numbers.

A quick glance over my shoulder showed Presley had cried herself to sleep. Thank God. She had dried tears on her rounded cheeks and her little mouth open. Every so often she took a shuddery breath.

Belatedly wondering if his phone was connected to the truck, I searched in quick glances for a voice control button. Finding it on the steering wheel, I spoke.

"Call Styx."

Except my voice didn't sound like Matlock's and it was shaking so bad, the damn truck said, "Did you say call Steven Exxon?"

Frustration welled.

"No!"

I repeated my request two more times before the bitch said, "Did you say Call Styx Mobile?"

"Yes!" I shouted.

"Calling Styx Mobile."

Each ring had my anxiety spiking.

Finally, after what seemed like the eightieth ring, a deep voice came over the speakers. "Yo bro, what's up? Where y'all at?"

"I-It's not Matlock," I stuttered.

The previously jovial voice suddenly became stone-cold sober. "Where's Lock? Who's this?"

"R-R-Raiven."

Once again, his voice changed. This time it was calming and easy. "Hey, Raiven, honey. What's going on? Talk to me."

"They—he—I...." My brain refused to cooperate with my mouth.

"Slow down, darlin', it's okay. Where is Lock?"

"They ran them off the road, they got in front of us. He... he...." As I started sobbing, I heard someone start talking rapidly in the background. The phone was muffled, but I heard Styx swear before the phone was uncovered and he spoke to me again.

"Okay. Raiven, who did they run off the road?"

"Yeah," I barely got out.

"No, who was run off the road?" He enunciated clearly and slowly.

"Um, Gunny and Soap." I sniffled.

"Where's Lock, Raiven?" he asked again.

"He got out and told me to go." I heard his sharp inhale at my answer. Then my tears escaped with a broken sob.

"Is Presley okay?"

I chanced a peek at her. Her eyes were open and she looked confused as she sniffled, but she was safe. For now. "Yes."

"Good. Now can you tell me where you are?"

"D-d-driving down the road. F-fast."

"Okay. Is anyone following you?" At his question, I glanced in the rearview mirror.

"N-no. Not that I c-can s-see."

"Good. Okay, listen to me. Take a deep breath, and slow down enough that you don't wreck but keep moving. You got me?"

Nodding, I didn't think about him not being able to see me.

"Raiven?"

"S-s-s-sorry. Yeah. Okay." My knuckles were white where I clenched the steering wheel for dear life.

"Can you tell me where Lock, Gunny, and Soap are right now?"

Now that Presley was awake, I swallowed the lump in my throat and took the deep breath he'd told me to take. "I don't knooooow. Back there."

It was whispered but he heard.

"Shit. Okay, are they—" He seemed to find some difficulty. "Are they alive?"

"I don't know." My answer came out thin and thready as my throat burned and wanted to close. So many things I didn't know, it was like being a broken record.

Silence.

"Okay. I'm tracking that y'all are on the Kansas Turnpike. Is that right?" his deep, calming voice asked.

Frantically searching the road in front of me, I finally saw a sign. "Yes." Then I wondered how the hell he knew that. "How the hell?"

"Need to know basis, babe. Trust that we're tracking you and we're loading up to head your way, but we're a long way away. I need you to keep your head. I'm going to make a few calls. I'll be calling you back shortly."

Words stuck in my throat.

"Raiven? You hear me?"

"Um, yeah," I croaked.

"Good. If you need me before I call you back, you call, yeah?"

"Okay." Immediately after my answer, the phone went dead.

Heart pounding painfully, I trembled. I had no idea what I was doing.

When the small voice came from the back seat, I wanted to cry but managed to hold my shit together.

"Waiven? Whewe's my daddy?"

Oh God.

Breaths coming in gasps, I struggled not to hyperventilate. Pasting on a smile, I gave a valiant attempt at sounding cheery.

"He's with your uncles." That at least wasn't much of a lie. "They're going to catch up to us."

Now that part, I prayed with every formerly non-believing bone in my body to be true.

"Otay." She didn't fuss, she didn't cry, she took me at my word without question, and I didn't know how to deal with that.

Checking the rearview, I was relieved that there was no black Charger barreling up on us. Except I was equally as distressed that there were no bikes behind me either.

"You okay back there, kiddo?" I looked at her in the mirror.

Her answer was a lingering sniffle, then a toothy grin, before she popped her headphones back on and her eyes focused on the video she had playing.

It terrified me that her innocent little life was in my hands. I didn't really know the first thing about kids, and I was a fucking wreck.

The first vehicle I'd seen in miles passed us on the opposite side of the highway, and I wondered if they'd be able to help. If they'd see everything going on back there.

Shit! Why didn't I call the cops? The thought hit me as quickly as the answer.

Because I didn't know how far Stefano's reach was and I didn't know who I could trust.

The phone rang and I saw Styx's name on the dash screen. I was shocked to see how much time had passed.

"Hello?"

"How you doin', sweetheart?" was the first thing he asked.

"Honestly, I have no idea." A fat tear tracked down my cheek.

"Everything's gonna be fine. You hear?" he demanded in a calm, commanding manner.

"Mm-hmm."

"Okay, in about thirty minutes or so, you'll see a group of about seven bikes pass you. They will turn around and come up behind you. You know what the Demented Sons back patch looks like, right?"

I nodded. "Um, yes." I remembered my uncle in his throughout the years.

"Perfect. That's what they'll be wearing but with an Oklahoma bottom rocker. One guy will ride up next to you so you can see their patch. If it's not one of our guys or you see a patch that says Demon Runners, you sideswipe them and keep going. Got it?"

"Yeah." I took a long, shaky breath. Jesus, it really was like being stuck in a living nightmare.

"They will escort you to us, then we'll take over."

"Okay. Umm, Styx? What about Ma—What about Lock and the other guys?"

Please don't lose it, please don't lose it, please don't lose it.

"We've got someone on that too, but right now you and that little girl are the priority. Don't worry about them. They are tough and they'll have backup soon."

Feeling a little better, I shook off my feeling of foreboding. "Thank you, Styx." It came out as barely a whisper.

"Hey. We take care of family. You hear?"

The lump in my throat was so big I could barely swallow, let alone answer. A small whimper was all that came out.

"Stay tough. We're gonna get through this. Later." He hung up.

I'd no sooner ended the call with Styx before the phone rang again. Tears broke through the dam, and I sobbed as my uncle's road name flashed on the screen.

"Uncle Carlisle." My words were a sloppy, snotty, watery mess.

"Blackbird? You stop that sniveling. You're made of tougher stuff than that. I got a phone call that filled me in on what happened. Are you hurt? Are you okay?" His gruff voice echoed through the truck.

Was I okay? Fuck no, I wasn't. I was definitely hurt. Decimated, even.

A man who'd stirred insane thoughts and feelings in me after barely over twenty-four hours might have sacrificed himself for me and his precious little daughter. How was I supposed to cope with that?

"No, I'm not hurt. Scared. Fuck, I'm terrified." A quick peek in the back seat showed Presley was sleeping again. Damn, that little girl slept well in a vehicle.

"You just stay moving, and the guys will be with you soon. Okay? How are you doing on gas?"

"I'm still good. We had filled up right before everything went to shit. But Matlock—" A shuddering inhale and sobbing exhale interrupted my ability to speak.

"He's going to be okay. He's tough too. Blackbird?"

"Yeah, Uncle Carlisle?" I tried to keep my sniffle quiet.

"You are strong. You take care of that little girl and yourself. The guys will take care of everything else. I wish you would've told me everything when we picked you up in Chicago, but I understand. I love you." It might have been my imagination but it sounded like his voice cracked before he cleared his throat. "I'll see you soon. I snuck in on a cancellation for my appointment this morning, so your aunt and I got on the road as soon as we heard from Styx and Snow."

"Thank you. Travel safe. I love you both, too." As the line went dead, I hoped that I'd live to see him again.

TWELVE

Lock

"SORRY"—THE ART OF DYING

E very-motherfucking-thing hurt. It hurt to breathe, it hurt to swallow. My eyelids were so heavy I had to fight to get them to crack open the slightest.

Groggy, I let my eyes travel over the room until I realized I wasn't alone. My heart sped up, and I wanted to jump to defend myself, but I couldn't move. Limbs like lead, I could barely turn my head their direction.

"Who are you? Where am I?" My voice was like sandpaper on gravel. My mouth was dry and my tongue stuck to the roof of my mouth. Blinking, I saw a woman next to me.

"Shhh. Try not to talk. Drink a small sip of this. Your stomach hasn't had anything in a while, and we don't want you puking on yourself." She gave a blurry half-hearted smile. "I've been giving you TPN since you've been out so your body got at least some nutrients, but they'd kill me if they knew. Thankfully they're too stupid to know it wasn't just IV fluids and antibiotics."

While I sipped slowly through the straw she placed at my lips, I studied her with clearing vision. Dark brown hair pulled up in a severe ponytail exposed huge brown eyes and a face devoid of makeup. At my confused look, she shook her head. "Sorry, I'm speaking Greek, huh? That's Total Parenteral Nutrition. Um, basically nutrients through your IV."

She pulled the drink away, and I watched her as she checked an IV bag, then the dressings on my chest and arm, causing me to wince.

"I'm sorry. I'm trying to taper off your pain meds so you're more lucid. I'll give you a little more," she said softly. The single door to the room opened.

I didn't know the guy but I sure as fuck recognized his cut. The Demon Runner barked at the woman, "Don't talk to him, sis. Just do what we pay you to do."

She snorted. "Pay me? You extort me. I don't have a choice."

The Demon Runner stepped closer. "Shut your fucking face, sis. Unless you want Viper to come down here and collect the money you owe us."

Her eyes widened, and I could smell the fear emanating from her.

Whatever she'd given me must've kicked in, because my eyes started to get heavy again and I slipped out of consciousness.

I had no idea how much time had passed, but the next time I woke, the same woman was changing the dressing on my chest, but this time her hair was wadded up on her head. The same Demon Runner who was in the room before was leaning against the wall playing on his phone.

It rang, and he looked up, so I closed my eyes. I heard him tell her, "Don't do anything stupid, sis. I'll be right outside."

Once the door clicked shut, I opened my eyes and whispered, "Who are you?"

"It doesn't matter." She refused to make eye contact.

Trying another approach, I asked, "You're a doctor?"

"Surgeon." She finished taping down the thick gauze and threw away the trash.

When I didn't think she'd say any more, I saw her glance nervously toward the door. "Look, I don't know why they have you or why they had me save you. But from what little I've overheard, you're in trouble and they won't mind wasting all my hard work once they get what they want from you." Whispering, she spoke quickly.

"I can't do anything else for you." She slid something under my hip. "That's the best I can do and I'll deny it until my dying day. Good luck."

The burly bastard stepped back in the room. "You done?"

"Yes. Dressing's changed, pain meds administered, and last round of antibiotics running. Can I go now? I'm expected at the hospital in a little over six hours. I need some sleep." Her dark hair was starting to fall out of the messy bundle she had it up in this time, and she blew it out of her face. Dark circles graced the underside of her eyes.

"He weren't supposed to get no more pain shit. Fuck. All right, go. Thanks, sis. You'll get paid soon. You come change his shit again tomorrow after you get off." She snorted at the guy, and I had a feeling he was the only Demon Runner with whom she'd get away with acting like that. He was either her actual brother, or possibly she was an ol' lady but I didn't get that feeling.

Whatever she'd given me for pain was starting to kick in, because my eyelids began to get heavy as fuck. I hated that shit, but if the cloudy memories I had were accurate, I'd be in hellacious pain without them.

My last conscious thought was to wonder if Raiven and Presley were safe.

The next time I woke, it was dark in the room, with only a small under-the-cabinet light on in the corner. I was surprisingly alone.

Taking the opportunity to catalog the room, I noticed cabinets that had locks on every door. I was on a stretcher like you'd see in an ER. I had an IV running, and the bag was nearly empty. Other than that, there was nothing sitting around the room.

"What the fuck?" Voice rusty, I croaked.

Trying to sit up was pure torture, but I finally sat on the edge of the bed with the blanket still covering me. I wasn't sure what was worse, the dizziness or the nausea. When I clutched the bed, my hand landed on something small and hard.

Blinking, I stared at it a moment before I realized it was a capped scalpel. The woman's words as she slid something under me came back. The problem was, I was weak as hell, dressed in nothing but underwear, and I had no fucking clue where I was.

A single scalpel wasn't going to be very effective.

Not one to dismiss the small things, however, I tucked it into the back of my underwear with shaking hands. That small movement sent a burning, sharp pain through my chest to my back. My arm was on fire, but glancing down, it appeared it must've been a flesh wound.

That was also when I noticed the discomfort in my dick.

"Oh please don't let my dick be gone," I muttered. Lifting the blanket, I saw a tube coming out of the leg of the underwear. Tentatively, I pulled the waistband of out and peeked inside.

Thankfully, my dick was indeed still there. Unfortunately, there was a fucking catheter shoved up it.

"Christ." I grabbed the tube with the intent of pulling it out, but before I could do anything, the door opened and a different Demon Runner came in shoving a sandwich in his mouth. Bits of the lettuce and God knew what else were falling out of his mouth and from the sandwich all down the front of his cut and to the floor.

When he saw me sitting up, his eyes went huge. "Trigger! He's awake!" More food flew out of his mouth as he shouted with his mouth crammed full. My lip curled at his disgusting lack of decorum or respect for his cut. Piece of shit Demon Fucker.

Rapid footsteps approached, and the chick's possible brother and a giant of a ginger that I hadn't seen before stepped in. "Have a nice sleep?" The guy from before grinned, revealing a broken front tooth.

The ginger made a phone call as he warily watched me. Like I could do anything.

"He's up. Come and get him the fuck out of our clubhouse. Our part of the deal is done." Vaguely, I heard a man's voice on the other end talking. "You're fucking crazy. We fixed him up and kept him here just like we said we would. Viper said you either get him when he wakes up or he's coming down here and finishing what you started without you."

The ginger ended the call, but before he could say anything, the woman shoved around him. This time she was in pale blue scrubs. "What are you doing? Lie down! You shouldn't be up!"

Her eyes worriedly traced the bed where I'd been lying, then I watched as relief registered in them. Still she came forward and helped me lie back. I didn't like it, because it left me feeling more vulnerable than I already was. Then again, I was so weak it wasn't like it mattered.

She'd obviously seen my intent where I'd been holding the tube coming from my junk, because she pulled her lips in her mouth. "Umm, trust me when I say you don't want to do that. Now that you're awake and moving, I'll take that out and get you a urinal."

"What are you getting so worked up for? It's not like it's gonna matter soon." The ginger chuckled as he stared at her ass.

Ignoring him, she tucked the sheet around my waist.

"I need to change this dressing and take care of my patient. Get out, Roja."

The ginger called Roja grunted then narrowed his eyes. "Don't tell me what to do, bitch."

"Hey! That's my sister you're talking to. Watch your fucking mouth!" the guy from before shouted. That answered that, she was his sister. So he could talk to her like shit but no one else could.

Fucking idiot.

The pig of a member stepped out, eating the last of his sandwich. Roja followed him, grumbling as he shoulder-checked the doc's brother as he went by.

"Trigger, I need supplies from the cabinet. I don't have keys. Remember? And grab a urinal from the last cabinet." She stood with her hands on her hips. Okay, the brother's road name was Trigger. I hadn't been able to read it on his cut before.

After digging a ring of keys from his pocket, he proceeded to rummage through the cabinets. One by one, he dug through shit then locked them again.

"We ain't got no more of them padded things," he finally said as he tossed her a plastic urinal.

She sighed as she caught it and set it on the stretcher next to me. "The bleeding looks like it's stopped. They may not need to be covered anymore, but could you please see if there are some in the storage room?"

Grumbling about it being a waste, he stomped out of the room.

"Look, he'll be back soon. I try not to get involved in their shit. I do what I have to in order to keep them out of my life. But I can't save your life only to let them do whatever they're going to do. I can't call the cops, though, so please don't ask," she whispered frantically.

"Then listen to me." I stared into her worried eyes. "You got a phone?"

She shook her head. "They take it from me before I come in."

"Can you remember a number?" Goddamn, the right side of my chest hurt.

She nodded, and I rattled off Snow's most recent burner number and the clubhouse number, because I didn't know Smoke's number by heart. "You tell them the Demon Runners have me. Tell them wherever the fuck I am. If you hear any more, let him know. Can you do that?"

She nodded.

"There were two other guys with me. Are they here?" Her confused look was my answer.

"Only you that I know of."

"A woman and kid?"

She shook her head.

My eyes closed, unsure of if that was good or bad news.

"Thank you for the scalpel. Not sure what good it will do. Where am I, anyway?" None of the Demon Runners I'd seen looked familiar, and I only saw the Kansas bottom rocker on their cuts as they'd walked away.

"Wichita," she whispered.

"What did you do to me?" I needed to know how bad the damage had been.

"Not much, honestly. Mostly stitched you up. You had a mild flesh wound to your arm, as I'm sure you can feel, but the shot to the back...." She huffed out a breath. "You were lucky as hell it was through and through. I can only assume most of it because I had limited equipment. I'm pretty sure it missed your scapula, but barely. Then it exited along your fourth and fifth ribs. Missed your lung and anything vital from what I could tell. Without opening you up or having an X-ray, I'm not one hundred percent sure. You could have some rib fragments in there if it nicked them. I sewed the chest wound up as best I could, but if I had to guess, it's going to scar pretty bad. I just took the stitches out, but the chest wound still has some open areas I couldn't stitch that are draining. They'll heal but it will take time. Exit wounds can be a bitch."

"I could give a fuck. Just please tell me these underwear were clean."

She pointed to the waistband of the underwear in question as she tried not to smile. "I'm going to lower the front of the underwear *I took out of the package* so I can take this catheter out now. Okay?"

I nodded, and she said, "Take a deep breath and let it out slow."

I nodded again and she slid it out.

"Motherfucker!" That was a feeling I didn't ever care to experience again. Saying it slid out is being nice. Really fucking nice.

She tossed everything in a trash can. "You'll need to pee within about four hours."

Footsteps approached. "Make that call. You remember the number?" I groaned.

She nodded.

I closed my eyes, feigning sleep.

"What did you give him?" Trigger's voice rang out.

"Nothing. I removed the catheter, then was checking his wound, and I think he passed out. I'm guessing it's still very painful."

106

"Pussy," the guy muttered, and I wished for my usual strength because I'd have jumped up and beat the fuck out of him. I'd show him who the pussy was. I'd choke him out with the piss tube that had been up my dick.

She quickly and quietly applied the dressing to my chest. "The back wound doesn't require changing. It healed up pretty good and I took the stitches out. I'll come back tomorrow and change the chest one."

"Don't bother. He won't be here. He'll be collected by then." The asshole gave a snort.

"Collected? Are his family members on the way then?" She was trying to sound like I was simply a friend of theirs when he had to know she knew different.

"Ain't no family coming for him, but don't you worry about it. He has information someone wants, and let's say he has a debt that needs to be paid. He's gonna wish you hadn't saved him." His laughter was sick and twisted.

"Trigger! What is wrong with you? How could you have me work so hard to save him if you're just going to let someone hurt him?" Disgust filled her voice.

"Don't you worry about it, I said. Go on. Get out of here. Tell Ma I'll be there Sunday for supper."

I heard her snarl under her breath.

"Whatever."

I sensed she had left the room, then I sensed her brother standing next to me. "I don't know how you pissed Viper and that Italian guy off so bad, but damn, I almost feel sorry for you." A menacing chuckle followed him as the door closed.

Shit.

THIRTEEN

Raiven

"I DON'T BELONG HERE"—I PREVAIL

I still couldn't believe we'd made it safely to Texas. For the last week and a half, Presley and I had been staying at what seemed to be a junkyard. At least that's what it looked like from the highway. What I'd learned was that it was the Demented Sons' clubhouse, which meant it was kind of like their home base.

Behind the rows and rows of pick-and-pull cars was a big metal shop. Behind that was what appeared to be another bigger shop but was more like a house. It had a big open room up front with a bar, tables, and some bathrooms, then in the back were several bedrooms.

"Pwincess Waiven? When my daddy gonna be hewe?" A frown marred Presley's pretty little face, and her fists were propped on her tu-tu'd hips. She stood in the doorway as I wiped the blood and excess ink from my work in progress with a gloved hand.

With a sigh, I blinked away tears. Looking up at Smoke for help, I shut off my machine.

"Hey, little Elvis. Your daddy is still working. Where is Mattie? Isn't she supposed to be watching you?" Smoke asked her. The guys had all taken to calling her little Elvis like Gunny did.

"Hers sweeping. I wanna caww him," the little munchkin demanded.

"Sweeping? What the hell is she sweeping?" His brows dropped, and a crease developed between his eyes.

"No, Unka Smoke. Hers swwweeeeping. On da couch." Her little blue eyes rolled in frustration at what she saw as his lack of intelligence.

Despite my earlier emotional response, I had to laugh at her.

"I'll be back," he announced, then stood and left the room. I set my equipment on the small work table and stretched my back. I'd started doing tattoos at the clubhouse out of boredom. The guys had supplied me with everything I'd requested and cleaned out a small storage room for me to use. I'd had no shortage of members wanting new shit when they saw my past work on my social media.

Peeling off the gloves, I slid the small table safely out of the way and sat sideways on the chair. I held out my hands to the sweet little girl.

"Come here, sweetheart."

Bottom lip stuck out, she dropped her arms and shuffled over to me. I lifted her into my lap, reveling in the way her hair smelled like the detangler I'd used on it that morning and sunshine. When she rested her head on my shoulder, my heart lurched.

"Daddy will call you as soon as he can. I know he loves you and he wouldn't want you to worry about him, so he must be very busy." Hugging her close, I fought the tears that hit me at random times throughout the day. There had been no word regarding Matlock, and I was beginning to give up hope.

Her small arms wrapped around my middle, and my stomach flipped. The past week had brought us very close. Something I never thought I'd have in my life. Especially with someone else's kid.

In fact, if I had to put a name to my feelings, I'd almost be willing to say I loved her.

"I miss him vewy much. What if he went to heaven like my mommy?"

I froze. I'd completely forgotten that Matlock had told me that

Presley's mom had died, for fuck sake! Then I realized the poor thing might have lost both of her parents before she was even three years old. It made my depression at missing and worrying over her dad seem insignificant in comparison.

It also made me realize something. If it turned out Matlock hadn't made it, Gunny would probably take her back to Iowa. The thought was so painful, it was suddenly hard to breathe.

Jesus.

Before I could answer, Smoke filled the doorway with his teenage daughter in tow. Looking properly chastised, she stood slightly behind her dad.

"Hey, Presley. Did you still want to go paint pictures?" the young girl said to the little one in my arms.

Presley's head popped up from my shoulder, and I missed it immediately.

"Wiff da big gewl paints?" Excitement shimmered in her words and the tense expectancy of her small frame.

"Of course!" Mattie smiled at Presley.

"Yay! I'm gonna paint my daddy a picture!" She jumped down and grabbed Mattie's hand. The two of them chattered all the way down the hall. I choked on my tongue at her happy exclamation. I barely heard Smoke talking.

"Sorry about that. She stayed up all night watching damn movies. Teenagers." He rolled his eyes and settled back into the chair.

"It's okay. I'm almost done." I quietly pulled on new gloves and got my machine going again.

The only sound in the room was the buzzing of the machine as I finished the last of the tattoo on the president's shoulder. Surprisingly, he had very few tattoos for a biker.

I was finishing up and letting him look in the mirror when Styx and Gunny came to the door.

"Prez, need you now." The seriousness in Styx's tone and the somber expression on Gunny's face left my stomach bottoming out.

"Thanks, Raiven. It looks great. I'll settle up with you when I'm done." I dumbly nodded.

He barely gave me the time to coat it and get the plastic seal on before he rushed down the hall, pulling his shirt on as he went. Styx gave me an empathetic look and was then on Smoke's heels. Gunny remained in the hallway, shuffling from one foot to the next.

"Gunny?" My voice quavered.

He shot a glance over his shoulder before stepping into the room and closing the door. Nausea grew as he scrubbed his face with both hands. I barely knew Matlock; I had no rational explanation for why his safety meant so much to me. Other than that I'd come to care immensely for his daughter and he'd likely saved our lives.

Regardless of why, I couldn't quit thinking about him, worrying about him, and insanely enough, missing him.

"Gunny, what is it? You're scaring me." Since he'd arrived here in Texas three days after I did with a skinned-up Soap and their wrecked bikes in tow, I'd asked about Matlock every day. Hollywood, Joker, and Hacker had arrived the same day with my aunt and uncle. Other than Joker and me bouncing ideas off each other since I'd found out he owned a studio in Iowa, no one had much to say.

"Snow got a phone call. Some chick who said the Demon Runners had Lock in Wichita."

Hope blossomed in my chest. "So he's alive? Is he okay?"

I had no idea who these Demon Runners were other than that they had been the ones asking for me in Omaha.

His Adam's apple jumped as he swallowed hard. "I'm not sure. It sounds like he was, but I didn't get the details. He wanted to talk to Smoke about it first."

"Oh." I wasn't sure how to take that. I didn't like the emphasis he'd put on "was." The little tendril of hope that had begun to unfurl slowly began to wither. "How is Soap feeling today?"

"Still whining about being stiff and itching under his cast." He gave me an indulgent tip of his lips.

I returned it with what I knew was a sad imitation of a smile. I'd been so glad to see Soap had been relatively okay and walked away from being hit by Stefano with only a broken leg and a lot of road rash. I'd overheard them say they reported it as a hit-and-run.

"He's going to be okay. I feel it in my guts." He ran a hand through his hair.

"Well, if he's able to bitch about itching and all, I'm sure he'll be fine." I gave a small quirk of my lips.

"No, I mean Lock." He spoke softly as he studied his hands.

Clutching his hands in mine, I crouched down next to where he'd sat in my chair. "I believe it too. I have to."

He looked up at me with a strange and questioning expression.

"What?" I asked.

Eyes slightly narrowed, he studied me. Then he gave a short shake of his head. "Nothing."

I heard a thump-click-thump-click repeating down the hall and I knew it was Soap hobbling along on his crutches. He'd taken to visiting with me in the afternoons, and we'd started the artwork for a leg piece for him. We wouldn't be able to do it until after his cast was off, but he still came by each day.

The door swung open, and at Soap's surprised, "Oh!" I looked over my shoulder at him. He was staring at where I was holding Gunny's hands. It dawned on me that he was misinterpreting the situation. I gave Gunny a fortifying squeeze, then stood.

"Hey Soap, how's that leg today?" I gave him a soft smile. He was a sweet guy, but he wasn't really my type. It seemed my type was the dark blond, broody type, with little girls in tow.

It was too bad, because Soap was a great person and good-looking. So was Gunny, but they didn't stir anything in me other than familial feelings.

"It sucks. That's how it is. If I see that fucker again, I think I'll break both his legs to get even," he grumbled.

Gunny heaved himself from the chair. "I'm going to see if Smoke is off the phone." He pressed a brotherly kiss to the side of my head. I nodded because I could barely swallow around the lump in my throat, let alone get words out.

Soap dropped unceremoniously into my chair, and his crutches clattered to the floor. He didn't say anything as I cleaned up my mess, so I thought he'd dozed off.

When I dropped the last of my soiled items in the trash, I jumped to find his bright eyes following my every move. "Jesus, Soap, you scared the shit out of me. I thought you were sleeping."

He shook his head. I could tell he was weighing his words.

"Raiven?"

"Yeah, Soap?" I leaned against the chipped counter and crossed my arms and ankles.

"You and Gunny? You, uh, I mean... well, are you two sort of a...."

"Spit it out, Soap. We're adults here. If you have something to say, just say it."

Huffing out a heavy breath, he rushed, "You two a thing now?"

"How did I know you were going to ask that?" I rolled my eyes but tried to soften my tone. "Look, Soap, nothing is going on with me and Gunny, but I'm not in a position to be involved with anyone. My life is in limbo until Stefano shows his face again and I can get him to promise to leave me alone."

He snorted in disbelief. "Honey, the only way that asshole is ever gonna leave you alone is if he's six-foot under. So you're saying there's no chance? For me and you, I mean." His actions made him look like a little boy as he fiddled with the edge of his T-shirt. He was definitely a grown-ass man, but unfortunately, I didn't feel anything but friendship toward him.

"No," I sighed. "I'm sorry."

He shrugged and plastered a broad grin across his face. "Well, you can't blame a guy for tryin'."

"I—" That was as far as I got before Gunny was at the door.

"Soap. At the table. Now."

Jumping up to one foot, he leaned over to scoop up his crutches and raced from the small room as fast as he could.

I'd learned they wouldn't let me in, but I couldn't help but follow. A thick arm shot out to bar me from getting close to the room, and I looked up into my uncle's eyes.

"Uncle Carlisle, what's going on? Please." No matter how hard I tried, my lungs wouldn't inflate. The inability to bring oxygen into my body was making me dizzy. "Uncle Carlisle?"

His head bowed and his eyes closed. "We need to wait until they're done."

"Why aren't you in there?" I clutched at his shirt. "It's Matlock, isn't it? Is it bad?"

When he didn't answer, panic closed in on me. "Is it?" I shouted.

"Yeah, Blackbird. It is."

One hand clutched his shirt tighter as the other covered my mouth. His bear-like arms wrapped around me as I fought to inhale. It hurt so bad. What if he was dead? I couldn't handle it if he had died because of my shitty taste in men. It wasn't fair.

"Come on, sweetheart, let's go sit down and wait for them." He led me over into the kitchen, where Aunt Jean was cooking massive amounts of enchiladas for everyone. He had me sit at the huge table in the giant kitchen.

It made me feel small, minuscule, insignificant.

My aunt slid the last pan in the industrial oven and sat next to me. "Raiven, honey"—she twined her fingers with mine—"talk to me."

I cast a nervous glance at my uncle.

"I'm going to see if they're about done." He rushed out of the room as if emotions might actually do him harm. I almost laughed.

Actually, I did, but it slipped into a sob.

"It's not your fault. You did what you needed to do in order to get Presley out of there. Regardless of how this turns out, I know he'll appreciate that his little girl is safe." My aunt thought she was being helpful, but she had no idea my emotions were way more tangled than she could've imagined.

All I could do was shake my head as I held my bottom lip tight in my teeth.

After being such a fool for Stefano and letting him dupe me, I couldn't believe that I so easily fell into bed with Matlock. Who the hell was I kidding, I didn't just fall in to bed with him, I had feelings for him. I must be a complete idiot, because, like I'd told myself a million times, I barely knew him.

As if my every thought had broadcast across my face, my aunt narrowed her eyes and studied me.

"Raiven? Please don't tell me you fell for that boy."

That boy. He was so far from being a boy, it wasn't even funny.

Shoulders slumped, I rested my elbows on the table and balanced my head on my fingertips.

"I honestly don't know. He was sweet. With both me and his daughter. I'd been prepared to hate him. Then I tried to get him to leave me behind to find my own way. If it wasn't for me, he'd be here with his little girl." A tear slipped free and rolled down my cheek before I wiped it away.

"Oh, honey." She shook her head. "Even if he makes it, he's never going to return your feelings. He was so damaged by the loss of Presley's mom that he locked that heart of his up tight. If I didn't see how he was with that girl of his, I'd wonder if he had one left."

"You're wrong," I argued, knowing I was being stupid, because I didn't really know that.

Pity swam in her eyes as she huffed and pulled me into her arms. I couldn't hold it together after that. I broke. Tears poured, and I cried my heart out because I knew whatever was going on wasn't good.

I couldn't have said how long we waited, but the whole time, my aunt held me and gently rocked me until my sobs became shaky sniffles.

Smoke, Styx, Gunny, Joker, and Soap came in, then a few more poured into the room but I'd lost track of who was there because I was focused on Smoke. He stood in the doorway and stared at me with an unreadable expression.

"Tell me," I demanded, then snuffled in an unladylike manner.

"The Demon Runners had Lock. The woman who called said they had her save his life." For a brief moment, relief settled in my bones. His next words washed it away. "Lock told her to call Snow. She thinks they're turning him over to some guy today or tomorrow. It sounds like Stefano."

My gasp echoed through the quiet room. I couldn't quit shaking my head

"Noooooooooooooo!" I don't know if I was actually screaming or if it was only in my head.

My body rocked, and I began to mentally disintegrate.

Someone scooped me up and carried me to the room I'd been sharing with Presley. When they laid me on the bed, I was shaking so violently that I wondered if I was having a seizure. Thick, strong arms wrapped around and held me from behind.

"Shhhhh." My mind barely comprehended it was Gunny who held me with his forehead pressed to the back of my neck. "We're gonna get him back."

The problem was, they didn't know Stefano like I did.

FOURTEEN

Lock

"HYSTERIA"—DEF LEPPARD

I'd lost track of how many days I'd been at Stefano's mercy. Not that I'd met him yet.

The black box that had become my normal was devoid of light, sound, or any belongings. Time didn't exist in there.

At first, I'd screamed and succumbed to panic. Waking up to pitch-black was akin to being buried alive. Then I'd centered myself and walked around like a blind man.

A weak as fuck blind man.

The room I was in was approximately eight feet square, if I'd paced it right. Concrete floor, textured metal walls and ceiling. The ceiling was barely over my head. If I had to guess, I'd say it was an old cooler with the inner release removed.

No furniture, no bathroom.

Once I'd walked the perimeter with my fingertips trailing the wall, I had to sit. I was exhausted from that little bit of exertion. I closed my eyes to fool myself into thinking it was only dark because I had my lids snapped shut tight.

Amazingly enough, the scalpel was still in the back of my under-wear band. I'd taken it out and rested it flat against the wall next to the door where I hoped they wouldn't notice. It was a chance, but I had no-where else to hide it, and it sure as hell wasn't going up my ass.

Every so often, the door cracked, blinding me with the splinter of light, and food was thrown in at me. Since I had no sense of time, I had no idea how often that was, only that I was starving by the time they finally fed me.

I'd been fed three times. I was assuming they were feeding me once a day.

Thanks to my exhaustion from healing and minimal nutrition, I fell asleep curled up on the cold, hard floor. Of course, like most nights—if it was even night—I woke from a nightmare.

Heart racing, hands shaking, I did my best to control my breathing, but I sucked at it. Putting my head between my knees, I sat up, leaning against the wall. My chest wound was aching like a motherfucker.

Trying to calm myself, I imagined Presley's smiling face in my mind.

Images of her as she'd grown flashed through my head, until sud-denly the images included Raiven. It wasn't lost on me that the night we'd slept together I hadn't had a single nightmare. It may have been coincidence, but I hadn't slept that well in years.

My head fell back to the wall.

The thought of never seeing them again was fucking with my head worse than the dark.

Seconds rolled into minutes, rolled into hours in my dark void, and I slept on and off. I also tried to do some sit-ups and push-ups, but it hurt so fucking bad and I was so weak. When I felt dampness on my chest over my wound, I knew I'd overdone it.

Out of breath, I lay flat on the floor. The room stank. Whether from my lack of hygiene options, what had been in there before me, or a combination of the two, I didn't know.

I was on the verge of dozing again when I heard a faint scraping and light flooded the room, temporarily blinding me as usual. This time was different though, because the door stayed open. My arms instinctively flew to cover my eyes, and the movement made me groan.

"Get up." The voice echoed in the small area.

When I didn't move fast enough, someone grabbed me by my injured arm and jerked me upright. My other hand shot out and grabbed him by the throat as I roared in pain, and my eyes began to adjust.

The whole time I wavered on my feet.

"Let him go!" The unmistakable cold of the end of a pistol barrel pressed to my temple.

Blinking rapidly, I let go of the neck I'd wanted to snap and jerked my arm free. The movement almost caused me to fall over. I also didn't know how long it had been since my body had any fucking food, because I was starving.

"Put those fucking cuffs on him! I told you to do it before you got him up, you stupid fucker!" After the one guy shouted at the other, they bitched back and forth.

The two assholes shoved and dragged me down a short hall, then through a door. Trying to catalog my surroundings, I made quick glances around. We seemed to be in an old slaughterhouse, and I didn't have to be a fucking genius to know that didn't bode well.

A lone chair was in the middle of the vast area. Broken windows high on the walls let streams of sunlight in. Dirt and God knew what else coated everything around us.

"Sit." They shoved me toward the chair. It went against my natural instincts to do anything they said, but I was exhausted. So I sat.

They didn't speak to me anymore. After the complete silence of the dark room, even though I didn't like them at all, I was dying for conversation of any kind.

I was also feeling like a snarky fucker by then.

"Well, this is fun, boys, but if we're playing musical chairs, we need another chair. Oh, and some music. Just sayin'. Unless we're gonna discuss the weather?" I grinned.

"Shut the fuck up," the Igor-looking motherfucker said. The other guy was pretty nondescript, other than being bald, and didn't answer me. He just glared and told the other guy to tape my ankles to the chair legs.

I sighed dramatically. "Well, don't expect your social media accounts to explode if all your parties are like this. Don't you think the abandoned factory is an overdone theme?"

The sound of a door opening and closing echoed through the high-ceilinged building. It was followed directly by the sound of hard-soled shoes and at least one other set of feet hitting the concrete floors behind me.

Turning my head to look over my shoulder, I saw two guys. A dark-haired pretty boy in a fancy suit who looked vaguely familiar, and one of the last fucking people I wanted to see.

Viper.

President of the Demon Runners in Omaha. What the fuck was he doing there?

"Well, look, the party is growing. You may be redeemed after all. Except you still need some tunes. Igor, Baldy? Do you know your two new guests? Because you may want to reconsider your guest list." Staying sarcastically cheerful was the only way I fought trying to break loose from the fucking chair and getting my ass beat.

Evidently Viper didn't appreciate my humor, because he caught me with an uppercut that sent my chair back on two legs. How I didn't fall over backward, I have no idea.

Turning my head to the side, I spit blood on the floor. "Well, good to see you too."

When he lunged toward me, the pretty boy I assumed was Stefano placed a hand to his chest. "Viper, enough."

"That's right, Viper. Be a good little pet." My mouth wouldn't stop even as it filled with blood again. I spit it toward his boots.

Viper's nostrils flared, and a vein pulsed in his forehead as he growled.

Stefano's dark eyes bored into me as the corner of his mouth quirked up. "Mouthy, aren't you?"

"What the fuck do you want?" I was tired of playing games. My stomach was growling and possibly digesting itself, I hurt, I was pissed, and I hated being trussed up and feeling helpless.

Like a cocky fucker, he leaned over, rested his hands on the knees of his fancy, dark suit pants, and tipped his head. Narrowed eyes studied me.

"All I want from you is where she is." His brows cocked, and he waited as if I would spill national secrets because he demanded it.

Instead, I played dumb.

"Where who is?" I drawled.

The condescending smile he gave me should have been a warning.

I was not prepared for the single finger he shoved into my chest wound.

Clenching my teeth, I fought to hold my shit together. I didn't want to give him the satisfaction of knowing he was getting to me.

By the time thick warmth ran down my chest, it was too much, and I screamed. He might as well have shoved a hot poker in my chest cavity.

"See, Viper? There are easier ways of getting to someone than busting up your knuckles." His tone was cold, calculating, and twisted as a motherfucker. What the hell had Raiven seen in this fuck?

"Now. Shall we start over? Where. Is. She?" He gave me a serene smile.

"Fuck. You," I gasped out.

Grabbing me by the hair, he jerked my head back until I swore my neck would snap. Then he got up in my face. Eyes so dark they looked black bored into me. I'd seen soulless people before, and this man was one. Again, I wondered how he'd fooled Raiven, because she was no idiot. Then again, snakes like him could be deceiving when they wanted to be. With me, he had nothing to hide.

By the time he was done with me that day, I hadn't given him anything. I could tell Viper and his guy I'd caught lurking in the corner of the building wanted a part of me. Stefano had made it very clear that I was his until he got his information and then Viper could have me.

I still didn't know what Viper's beef with me specifically was.

"Enjoy your dinner." Igor shoved me into my cell that I'd learned actually was an old walk-in cooler. Weak and in agony, I fell to my hands and knees. He tossed a sandwich in on the floor. It fell apart and scattered. Then he threw in a bottle of water, hitting me in the back with it.

"I wouldn't even fucking feed him if it was me," muttered Baldy.

"Stefano wants him to last long enough to get what he wants out of him, so he eats enough to keep him alive." The dickwad I'd dubbed Igor laughed.

I didn't know if I'd get out of there alive, but if I did, I'd never forget their faces. Fucking assholes.

Their cackling and the light ended as they slammed the door.

So goddamn hungry I didn't care, I blindly searched for every fucking piece of food on that floor. Then I sipped the water, wincing as I raised my arm. Unsure how long I'd be in there, I wanted to save some.

My chest wound was killing me, and the coughing I'd done from Stefano's version of waterboarding wasn't helping. There was going to be a special place in hell for that motherfucker too.

If I had my way, I'd be the one to send every fucking one of them there.

FIFTEEN

Raiven

"GOOD DAY TO DIE"—GODSMACK

"I've missed you so fucking much." His lips crashed into mine as his hands fisted my hair. I'd missed everything about him, and it was insane. The smell of him, his taste, his hands on my skin. I'd take it all.

Teeth grabbed at my bottom lip as he broke from the kiss. It was as if separating was painful.

My hands slipped up under the back of his shirt, nails skimming over each flexing muscle. They traced and memorized every curve, dip, and movement.

It wasn't long before our hands roamed, clutched, and ripped at our clothes. My shirt went flying, and my bra went sailing.

One nipple, then the other was pulled into his mouth. He tugged on my nipple piercings as my back was pressed to the cool wall. His tongue laved my chest while his fingers slipped into the waistband of my jeans and under the lace of my panties.

"So wet." The words caused his breath to blow across my nipples, and they tightened in anticipation, begging for his warm mouth to return

His fingers barely dipped into my core, teasing me as I pulled him back to my chest. Laughing, he broke away. Strong arms hefted me up until my clit rubbed on his hardened cock.

Even wrapping my legs tight around him, the layers between us were aggravating, and I tried to unfasten his pants. The need for him to be buried deep inside me was driving me fucking crazy.

"Raiven." The voice was interrupting my time with Lock, so I ignored it.

When my shoulder was shaken and the image and feel of Matlock disintegrated into dreamland, I was pissed.

"Dammit," I whined, not wanting to wake up.

"Shhh, you'll wake Presley."

At the mention of the little girl of my heart, I jolted awake. Sitting up in bed, eyes wide, my heart raced. Searching her toddler bed against the wall, I saw her cuddled up with her stuffed dragon. Knowing she was safe, I let out my worried breath.

Blinking rapidly, I wrinkled my nose and yawned. That's when I realized it was Styx who'd woken me.

"What are you doing? What time is it?" If Presley was still sleeping, it was early.

"Real fucking early. Get dressed and come to Smoke's office." He was vague and looked angry.

"Okay." Not sure what I could've done wrong, I climbed out of bed as Styx softly closed the door.

I dressed quickly and padded quietly down the hall to where Smoke had his office. Knocking, I waited as the voices inside ceased and the door swung open.

The dark-haired, ice-blue-eyed man who'd been introduced as Reaper the night before answered the door. All I knew of him was he was from Iowa and my uncle's old chapter. He stepped to the side, allowing me to pass.

I was shocked to find the room crammed with all the members that were down from Iowa, including my uncle, whose face resembled a human storm cloud. In fact, they all seemed pretty pissed off.

Smoke and some of the other guys looked resigned.

"What's going on?" My brow furrowed as I tried to make eye contact with any of them, but none of them would look at me. "Did I do something I don't know about?"

"No." Smoke ran a frustrated hand over his mouth. "Have a seat. I need to ask you something. If you don't want to do it, all you have to do is say so."

Nervous as hell, I sat at the lone chair across from him.

"Well, how about if you tell me what's going on, then I can decide?"

"We finally heard from Gabriel De Luca." I shrunk a little in the chair. They were a powerful family in Chicago. Though they were prominent business owners, everyone knew his family was part of the Sicilian Mafia in America. I'd since found out from Gunny that he was essentially Stefano's boss.

"What did he have to say?" It was difficult to form words, because my tongue was thick and dry.

"He proposed a plan. We don't like it. But it's already been nearly five weeks since everything happened. We don't know what kind of shape Lock's actually in. The doc that called said he was stable the last she saw him, but that's been nearly three weeks now. We don't even know if he's still alive." He swallowed hard, and I jumped when Gunny punched the wall and roared.

Without another word, he stormed from the packed office.

Everyone looked uncomfortable. "Should I go after him?" Hacker asked. Smoke nodded, and he left.

"What was the plan?"

"He wants to use you as bait. Offer to trade you for Lock." His gray eyes stormed. My uncle growled; feet shuffled. Fear seeped deep inside me, penetrating my bones.

"T-trade me?" I stuttered.

"Not really, but we'd let them believe it. We'd have everything set up. Reaper here is the best sniper that I know, and Hollywood was his spotter. They'd be among many who'd have eyes on y'all. But this is

125

your choice, and if you say no, then the answer is no." Smoke spoke softly but held eye contact with me through his entire explanation.

"Umm." I glanced around the room, looking at all the faces. Many I'd become friendly with and several had my ink on them already. In fact, most of them.

Joker had even inked me before he'd left last time. I'd offered to trade, but he'd declined. He and the rest of their crew had gone home for about a week and a half and arrived back last night.

Sitting there thinking about what they were proposing had a few realizations setting in. I'd run from Stefano out of fear for my life. I never thought he'd actually chase me down. Nor did I think my actions would pull someone else into this. A lot of someones, but specifically Lock. A man who had a young girl. I really had no one. My aunt and uncle, but no children or significant other who needed me.

Nodding once, I firmly said, "I'll do it."

"Raiven!" my uncle pleaded.

"Pops, this is her decision," Smoke reminded him.

My resolved gaze held his. "I love you, Uncle Carlisle, but Presley needs her dad. Besides, I'll be okay."

His head dropped, and a shuddering sigh left his big, bulky body. We both knew there was no guarantee that was the truth.

"What do I do?" My jaw clenched as the possible outcomes ran through my head.

"We're going to call Stefano. Tell him we have something he wants. Tell him we want our guy back and he can have you. We'll make it sound like you're some chick that doesn't matter two shits to us. It's going to sound bad, but I swear to you, and to you, Pops, we'll do everything in our power to keep you safe." Smoke leaned back in his chair and observed me. His eyes were calculating but patient.

"Make the call." Inside, I worried that it may be too late for Lock, but I prayed I was wrong. I clenched my jaw and fortified my resolve.

"Done. All of you clear out except for Check, Styx, and Raiven." Without so much as a mutter, they all filed out of the room. My uncle

126

wouldn't meet my eye, and it hurt, but deep inside I knew I was doing the right thing.

Once everyone was out, Styx stepped up behind me and placed a hand on my shoulder. "Forgive me for anything I do."

I nodded, wide-eyed and unsure.

"Let's do this." Check handed Smoke a cheap-looking phone.

"It's clean?" Smoke asked him.

"You doubt me?" Check asked with a raised brow. Check was their techno guy and road captain. I'd slowly been figuring out the different positions and their names since I'd been there. He looked way younger than his midtwenties, and he was really damn pretty, but fuck could his eyes be hard.

Smoke grunted, "No," then put it on speaker and dialed the number I guessed was Stefano's. I assumed he got it from Gabriel, because they hadn't asked me for it.

It rang several times before I heard Stefano's voice come over the speaker. Where it once sent chills down my spine for another reason, those chills were now out of fear.

"Who is this, and where did you get this number?" He was curt and suspicious.

"My name and where I got your number are irrelevant. You have something we want, Stefano, and we have something you want." Smoke sounded as cold as hell, and it was a little unnerving.

"What might that be?" Quickly, Stefano's tone turned sarcastically smug.

Smoke's gaze flickered to Styx, who suddenly grabbed my hair, jerking my head back. I shrieked in surprise. He quickly let it go, and I read the apology in his eyes.

"A certain dark-haired person. Lots of tats. Mouthy." Smoke grinned at me, and despite the shock of Styx pulling my hair, I bit my lip because he was right.

"That could be anyone."

Smoke looked at me and held a finger over his lips. "Tell your boyfriend you miss him." He shook his head, implying I shouldn't say anything.

He then slapped his arm hard enough to leave an imprint. It scared me, and I jumped and squeaked again. "Tell him!"

"H-he's not my b-boyfriend." Even trying to act, there was no way I'd say he was.

There was a moment of silence over the phone. "Raiven? Is that you?"

I could hear the evil grin in his tone, and I wanted to vomit. Speaking with him again was making me physically sick.

"I don't want anything to do with you, Stefano. No one knows what happened. I-I haven't said a word. Can't you please just drop this? Let me live my life."

His sinister chuckle made my skin crawl. "Oh, Raiven. I know you never said anything. I'm still alive. If you had, I wouldn't have made it twenty-four hours. You never got it, did you? I could have killed you at any time while you rode the trains that night. This wasn't about killing you. This is about you being mine. Your life is mine."

"No!" My shock and fear poured through that single word.

"Alright. When do you want to make this trade? And how do I know I can trust you? After all, you won't even tell me your name. That seems unfair, since you know mine." He was obviously done talking to me.

I slapped the palm of one hand over my mouth and wrapped my other arm around myself, nails digging into the back of my arm. Nausea welled, churning in my stomach at the realization that Soap was right. He'd never let me go. I'd been so naive.

"Since I'm sure you know you have my SAA, you know I'm with the Demented Sons MC. Which, by the way, you really fucked up when you did that. But as long as you uphold your part of this trade, and of course provided my guy is still alive, we're willing to call this situation even and done with. With that being said, as soon as possible for the trade. We're not sure where you are, so where do you suggest we meet?"

Stefano laughed. "*I* fucked up? Do you know who I am?"

"We know exactly who you are. Do I need to say it over this line?" Smoke spoke with deadly calm.

"Well, I'd like to say somewhere public, but your friend here… let's just say he may draw unwanted attention. Where do you want to meet, since you seem to be calling the shots here?" His question was snide, and I could tell he didn't like the situation.

"Where are you?" Smoke asked.

"I'm in the lovely state of Kansas. You coming here then? Because I'm sure as hell not driving up to your little *play*house." Stefano's chuckle made me want to hurl.

"We're actually in Texas," Smoke answered, and I noticed he didn't specify where we were.

"That's right. A little birdy did tell me you were heading that way. So how about you drive to Dallas? Call me when you get there, and I'll have further instructions." Without giving Smoke a chance to say another word, the call ended.

Smoke motioned for Check to get rid of the phone. Check quickly disassembled it and left the room with the pieces.

"You ready to travel?" Smoke asked me.

"Now?" I squeaked as my eyes bugged.

"Time is not Lock's friend." Despite their levity, the truth of his words hit hard.

Brow furrowed, I nodded.

"As ready as I'd ever be to see that piece of shit again. But what do I tell Presley? She knows I'm always here. She sleeps in my room. How is she going to handle me being gone?" It was that little girl I worried about more than myself and my safety.

"We'll tell her your aunt Jean and her poppas are going to be with her while you go get some things for her. I don't know. She's a kid, she'll be okay." Styx shrugged, and I looked at him in disbelief.

"Do you not know that child at all?" Incredulous, I asked.

"You haffa take me wiff you, Pwincess Waiven. Yous my fwend, so you can't juss weave me here! What if you no come back wike my mommy and daddy?" Fists propped on her purple tutu, she glowered at me. She had at least seven of those crazy, goofy skirts, all in different colors. She loved the damn things.

Her words tore at my heartstrings, which was why I'd hoped we'd be out of there before she woke up. No such luck. The guys had been sequestered in their meeting room longer than I'd expected.

Crouching down in front of her, I loosened her hands from her hips. I held them snugly in mine. Her big blue eyes stared at me, full of fear and things a little girl her age didn't understand. Things she shouldn't have to worry about.

"Presley. I'm going to try to bring you a super surprise." That was her thing lately. If it was something she deemed really amazing, it was a super surprise. If it was something small then it was simply a surprise. She made me laugh at times. Something I worried I'd never do again after we'd lost Lock.

"A supah supwise?" Her eyes popped open wide.

"Yeah, sweetheart, a super surprise." I tried my best to smile, but I was pretty sure it came off like more of a grimace. The fact that I may not be coming back to her hurt my heart, but I shoved it to the back of my mind.

She jumped up and down in excitement and threw her arms around my neck. My emotions went haywire like they had been doing since we'd arrived in Texas.

Without Lock.

Tears welled as I hugged her tight.

SIXTEEN

Lock

"THE VENGEFUL ONE"—DISTURBED

I didn't need a mirror to know I was a mere shell of myself. Regardless of how much I'd wasted away, I still could barely hold my own body weight up. Clutching the hook above me to keep the weight off the raw skin around my wrists, I stood on my tiptoes. Every muscle in my body was shaking. I'd moved past muscle failure.

For days Stefano would disappear and I would be subjected to Viper's vicious brand of torture.

Like that day.

That day was a Viper day.

Fuck. My. Life.

Another punch landed on my already aching ribs. He'd been using me as a human punching bag for the last fifteen minutes. Thankfully, he was busy running his mouth so it wasn't a solid fifteen minutes of hits. It was better than the day before, when he'd hung me from the hook the same way, then hosed me down and shocked me with jumper cables.

"Not so fucking tough now, are you?" he jeered.

My head hung, and sweat dripped as if I was the one getting the workout. It was hard enough to breathe, let alone try to talk.

When he grabbed my hair and jerked my head up, I swore I was shaving my fucking head if I made it out. When. When I made it out. I also swore a vicious retribution against each and every one of the pieces of shit who'd kept me locked up worse than an animal. It was the only thing that keep me alive.

The memories of Presley and Raiven only kept me going for so long before that began to hurt more than drive me. It took digging deep for that simmering anger and hatred in order to keep the desire to live burning.

"You know, it's funny. You've never asked me why I hate you." He gave me a quick jab to my left ribs. "Not once. Aren't you even the slightest bit curious?"

Still holding my head up with his left hand, he stared at me, expecting me to look away. The hatred in my eyes burned bright, and I saw it reflected in his dark ones. Yet I held my tongue.

Viper was a braggart. I knew he'd tell me eventually, but it really didn't matter. I gave less than two shits about him or his hatred for me.

"I'll tell you anyway. One word. Letty."

Keeping my face emotionless was difficult, because he'd actually surprised me.

Letty? What the fuck did he know about Letty?

"The little accident?" He smirked, then rasped out, "You're welcome," as he stood there with my shaggy hair in his hand.

Things began to click as I remembered Gunny telling me about the message they'd received. We'd had problems with a bunch of the Demon Runners nomads for a while, but never with his crew. At least I'd never suspected we did. There was no love lost between our clubs, but how did his crew from down in Omaha get involved with the nomads' bullshit up by us? And what the fuck did Letty have to do with it?

Rage began to build as I realized he was saying he'd been responsible for her death. Simmering, and chest heaving, I held my tongue.

"Did you ever wonder why she wouldn't marry you?"

What the actual fuck? How the hell did he know that?

My face must've given something away, because he let out a dark laugh.

"Because she was already married to me," he whispered in my ear.

The rage finally erupted, and I roared in disbelief. He had to be fucking with me.

"That's right. You were fucking *my wife,* you piece of shit. But the only reason you were able to stick your dick in her tight cunt was because I sent her to you." His lip curled, and I read the hatred for me on his face. It appeared to run nearly as deep as mine for him.

I lunged at him, but strung up the way I was, I only succeeded in losing my footing. All of my weight landed on the cuffs around my wrist, and between them, my shoulders, and my ribs, I screamed through gritted teeth.

He stood there and laughed at my pain and helplessness. I wanted nothing more than to get loose and choke the life out of him.

"Oh yes, I know all about her going up there to see her friend, how she got drunk and fucked you. Here's another bombshell for you: she actually tried to pass your brat off as mine." At my building incredulity, he sneered.

"Oh yes, your precious Letty was going to keep your brat from you. The thing is, she didn't know I'd had a vasectomy after one of the club whores tried to tie me down with a kid. When I told Letty I knew she was a liar, she broke down and told me the truth. Well, maybe it took a little, um, convincing, to get her to admit to whoring herself out to you." His dead eyes watched me for a further reaction.

My jaw was ready to crack, I was clenching it so hard. Anything to keep from giving him any further satisfaction.

"Turned out to be a good thing she didn't lose the kid after the convincing conversation. Once she was presentable again, I sent her up to you to gather information. You being the noble schmuck you were, fell right into it. Didn't any of you wonder how our nomads knew so much about your club business? Your habits, your families? That's right, it was your precious Letty. Stupid rookie mistake, Lock. Never fall for the pillow talk bullshit." Without warning, he hit me again.

"You're," I gasped, "a… fucking… liar." It was so hard to get the words out, I started coughing, which made things worse, and I involuntarily flinched.

"Oh, you wish I was. The only consolation I'll give you is that she fell for you. The bitch told me she wasn't going to supply us with info anymore and she wanted a divorce. Fucking idiot didn't realize her usefulness had ended as soon as she said those words. YOU STOLE HER FROM ME!" he shrieked in my face, spittle flying from his mouth, veins popping out in his forehead, tendons straining in his neck. "I won't be happy until every single one of you Demented Sons is gone. But I'll get great satisfaction from starting with you." His expression was psychotically calm.

He dropped my head from his hold, then landed punch after punch to my ribs and abdomen. Shoulders screaming, I hung there, unable to maintain my balance on my toes as he hit me over and over.

"Viper! What the fuck do you think you're doing?" I'd never been so glad to hear Stefano's voice in my life. It echoed across the warehouse, bouncing off the old walls and rusty machinery.

Viper stepped back, chest heaving as he flicked his gaze to Stefano. "Trying to get your answers."

"You stupid fucker. I have my answer. I know where she is. They are going to trade her for him, but I assured them he was alive." Fury spun from his tone.

"What? You promised him to me after you were done!" Viper shouted.

"Well, it would seem that while I've been away, you've been having your fun. Do you think my guys don't report back to me? Evidently, they neglected to tell me the extent of your entertainment. Besides, they have his kid too. You can have at him and her after I get Raiven. Hell, go down there and kill them all as soon as I get what I want. I don't care.

But you better not have ruined my bargaining chip. If I'd known they'd be so willing to trade, I may have done it in the beginning. Then again, I get so much enjoyment out of persuasion techniques." He chuckled.

There was no way my brothers would let him get to Presley, so I contained my rage. I prayed that it was some kind of trick and that they'd never let Raiven within a hundred feet of any of these pieces of shit. They better have a fucking foolproof plan, because the thought of Stefano having her again made me ill.

"Get him down and chain him to the chair. Hose him down to clean him up. We need to leave with him soon, and I don't want to smell him." The demands were followed immediately by Igor and Baldy.

They needn't have bothered chaining me, I was too weak and sore to fight them. However, when the cold blast of the water hit me, I was almost grateful for the chains. I'd have probably fallen out of the chair otherwise.

It took my breath away, and the force pushed me to the side. When they stopped, there was nothing but the sound of my ragged breathing and dripping water echoing through the old building. I couldn't lift a finger, let alone my head. I was physically and mentally exhausted.

When they unchained me and told me to stand, I fell to the floor. Everything was blurry and tipping before it went black.

By the time I woke again, it took a minute for my vision to clear enough to see I was in an old barn. The wooden complete-with-hayloft kind. It smelled of musty hay and disuse. Gaps between the wall slats let in muted sunlight, and dust motes danced in the beams of light as my head lolled around, trying to see if I was alone.

I could barely hold my eyes open.

"Good morning, sunshine." I moaned at Igor's chipper comment.

Great, good ol' Igor was there. Fun times. Thankfully, I didn't see Viper anywhere at that moment.

"You should be happy, your people should be here shortly."

"My people?" My voice sounded rusty and creaky. Clearing my throat didn't help.

That was when I heard a vehicle pull up behind me. The old doors groaned as they opened.

"They're on their way," Stefano announced. He rattled off orders to the men with him. The ones I could see were armed to the teeth. I couldn't see how many there were in total because most were out of my line of sight.

One went up into the questionable hayloft, and I wondered if he'd fall through. The rest dispersed, leaving Igor, Baldy, and Stefano.

Time ticked by as I sat chained to the same fucking chair from the slaughterhouse. Off and on, I dozed, no matter how hard I tried to keep my eyes open.

The doors in front of me were rolled open by Igor and Baldy, and I watched as a black SUV drove up.

The vehicle sat there as the dust settled. No one got out, and I could feel the tension of the men in the barn.

Finally, the passenger door opened, then the other doors. I recognized Styx, Smoke, Check, and Hacker. The last person to climb out set my heart racing, and I wanted to shout at them not to let her come in there.

I wasn't prepared for her. My memories of her hadn't done her justice. Even dressed casually in snug-fitting skinny jeans, Chucks, and a red T-shirt, she was beautiful. Her blue-black hair glinted in the sun, and I almost smiled at her signature pinup-style curls. Ink flashing, she stepped forward with Styx holding her colorful arm as he jerked her forward.

My eyes narrowed at his treatment of her.

She stumbled, and he yanked her upright. My fists clenched.

They stopped a good ten feet from where I sat. Her gasp filled the old space.

Though I tried not to look at her face, I couldn't help it. The tears streaking her cheeks sent a stabbing pain through my chest that rivaled all of the abuse they'd subjected me to. Her lower lip trembled as she trailed her gaze from my head to my bare feet. I hated to think of what she was seeing.

Not only was it embarrassing knowing I looked like shit, but I could tell by her eyes that it upset her. I hated that.

"Raiven. My darling Raiven. It's been far too long," Stefano crooned from behind me. Fuck, I hated hearing that almost more than I hated seeing her upset.

Her gaze left me and shot to him. The fear and revulsion that battled on her face fed my rage. I wished for a way to get free. I wished for that useless scalpel I'd never been able to use. I wished for anything to protect her and keep her away from the piece of fucking shit talking to her.

"You said he was good." Smoke growled as he spoke to Stefano.

"He's alive. If you remember, I did say we couldn't meet in public due to his, uh… appearance. Gino, bring her to me." Ahh, Igor's name was Gino.

"Not so fast." Styx shoved her behind him as Smoke demanded, "Unchain him."

Gino glanced at Stefano for guidance.

"Do it," Stefano said softly. Gino unchained me, and it left me feeling like I'd float away.

Styx handed Raiven off to Hacker as he stepped toward me.

"Don't move!" Stefano's men raised their guns, and everyone but Styx whipped out a gun too.

"You were supposed to be unarmed," Stefano hissed.

"Yeah, so were you. I guess we all lied, huh?" Smoke's response was snarky and sounded like something I would've said. I almost laughed.

"I'm only coming to help him up. I'm not armed." Styx held his arms out.

"He's not," said Smoke.

"Check him," Stefano instructed someone.

The guy patted him down, and Styx grinned. "That's my dick, asshole. Want another feel?"

After rolling his eyes, the guy nodded, and Stefano agreed to Styx helping me.

"You." He pointed at Hacker. "Drop your weapon to the ground. Then bring her to me as your friend here gets your man."

Legs shaking like a newborn colt, I stood with Styx's aid. "Jesus, bro. I've got you." He crouched slightly to allow him to put one of my arms over his shoulder.

I winced at the pain in my shoulder from the movement. Each step forward was agony, and as I passed Raiven I paused. I wanted to reach for her. Touch her. Save her.

But Styx urged me forward until we stood next to the rest of my brothers.

I waited for the moment when all hell broke loose and the plan they'd hatched came to fruition, but nothing happened. Hacker simply handed her off and backed away.

"We're done then." Stefano grinned evilly as he slid a hand up, brushing Raiven's hair off her shoulder. Her shudder sent waves of disbelief and fury coursing through my veins.

"No!" I shouted in my creaky voice.

"Stop. Not now," Styx said quietly in my ear. We all began backing out toward the SUV, and I tried to fight the hold Styx had on me. All I could think was we couldn't leave her with him.

Besides my promise to Pops, she was mine!

"Get in the SUV. We're going to have to move fast." Smoke spoke low, and I couldn't believe what I was hearing.

Though I wanted to, I was in no condition to fight as they essentially forced me into the SUV. Still waiting for something to happen, I yelled at them as they shut the doors and we whipped around to leave. "What are you doing? You can't leave her there!"

"It had to be this way. I need to get you somewhere to check you out," Styx said, and I wanted to knock his teeth out.

I couldn't believe what had happened.

It was like my nightmare had no end.

SEVENTEEN

Raiven

"THE KILL"—THIRTY SECONDS TO MARS

"I've missed you, my little bird." Stefano fingered my hair, and nausea welled to the base of my throat.

"Funny, I've missed you too." A voice I didn't recognize came from behind me, and Stefano jerked me in front of him.

"Gabriel! What are you doing here?" He tried to sound normal but I could not only sense the tension in his body behind me, but hear the slight waver in his voice.

The man who'd joined us was tall with dark hair, dressed immaculately, and flanked by several burly suited men with hard eyes. Much like Stefano.

The difference between them was the newcomer had a suit that had obviously been tailored to fit him like a second skin. It was pure money and power.

It was then that I knew I was looking at Gabriel De Luca. The few pics anyone had ever captured of him didn't do him justice.

My heart rattled and my inhale was shaky as I waited to see what would happen.

"The better question is, what are you doing here? This doesn't look like a sick aunt." His brows rose and he motioned toward me.

"I...." Stefano stepped up next to me. He was speechless and intimidated for the first time since I'd met him.

"You what? That's what you told me, right? You had to leave town because your aunt was ill. Your only living relative. Surely you remember what you said. So you lied to me?" It was unmistakably a rhetorical question. He turned his head toward the massive man next to him without taking his eyes from Stefano. "Go get her."

"Gabriel. She's my girlfriend. We had a disagreement. I was only coming down to get her. Bring her to heel and back to Chicago. I only made up the story about an aunt because I didn't want you thinking I was pussy-whipped." His hold on my arm tightened before the other man reached us and pulled me free. He motioned for me to go toward the door by Gabriel.

The deep chuckle that left Gabriel De Luca held little humor. "Is that so? In the middle of Nowhere, Texas? In an abandoned barn? Oh, and the obvious trade I witnessed? What was that, Stefano? Do tell."

"It's not what you think. She was hiding out with them. I-I was just getting her back," Stefano stammered. I'd never seen his composure crack like it was in front of Gabriel. It was interesting to find out the situation with me and Lock had gone on behind Gabriel's back.

"You had dealings with a motorcycle club that weren't sanctioned by me!" he roared. Then quieter, "And they weren't the first ones, were they?"

Stefano didn't answer, he only stood there wide-eyed. Once we were with the rest of his crew, the burly guy stopped me.

Gabriel made a valiant effort to rein in his emotions, but I could see the fury storming through his dark brown eyes. The muscle that jumped in his jaw ticked twice. The burly guy moved me behind himself and Gabriel.

"Get out here! All of you, or I'll hunt you and your families down!" he called, and I jumped. Men I hadn't known were hiding came out of the woodwork. One climbed down a rickety ladder.

They all stood, uncertain and wary. Six men including Stefano, to Gabriel's four.

"Toss the weapons to the side." They obeyed the commanding man without hesitation.

No one said a word.

Finally, Gabriel spoke with a calm that was carefully cultivated. "Stefano. You betrayed the family. You think I don't know what you did? You think I'm stupid? That my men are stupid?"

"She's just a girl. She's nobody. You can have her if you want, then this is done," Stefano bargained, and I gasped as my eyes nearly popped out of my head. I looked at Gabriel. Sure, I could appreciate he was a beautiful man, but Jesus. I wasn't property to be traded or handed off like a secondhand shirt!

"Hmm, then this is done?" Gabriel sounded curious.

"Sure. You know I wouldn't cause trouble. She's not worth that much hassle. She's yours. My gift." Like that was supposed to appease the second-in-command of the most powerful fucking mafia family in Chicago.

"Ah, Stefano. You know what I was talking about, and it wasn't this girl or your obsession with her. It wasn't even your not-so-secret drug dealings with the Demon Runners. No. You killed Giacomo and believed you'd get away with it." Gabriel's tone was flat, emotionless.

Stefano's face went white as a sheet.

There was only the slightest movement as Gabriel reached in his jacket. He withdrew a pistol with something long on the end. It looked like the one Stefano had used the night he killed that man in the restaurant. Suddenly, it all made sense.

The man he'd killed wasn't some random guy, he was connected. Holy shit.

Every movement was fluid as Gabriel raised his arm and pointed it at Stefano. He looked like a dark avenging angel, and it sent a chill through me.

"No one betrays me. No one betrays the family." His chin tipped up.

With only the slightest sound, a hole appeared in Stefano's head, and he dropped like a stone. One by one, all the men with Stefano fell. Blood, dark and shiny, spread from their lifeless bodies before sinking into the dirt.

In shock, I could only stand there and shake.

Gabriel turned to me, and I nearly hyperventilated. The guys had said I would be safe, but this guy didn't look like he was my friend.

"Please don't kill me, I didn't know. I swear. I won't say anything." Pleading, I fought the tears and nausea. It was like déjà vu. The night Stefano had killed that man came back like a nightmare.

"I know you won't say anything. You haven't said anything yet, though I wish you'd contacted me." He returned his gun to the inside of his jacket, then brushed a speck of the dust from the barn off his dark sleeve.

"I didn't know. He always said he was a businessman. I foolishly never questioned. I… I don't know what else to say," I choked out.

He studied me in silence. It was unnerving the way he appeared to be reading my mind. "Don't worry, I believe you. Your friends, they are friends of my family. They brought Stefano's betrayal to our attention. For that, I owed them. I don't like owing people. I believe if I return you to them, we'll be even. Don't you think?" The corner of his mouth raised imperceptibly.

Heart hammering in disbelief, I could only nod.

"Good. Tony and Joseph will return you to your friends and family. Then everyone is satisfied." Without another word to me, he turned to one of the men.

"Get this taken care of." He waved dismissively at the bodies on the floor.

Like what had happened was no big deal, he walked out of the barn followed by one of his men. The other two motioned for me to leave.

One last glance at Stefano, and I puked all over the grass as soon as I cleared the doorway.

Gasping, I looked to the man closest me. "I'm so sorry."

I was terrified I'd gotten it on him. He simply shrugged. "It happens."

It happens. Fucking A, what the hell kind of dream am I stuck in?

As we pulled onto the main road, four bikes pulled in behind us. The two men seemed completely unconcerned. As I glanced back, I recognized the Demented Sons cuts. Relief flooded me.

The drive back to the Demented Sons clubhouse took about two and a half hours. Two and a half hours of silence from the suits in the SUV we traveled in. They did stop once for me to get a drink, to wash out my mouth, and to pee. For that I was grateful.

The four guys who'd been following us were Reaper, Hollywood, Gunny, and a guy I didn't recognize by name, only his face. Reaper, Hollywood, and Gunny all hugged me. The other guy gave me a nod.

"Damn, doll, I was worried for a bit there. Lock didn't want to leave you, and I thought he was gonna fuck everything up." Gunny grinned, and I burst into tears. The images of the man Stefano had killed and then Stefano and his men bleeding into the dirt kept flashing through my head on a repeating cycle.

"Aww hell, babe, I'm sorry." He held me until I gained a semblance of control and then we loaded back up and finished the last leg of the trip.

We arrived not long after Lock and the guys had returned. Everyone was still in the common area of the clubhouse, except Lock. Gabriel's two suits went into Smoke's office with him briefly, then they left.

"Where's Lock? And where's Presley?" I questioned Styx.

"He's taking a shower. He wanted to get cleaned up before he saw her. Smoke's daughter took Presley down to the park with a couple of prospects to give him time. She doesn't know he's here yet. You may want to check on him. He's weak as fuck, but refused to let anyone help him," Styx replied.

Gunny appeared worried.

Without answering him, I rushed down the hallway to the room I'd called home for over a month. The water wasn't running, and I tentatively knocked on the door to the bathroom. It wasn't latched, and at my touch, it swung open a bit.

Crystal-blue eyes met mine in the mirror, and I hesitantly stepped in the room. He held clippers in his hand as he shaved one side of his head. Dark blond hair was scattered around him and on the floor.

"Um, do you want help?"

He shut the power off. "I'd like to say no, but I can barely hold my arm up anymore." Defeat reigned on his features, and I ached for the man I'd known so briefly before. He gestured for me to take them.

Slowly, I took the warm, shiny clippers and flicked them on. The vibrations shot through my hand as I raised them to his head. I started to follow the separation from where his hair was longer on top and where it had grown out on the sides.

"Cut it all off."

"What?" I was sure I'd heard wrong.

"All of it. Cut it off."

"But...."

"But what?" His eyes were tired.

"I kind of like it longer on top." I spoke softly. I wasn't even sure if he heard me above the soft buzz of the clipper.

"Cut it off." His voice was broken but firm.

Lips pulled between my teeth, I fought begging him not to do it. I'd wanted to run my fingers through it so bad. I'd dreamed of it wrapped around my fingers as I pulled him into my heat. The thought of getting rid of it all made it hard for me to swallow.

Hands trembling slightly, I took a deep breath to steady them. The first swipe of his long locks left them slowly drifting to the floor. Row after row, the dark golden lengths fell. Some of it was clumped and matted, causing me to have to work slowly to get the clippers through it.

Finally, his entire head was sheared down to less than a quarter of an inch. I wanted to cry.

"Thank you."

I nodded but couldn't speak around the giant lump in my throat.

Though he was still beautiful, he looked gaunt, bruised, scarred, and haunted. He pulled his icy eyes from mine, his head dropped, and his shoulders heaved. It was damn near like staring at a living, breathing image from a POW camp.

Heartbreaking and disturbing.

Tentatively, I reached out to lay a hand on his shoulder. He flinched but then relaxed somewhat. When he didn't push me away, I gently maneuvered him so I could hold him.

He didn't speak, he didn't make eye contact, but his once massive arms wrapped tightly around me. His face buried in the crook of my neck as his body shook with silent but tormented sobs.

I hated to think of what he had endured at the hands of Stefano, and I nearly buckled under the weight of the guilt. If not for me, this man, this amazing father, would have been in Texas safe and sound with his daughter.

My own tears ran unchecked down my face and neck to pool with his. As I stroked his back, I mentally cringed at the ability to feel his ribs. Those glorious muscles I remembered so well in my dreams were but a memory.

"Hey. How about if we get in the shower? For old times' sake?" I tried my damnedest to lighten the mood.

Nodding against my skin, he stepped back, arms falling limp to his sides.

"Sorry," he whispered. He wouldn't meet my gaze, so I gave him few moments to regroup while I cleared Presley's toys out of the tub, then started the water. Using the excuse of waiting for the water temperature to stabilize, I wiped my tears with the shoulder of my T-shirt.

Unashamed, I undressed as he waited. Once I was naked, I reached to help him untie the hospital scrub pants that hung low on his narrow hips. Surprisingly strong, though shaky, his hands closed rapidly over mine, and he slowly pushed my hands back.

Fumbling, it took him several tries to get the simple tie undone.

Frustration colored his face red by the time they loosened and dropped to his ankles.

I desperately wanted to reach for him to offer him a steadying hand as he wobbled when pulling each foot free of the pant legs. Deep down, I knew he wouldn't welcome it, so I waited.

"You climb in first," he rasped.

"Sure." Standing at the edge of the warm water, I allowed him to use my shoulder to steady himself.

"I meant to ask you how you got that brown spot in your eyes," I asked to make conversation. I'd noticed it that first night. The one that seemed a million years ago, but there'd never been a time to ask.

"It's called heterochromia iridis. Basically, a variety of color in a single iris. My dad has it, Gunny has it, I have it. Came on when we were about six, I think. Genetic shit." He shrugged and closed his eyes.

Evidently, that conversation was over.

Tipping his head back in the water, I watched as the hot streams washed over his head and flooded down his face. For the first time since I saw him sitting chained to that chair, he looked at peace.

Loath to interrupt, I grabbed the shampoo and poured some in my hand. "Turn around?"

While he did what I asked, he braced both hands on the wall. The soft moan that escaped him as I lathered the bristly, short hair did stupid things to my body. It hadn't gotten the memo that Matlock wasn't the same man, nor was he in any way prepared for what it wanted.

Trailing my soapy hands down, I massaged his neck and shoulders. When my hands tried to work their way down his arms, he pulled away and dropped his head into the water. The foam had taken a faint pinkish-brown tinge, and I knew it had to be from dried blood. I hated it.

He remained that way until the water ran clear. When I tried to wash his body with a scrubby, he took it from me, held the wall with one hand, and scrubbed himself with the other before switching.

Standing there doing nothing left me feeling overwhelmingly useless. I washed myself for lack of anything else to do. Except, instead of allowing him to switch spots with me so I could rinse, I stepped under the water with him.

"Lock. Please let me be here for you. Let me help you the way you helped me," I pleaded, and his eyes clouded.

His snort of derision startled me. "If I'd helped you, you wouldn't have witnessed any of that today."

"If it wasn't for you, I may not have even been alive to see anything today, goddammit!" Not wanting to fight with him, I reined in my temper and ripped the shower curtain open. He was so frustrating, but I knew he'd been through hell. I needed him to let me be there for him. It was the only way I could see myself being able to compartmentalize everything that had happened and all the shit I'd witnessed. I needed a fucking purpose like I needed my next breath.

Dripping water on the floor, I jerked two towels, one after the other, from the small cabinet and slammed the door.

During my brief moment of anger, he'd shut the water off. Not trusting myself to be kind, I handed him his towel and dried myself with furious motions.

Warily, he watched me as he slowly dried himself. The towel wrapped tight around him, he held the edge of the shower to step out of the tub.

My anger quickly faded as I stepped closer to be his shoulder for support.

"Jesus, Raiven. Please put a towel or some clothes on?" At his hoarse request, I looked to him in confusion, to see him staring intently at the ceiling. The bulge in the front of his towel gave away the problem.

Honestly, I was surprised he had it in him to be turned on. That surprise didn't stop the little zip of satisfaction that sped through me. Ever so slowly, I dried myself again, even though I'd already done it, then wrapped the towel, securing it over my boobs.

"Oh, I'm sorry. Do I embarrass you? Repulse you?" Eyes wide, I blinked innocently.

When he growled, grabbed my hand, and pressed it to his massive erection, I gasped and my lips formed a silent O.

"I think you know exactly what you do to me, but I'm in no condition to do a motherfucking thing about it." His blue-gray eyes seemed to glow as they bored into mine.

"Lock," I whispered, part chastisement, part plea.

"I hate to ask, but will you help me get dressed? I want to see my daughter."

Embarrassed that my anger had made me forget he had yet to see Presley, I ducked my head. Trying not to make it obvious that I was aware of how drained he was, I helped him to the room, where he sat wearily on the edge of the bed.

"What do you want to wear?" I asked as I dug through the drawers I had filled with the clothes he'd brought with him initially. There was no rationale for why I'd unpacked, washed, dried, and put away his clothes in the drawers next to mine. Except for my unwavering hope that he'd make it back here.

"Jeans and a hoodie. Grab me a T-shirt too. Please," he tacked on almost as an afterthought.

"Lock, it's damn near a hundred degrees out there. This place is like a fucking oven in the summer. I don't know why no one ever told me that before I agreed to move here." I muttered the last to myself, but he heard.

He actually chuckled. Though it sounded rusty, the sound was music to my ears, and I glanced up from digging through his clothes to shoot him a small grin.

"It's not like I'll be going outside and running laps. We'll be in the AC, so we'll be okay. I don't want Presley seeing me... like this." His gaze dropped to his lap, his humor quickly fading. It wasn't like he was skin and bones, but he'd certainly lost a significant amount of his bulk.

"Of course. Sorry." I pulled out a pair of cut-off shorts and a tank top for myself, pulling them on.

"You have got to be fucking kidding me." A look over my shoulder showed his mouth hanging open and his eyes as wide as mine had been.

"What?" My brow furrowed, and I tipped my head in question.

"You didn't put a bra on. Hell, for that matter, you didn't put any fucking panties on! There is no way you're going out there half-naked in front of a bunch of horny-ass bikers."

Propping my fists on my hips, arms akimbo, I glared at him. "You, Matlock Archer, don't get to tell me what I will or won't wear." I raised a brow. "I've been wearing these clothes for weeks, and I've survived just fine."

His storm-cloud eyes narrowed at me as his jaw worked back and forth. Thankfully, he chose to keep his further opinions to himself.

Plopping his clothes on the bed next to him, I leaned down and placed my hands on my knees to look him in the eye. I didn't miss how his gaze flickered down the front of my shirt. With a smirk, I asked him, "Do you want boxers on? Or do you prefer to go commando?"

"Give me the goddamn boxers. I need something to help hold this thing under control." He motioned to his dick, and my smirk curled wider.

Trying not to make a big deal of his weakness, I dressed him as he helped the best he could. "You're going to need a belt," I mumbled as I buttoned his jeans. Not realizing he'd heard me, I was shocked to hear him answer.

"No shit."

When I looked at him in disbelief, he gave me his own twisted smirk, though his held little humor. "When you're locked in the dark for weeks on end, you learn to rely on your other senses. I can hear very well."

Blanching at the small snippet of what he'd been subjected to, I inhaled deeply.

"Right." Grabbing a belt, I threaded it through the loops. Continuing to be so near to him was making my belly flutter.

Determined to nurse him back to health, I tried to gain control of my emotions.

It would only be repaying a debt. Once he was better, I would leave.

Fuck, this is going to suck.

EIGHTEEN

Lock

"BEGIN AGAIN"—SHINEDOWN

Before we even made it to the main room of the clubhouse I'd only been to a handful of times since becoming a Demented Son, I heard it. The sweetest sound to ever hit my ears.

My daughter's beautiful giggles.

It sucked that I had to stop halfway down the short hallway to rest, but each step was a struggle. Raiven stayed by my side the whole time. Patiently waiting.

God, I didn't deserve her sweetness. Not to mention, it embarrassed the fuck out of me to have her see me like that. If I hadn't been strung up and getting the shit beat out of me right before I'd been released, I might not have been so bad. I also hated that she'd quit calling me by my name and started calling me my road name. Except for when she'd chewed my ass.

Once my head quit spinning and my legs quit shaking, I moved forward. Seeing Presley riding around on Gunny's shoulders as she squealed made me smile. It also gave me time to make it to a chair before he put her down. I'd never be able to stay upright when she barreled into me like I knew she would.

"Daddy!" Her shout was ear-piercing, but I loved it. Gunny set her down, and true to form, she ran at me, launching herself into my arms.

"Baby girl. God, I missed you." Breathing in her sweet, soft hair, I held her tight. I never wanted to let her go.

"Oh Daddy! I missed you so vewy much!" She leaned back, and her small, chubby hands framed my face. "Why for you gone so wong? And where you hairs go?" Her pretty pink mouth flopped open when she realized my head was shaved. Blue eyes bugged damn near out of her head.

"Uh, it was hot. So I cut it off." Proud of myself for my quick thinking, I grinned at her.

She frowned. "I no wike it. You grows it out."

Raiven hid her smile and laughter behind the hand that had gently slid over my skin. Pulling my gaze from the beautiful woman hovering next to me, I smiled at my bossy daughter.

"We'll see."

"It's good to see you, little brother." Gunny spoke low.

"You too, brother. You too. I can't thank you enough for staying down here and taking care of...." My eyes moved from Presley to Raiven. Though Raiven didn't catch it, Gunny did.

He grinned, but where I may have once felt humor, I suddenly found myself questioning if I was worthy of her. I had issues before. Now my mind was teetering on the edge of insanity. Instability hovered in the wings.

Waiting.

Lurking.

It wasn't long before everyone else who'd been holding back came forward. They'd been making sure I had a few moments with my daughter, and I appreciated that.

"Lock, bro. It's good to see you." I had no idea who had said it. There was a chorus of greetings from all my brothers, old and new. One faded into the next.

On the way back to the clubhouse, Styx, Smoke, Check, and

Hacker had ridden in the SUV with me. They'd filled me in that my brothers from back home would be leaving tomorrow. I knew they had lives and families to get back to, but fuck, it burned seeing them and knowing it was going to be so short. I'd barely said my goodbyes and I'd be saying them again.

"Can I have a minute, everyone?" Styx spoke up. Knowing glances had my brothers patting me on the back or shoulder and saying they'd see me at dinner.

You'd think after being damn near starved for weeks, I'd be famished. The weird thing was, I had very little appetite.

"Hey, little Elvis, we need to go get all those pictures you made for your dad," Gunny said, coming to the rescue.

"Otay!" She kissed me and hugged me one more time before jumping from my lap. She'd made it about five feet before she spun around, jerked from Gunny's hand, ran back, and hugged me again. "I wub you so much, Daddy!"

"I love you too, princess." Her smile, fuck, it was everything.

As soon as she returned to my brother, Styx spoke up again. "Lock, we need to discuss your recovery."

I rolled my eyes. I didn't want to talk about anything. I'd get better, and I was going to bust my ass not to feel the way I was at that moment.

"Don't," he warned. Then he proceeded to give me and Raiven instructions on eating frequent small meals, whether I thought I was hungry or not. There were lists of things I should eat, things I should do, things I should not do, workout programs and schedules. It went on and on.

"I got it, Doc," I interrupted.

"Jesus, you're a stubborn fucker. Raiven? You got all that?" He crossed his arms as he turned her way.

"Yes."

"What, is she my keeper now? I need a babysitter?" Deep down, I knew I was being an asshole, but I couldn't help it. In my peripheral vision I saw the hurt flash across her face before she schooled her features to her tough-as-nails persona she tried to pull off with everyone else.

Another reason I hated myself at that moment. I'd been weak. I'd let go of the two of them and used anger and hate to stay alive instead of the thoughts of seeing them again. Even though the tiny sliver of my rational side knew it didn't matter what kept me alive, it still seemed wrong.

"No, she's not your babysitter, but let's just say she's going to be there to prevent you from being a stubborn ass. Unless you want me to arrange for a home health nurse to come in and crack the whip?" He raised an eyebrow and smirked.

Fucker.

"Fuck no, I don't want a goddamn nurse." Surliness poured from me. I wasn't that bad off.

"I'll have it all printed up for you, Raiven, in case he tries to give you a hard time. That way you can show him the black-and-white proof."

"For fuck's sake," I complained.

His expression went serious. "We need you as our SAA. You can't do that until you're in top shape. I'm pulling double duty as enforcer and SAA on top of working full-time. We're too small of a chapter. We agreed to your jump because we need you. So I'd really appreciate if you'd not fuck around with my recuperation program for you."

"It's gonna really suck to have a nurse in the club, isn't it?" I grouched.

Styx simply grinned. "That's trauma nurse to you."

"What-the-fuck-ever."

Presley came running back.

"Daddy! Wook what I made you!" She had page after colored page for me. Seventy-five trees must've died for all that.

"Thanks, sweetheart. I love them." Like a good dad, I looked at every single one of them and treated them like the precious gifts they were. She grinned from ear to ear at my praise.

Presley talked nonstop, dragging me around and showing me where she played, slept, and colored. She introduced me to Mattie, Smoke's daughter. The young teen was quiet and bashfully waved at me before returning her gaze to my daughter.

While I was enjoying myself, I was struggling and fading fast.

Raiven must have sensed it, because I saw her look at her watch, then brightly announce, "Okay, Presley, let's have our snack and then it's nap time."

Presley stopped, crossed her arms, and glowered.

"I don't wanna nap."

Watching her, I had a sneaking suspicion that's how I'd looked when Styx was telling me about my new routine. Chagrined, I stepped in to back up Raiven.

"Come on, pipsqueak. I'm hungry." I wasn't.

We took a seat at one of the tables, and I was thankful because I couldn't have made it much further. Exhausted, I dropped to a chair. Presley climbed up into the chair next to me, and Raiven went into the kitchen.

She brought out a tray of snacks and drinks and doled them out to us. I glared at the shit she put in front of me.

"Eat up!" she cheerily announced as she sat and started to eat the grapes she had in front of her.

Sighing, I forced myself to eat. As each bite hit my stomach, I battled with the nausea that churned. I also took the fucking vitamins Styx had "prescribed." He hadn't really, I was just feeling snarky and shitty. He'd simply made the recommendations based on what he knew and his discussion with a doctor friend of his. It didn't make it sit any better with me.

After having no choices or freedoms for the time I'd been captive, being told what to do pissed me off.

Once we were done, Raiven rounded us up and we headed back to the room we were in earlier. I'd recognized Presley's princess toddler bed in the room when they'd brought me there after we arrived.

"Daddy, tuck me in!" Shit. I didn't know if I'd get back up off the floor, but I couldn't tell her no. I hadn't seen her in God knew how many horrific days. I'd lost track. There were so many of those days I never thought I'd see her again.

So I lowered myself carefully to the floor, snuggled her in with her blanket, and rested my hand on her until she fell asleep. Then I didn't want to leave her, but I knew I needed rest too.

Frustrated, I tried to get up on my own several times. Finally, when Raiven tried to help me, I shoved her hand away.

"Fine. Be a stubborn fucker," she whispered. Then she left me on my hands and knees next to Presley's bed as she went into the bathroom.

In desperation, I ended up crawling over to the bed, where I tried to pull myself up. By the time I got myself upright, I was aching, sweating, and panting. It was fucking ridiculous.

"Why do you have to be so damn bull-headed?" I looked up from where I was watching my feet shuffle to the bathroom. She stood in the doorway, arms crossed, until I reached her, then she stepped back to allow me to pass.

"I hate feeling like this. I hate relying on you or anyone else to take a fucking shower. I need to piss and I don't want you to watch. So do you mind if I have a little privacy?" Resigned, I decided to pick my battles.

"Okay, but I'll be right outside the door." She gave me a sympathetic glance, and I hated it too.

Who knew taking a fucking piss on your own could be so draining? No fucking pun intended.

I'd had to hold on to the wall with one hand so I didn't lose my balance. Washing my hands required locking my knees and leaning against the edge of the sink with both legs so it could hold me up. By the time I got the soap washed off, my arms and shoulders ached. Thanks to Viper, my shoulders were so sore I couldn't raise my arms to dry my hands.

Hanging my head, I gave in. "Raiven?" I spoke softly.

155

Immediately, she was in the room and handing me the towel. That told me she'd been watching through the crack in the door.

"Thanks," I begrudgingly offered.

"You're welcome. Come on." Trying to be helpful, she lifted my arm to put it over her shoulder. She didn't know, but it hurt like hell thanks to being stretched from my arms and having Viper use me as a punching bag. It caused me to wince, which made her apologize. "I'm so sorry."

"Stop. Quit being sorry. I can't stand the thought of you feeling sorry for me," I grumped. It took longer than it should've, but we made it to the bed, and she helped me work my way up on it. I couldn't be bothered to pull the covers back first.

Weary beyond belief, as soon as my head hit the pillow, my eyes began to close. The bed dipped behind me, and her warmth scooted close to me, though she wasn't touching me.

"Come here." I needed her, but I didn't want to admit it. "I'm cold."

"Cold?" She scoffed, but she did as I said and her front pressed to my back. Her arm snuck around my waist, and I lifted mine enough for her to slip hers under. Taking her hand, I tucked it up close to my chest.

Finally feeling complete, I fell asleep.

Grabbing Viper by the throat, I threw him back. His nails dug into my wrist, and he whimpered as he gasped for air.

Blinking when something seemed off, I cleared my vision and realized I had Raiven pinned to the bed and she was clawing at my hand around her throat. Startled, I jolted off her and fell to my back. Chest heaving, heart racing, limbs shaking, I lay there staring at the ceiling until I had myself under control. My head warily rolled her way, and I reached tentatively for her, worry heavy in my heart.

When she flinched, I died a little inside.

"Are you okay? God, I'm so fucking sorry. I don't know what happened." But I did. That was why I'd never shared a bed with Presley. No matter how scared she'd ever gotten in the night, I never let her climb in my bed. I'd lie on the floor next to hers, but never did anyone sleep with me.

Letty was the only one, but even that had been hit or miss. I often ended up in the guest room.

Then there was Raiven that one night.

Fuck… that one fucking night. That was all I'd had with her before everything tanked.

I'd thought I'd be okay. It was only going to be a nap. Maybe if the last several weeks hadn't happened, I might've been.

Eyes huge, her hands on her throat, she stared at me. If anything could've made me feel worse, it was that look.

Except, instead of jumping out of bed and running for her life, what did she do? She fucked up my world by pulling me close. She rested my head on her unbound breasts and held me. It wasn't sexual, even though I could've pulled her nipple into my mouth through her tank top. They were right there.

Feeling her compassion as she kissed the top of my head nearly sent me into another fit of tears, and I fought it like a motherfucker. Breaking down in front of her earlier already had me listed as a class A pussy in my book.

Comfort and wordless support were what she was offering. My arms wrapped around her, and my fingers clenched the back of her tank tightly.

I clung to it like a fucking lifeline.

"I'll be here as long as you need me," she whispered.

It was on the tip of my tongue to answer with "forever."

NINETEEN

Raiven

"WOLF MOON"—TYPE O NEGATIVE (INCLUDING ZOANTHROPIC PARANOIA)

Lock had been back for three weeks. Every day of those three weeks, he'd grumbled like a son of a bitch about the strict recuperation regimen that Styx had outlined. The man was a surly, assholish dickwad.

"Styx, I swear I'm going to punch him in the nuts." I was pretty sure steam came from my ears.

"Cut him a break, hon. He's been going above and beyond to get his butt back in shape. He went through a lot." Styx probably thought he was helping. He really wasn't.

I rolled my eyes.

My patience was running thin with him. The fan-fucking-tastic icing on my cake of life was I'd been sick and trying to keep his ass on track too. I wasn't sure if it was because I had yet to process the last few of months of my life, or if I'd intentionally buried all my shit to help him. Either way, it was catching up to me.

Exhausted, moody, nauseous, I continued to trudge through. On top of working half days at the tattoo shop the club owned, I helped with Presley, kept Mr. Grouch-Ass in line, and did my best not to lose my shit.

Finally, I couldn't stand it anymore, and I'd made a doctor's appointment for after I got off work. I was tired of feeling like crap. They'd wanted me to go get labs done the morning after I called. Maybe I needed some vitamin B injections or some shit. Maybe I needed sleeping pills. Fuck, maybe I needed my head read. That was highly likely.

Whatever it was, three days later, I was chilling in the doctor's office scrolling through social media on my phone. The "few minutes" the nurse had said it would take the doc to come in had come and gone. Glancing at the time, I rolled my eyes for about the five-thousandth time.

The door opened, and I heard, "Ms. Knight?"

I looked up from my phone and dropped it in my purse.

"Yes, that's me." I gave a weak smile.

"Well, we may have an idea of what's going on with you." The doctor scrolled through some shit on her laptop as I waited.

"Umm, okay?" I really wanted to say, "Spit it out!" but I didn't.

"Well, for one you are a little on the anemic side, so I'm going to prescribe some iron supplements along with your prenatal vitamin." She clacked away at the keyboard.

"Okay. Whoa. Wait. Excuse me?" I held both hands up with my pointer fingers extended. "Prenatal vitamins because they are good for me, right?"

She gave a small, understanding smile. "Yes. They are good for you and the baby."

I choked. Arms flailing, I struggled to suck a minuscule amount of oxygen into my deprived lungs. She calmly stood up as if I wasn't dying in her exam room and rubbed a soothing hand on my back.

Once my body quit gagging and coughing, I placed a hand on my heart. It was pounding so hard, my hand was jumping. Then I laughed.

"Sorry about that. I thought you said baby." My heart rate was starting to slow, and the panic was subsiding. I'd clearly heard her wrong.

"Yes. You're definitely pregnant, Ms. Knight. When was the first day of your last period?" Returning to her computer screen, she waited for my answer.

"Uh." Panic mode returned because I couldn't remember. I did remember telling Lock we'd been safe in the hotel that night, so it had been before that. But shit, that didn't always mean anything, and I cursed myself for being so stupid and getting carried away.

Then a worse thought process began, and I jumped off the exam table and vomited in the trash can. Dry heaving, I trembled from either the puking or the news the doctor had delivered.

"Doc. How far along am I?" Nervous and unsteady, my hands rubbed shakily over my face and around to the back of my neck. Feeling on the verge of collapse, I leaned against the counter by the sink after rinsing out my mouth.

Please God, don't let this be Stefano's baby. "We used a condom the last time. Right? Of course we did. We always did. Jesus, I'm talking to myself."

Acting like I wasn't puking in her trash can and talking to myself, the doctor continued, "Is the father still in the picture?"

Wide-eyed, I didn't know how to answer that. "I don't know," I whispered. On weak legs, I returned to the exam table and dropped to my ass. She bit her lip.

"I'll tell you what. Why don't we schedule an ultrasound so we can get some measurements, and that will give us a better idea of where you're at," she responded softly. She was trying to sound reassuring and calm, but it wasn't helping.

"Uh, yeah. Yeah. Okay. When?" My hands were rapidly tapping the side of the table.

"I'll be right back. Let me go look at our schedule." A sympathetic tip of her lips had me wanting to cry. She closed her laptop and exited the room.

"She had a laptop, why couldn't she look that up in here? Shit. Maybe she's calling in the men with the white coats. I'm losing my

160

fucking mind. Look at me! I'm talking to myself again!" Hands waving in the air, I grasped my hair to steady them.

The nurse came back instead of the doctor. "Ms. Knight? So we've had a couple of cancellations. We can get you in on Thursday of this week or Monday."

She'd barely gotten my options out before I blurted out, "Thursday!"

"Okay, I'll be right back."

Oh my God, why does everyone keep leaving? Don't they understand this is an emergency situation? Christ on a cracker!

All could see was a calendar in my mind showing it was only Monday. Three days. Fuck, I'd have to wait three damn days. Three days to find out if my baby's father was dead and I'd watched his brains blow out or if it was a man who acted like he could barely stand me anymore.

For fuck's sake, he'd had a goddamn cot brought into the room after the nap incident that first day. I hated it. I missed the warmth of his body behind me.

Thinking about the possibilities, I began to dry heave again. Thank God my stomach was already empty.

Then I prayed I wouldn't be one of those women who had morning sickness through their whole pregnancy. Slapping my hand to my forehead, I realized that was why I'd been nauseous so much.

Shit.

Shit, damn, fuck, fuck, fuck.

"Okay, here's an appointment reminder card. If you go to the pharmacy waiting room, they can fill your prescriptions." When I looked at her like she had a dick on her forehead, she gave me a raised-eyebrow, nervous grin. Like I was crazy.

"Um, we have an in-house pharmacy for non-narcotic and basic prescriptions. It's up front and to the left of the doors you came in. Was there anything else I could help you with? Any questions you had?" Expectantly, she stood there with her hands in her pink scrub pockets.

Brain reeling, coming apart at the seams, I shook my head. "No, I guess I'm good."

What a crock of shit. I was so far from good it wasn't even remotely funny.

Grabbing my purse, I slung it over my shoulder and held the handle in a death grip with both hands. Unable to think clearly, I had to rely on her for directions back to the lobby.

In a daze, I waited again, collected my prescriptions, which I absently shoved in my purse, and then I stumbled out into the bright afternoon. The heat radiating off the asphalt rivaled the sun's warmth, creating a veritable inferno.

Christ, Texas was hot.

I didn't have a car yet, so I walked back to the tattoo shop. I'd found the clinic down the road from the shop because I didn't want to have the club guys running me all over town. After what I'd found out, I was glad I hadn't mentioned it to anyone.

Initially, I'd been escorted anywhere I needed to go because they were worried about Stefano finding me. I'd had armed escorts everywhere I went. Then when Lock got back and Stefano had been taken care of, it didn't occur to me to drive his truck. It was his, not mine.

By the time I'd returned the block and a half to the shop, I was soaked in sweat and wanting to die. The cool AC as I pushed open the door was blissful nirvana, and I dropped to the black leather couch in the waiting room.

"I thought you left for the day?" Justin, one of the other tattoo artists, was showing his latest client out. He stopped by where I was sitting and tipped his head to the side in question.

"I... uh... I needed to... I mean, I met a friend for a coffee down on the corner." Stammering, I sounded like a moron. It was a hundred and ninety-five in the shade.

"Coffee?" He looked at me like I was a fucking weirdo.

"Um, iced coffee. Yeah." A big smile spread across my face until my cheeks hurt.

"Okay." He drew out the word and pursed his lips. "I'll see you to-morrow then."

I was sure he didn't mean for me to see, but as he walked away, he glanced over his shoulder at me and shook his head. I was acting like a weirdo and I knew it.

My head fell back on the cool leather as I texted Smoke that I was done so he could send one of the guys to get me. Now that I'd found this shit out, I was going to have to look at getting a car. My life was about to change drastically, and I wasn't sure what to make of that.

"I'm gonna be a mom," I whispered as I placed a hand lightly on my belly. As I waited for my ride, my mind rambled and rolled aimlessly from thought to thought.

The bell over the door rang, and I looked up to see Slice walking in. A newly patched member, he seemed to get the short end of the stick, along with one of the prospects, Truth. They were my designated drivers.

"Hey, gorgeous. You ready to head out? Presley was mad because I wouldn't let her come with me, but I'm on my bike today." Broody, he stared at me with his unnerving green eyes.

He was big, but not 'roided-out big. Most of the guys seemed to come by their muscles honestly between the gym at the clubhouse and their jobs. Also like the most of the guys I'd met from both chapters, he was gorgeous. There were a couple, like my uncle, that were what someone might call a "typical" biker, with big beer bellies and bushy beards. Most of them were like… well, like Lock or the handsome devil in front of me.

Nodding, I gathered up my purse and waved bye to Nikki as she sat at the reception counter. At first, I'd thought she was going to be a bitch and we were going to be walking around on eggshells with each other. It didn't take long to figure out that the piercer was pretty introverted despite her mermaid hair, tats, and piercings that screamed wild child. She was sweet, and we got along great.

"See you tomorrow, Raiven."

Stepping out into the blazing oven, I grimaced when he handed me the extra helmet. God, it was hot enough as it was without wearing a helmet, but it was a club rule or some shit.

After I shoved my purse in his saddle bag, I put the helmet on. It was a struggle to get it fastened because I was shaking again, thinking about facing Lock.

The ride to the clubhouse took about twenty minutes. Twenty minutes of feeling like I had a hairdryer blowing in my face.

By the time we parked in front of the clubhouse, I was roasting, sweating like a stuck pig, and beginning to feel nauseous again. Seeing Lock standing in the shade with Styx, Smoke, and Check didn't help.

Dammit.

With narrowed eyes, he watched me get off Slice's bike. Between him watching me and thinking about what I'd found out, my hands began to tremble, and I fumbled with the strap of the helmet.

"Here, let me help." Slice gently pushed my hands away and crouched to see what he was doing, because my hair had become tangled in it.

The relief of getting the damn thing off was incredible. He laughed as I sighed.

Approaching the trio, Slice gave them each a handshake and their little bro-hug before I caught up. Of course, I may have been dragging my feet.

Lock had made great strides and he'd been going above and beyond with his recuperation despite his bitching. He was working out more than Styx approved of, but there was no reasoning with him. In the few short weeks he'd been back, he'd shown significant improvement.

He was still much leaner than when I'd first met him, but he was filling out and his muscles were slowly coming back. Unfortunately, he was still as sinfully hot as he always had been. My eyes rolled.

Oh and be still my heart, he was growing the top of his hair out again to make Presley happy. I hid a grin, because it sure made me happy too. Then I remembered my afternoon, and my grin wilted in the blazing summer sun.

"Hey, Raiven. What do you think of Lock's new scoot?" When Check stepped back, I realized they were standing around a black bike very similar to the one I'd ridden on with Slice. It was gorgeous.

"Wow. It's beautiful, but are you sure you're okay to ride?" I worried that a heavy bike like that might be too much for him so soon.

"Why? You'd rather ride with Slice?" His snark was unexpected, and I was speechless. Slice raised an eyebrow and cocked his head.

"Whoa, whoa, whoa. I only gave her a ride from work. I ain't poaching, bro." Hands held up with his palms facing Lock, Slice went wide-eyed as I uncomfortably stood there.

"Make sure you don't" was Lock's quiet reply.

"Lock. Chill, bro. I sent him to get her." Smoke gave Lock a look I couldn't decipher. Without answering Smoke, he shook his head, turned his back to me, and went inside.

"What the heck was that? Am I missing something?" I asked the remaining guys.

Styx spoke up first. "He's been struggling. Doesn't want you to know. One thing I will tell you is he's doing really well, all in all. But it's going to take time for him to be back to one hundred percent."

"Styx is right. Lock's being pissy. You know that. Same old, same old. He's also frustrated because when he told me he got the bike today, he said he was going to pick you up, but I told him to come here first. Honestly, I was worried he wasn't ready for a passenger but I didn't want to point it out and make him feel shitty. He's already struggling, and I didn't want to add to it." Smoke shrugged and ran a hand through his hair.

"I didn't even know he was getting a bike today." After I spoke, I realized I sounded like a pouting child and I was embarrassed as hell. But dammit, I would've liked to have gone with him to pick it out.

"I'm not so sure he did either." Check laughed.

"What do you mean?" My brow rose in question. That didn't make sense.

"Well, he took me down to drop my bike off for some warranty work. Instead of driving me back here, I drove his truck and he rode that home." He nodded toward the sleek beast they'd been checking out.

Taking the time to really look the bike over, I realized it was more than a little different than Slice's. It had a fancier seat and several details that were changed.

"It's beautiful," I murmured. It really was. While Slice's bike was black with chrome pipes and stuff, Lock's new ride was all black. Every piece of it was black. Sexy-as-fuck black.

"It should be. It's a Street Glide CVO. Sweet-ass ride. He's a lucky motherfucker." Check stared at the bike with longing, though he was talking to me.

"Um, yeah, you're speaking Greek to me. All I got out of that was it's a beautiful machine."

They all laughed and nodded as Check grinned and said, "That's pretty much what I said."

"I don't understand why he's so pissy if he got this today. He should be in a great mood. Instead he acts like I piss him off by breathing. I think all I'm doing now is putting him out. Maybe it's time for me to find my own place. He's doing better and doesn't really need me here." The thought of leaving him and Presley made my chest ache. Then there was my new situation.

"Raiven, why don't you talk to him before you decide to leave?" Styx had pulled his attention from the bike and was giving me a concerned look.

The last thing I wanted to do was talk to him in his current mood. I also had no idea if I should tell him about what I'd found out earlier. Telling myself I'd wait until Thursday when I knew more, I sighed. "I'm going in the AC. This heat is ridiculous. I don't know why I let my uncle convince me to come here. Fuck."

They all chuckled as I walked off, and I shot them the middle finger over my shoulder.

The cool air hit me as I stepped into the dim main room, and I moaned in relief.

Lock was nowhere I could see, and I wondered if he'd gone back to our room. His room. It had been easy to forget it was really his room, since he was the member. It was only mine because I was there as a guest. Well, and because my uncle was a retired member. First I was there to keep me safe until the club knew what was up with Lock and Stefano. Then it was because I was there to take care of him.

Which seemed to be coming to an end.

Shuffling my tired ass into the room, I was surprised to see a couple of boxes packed. Lock was taping one shut as I closed the door. Cautiously, I glanced around, looking for a clue as to what was going on. All of his things were gone from the dresser top. Something told me if I looked, his shit would be gone from the drawers and the closet.

"What's going on?" I tentatively questioned.

"Packing" was his curt answer.

Exasperated, I plopped my purse on the bed. "I can see that. What I mean is, why are you packing?"

"We're leaving."

Though I could see it, I wasn't truly prepared to hear it. A raw ache began to fester in my chest.

"Oh." Of course, I knew it would end eventually, but I didn't realize how bad it would hurt. The pain when I tried to breathe deep was nearly debilitating. I sat on the edge of the bed and stared at my hands, willing my inner badass to get her ass out there.

"Um, do you need help packing Presley's things?" It was impossible to meet his eyes.

"Already done." At the clipped words, I glanced at the small bed. How I hadn't noticed it was piled with her bags, I didn't know. My only excuse was I was overwhelmed and tired.

"Oh." I was like a broken record.

"There's boxes there for you too." He gestured to the flattened boxes leaning against the toddler bed.

Confusion and worry wrinkled my brow. "They're kicking me out since you're leaving?"

When I'd seen him packing, I'd hoped that since my uncle was a retired member, they'd let me stay until I found a place with reasonable rent.

"What the hell are you talking about? You're going with us. I found a house not far from here to rent for a while." Stacking the boxes, he didn't make eye contact.

"Excuse me? You don't need me to take care of you anymore." He was confusing me with his back-and-forth shit. I got the cold shoulder one minute but then he was telling me I was moving in with them.

Me being off my game didn't help. I'd been moody, and my clothes were feeling a little snug, which was really a hit to the ol' self-esteem. My back had been killing me, and I'd attributed it to all the leaning over from tattooing but after my news, I wondered if it wasn't the baby.

"I'm better but not all the way there yet. I could still use your help. I assumed, but I should have asked. Would you be willing to help me with Presley until I'm back to one hundred percent? Sometimes I still get tired, and she's a handful." Though he tried to act nonchalant, I thought I saw a flicker of something pass over his face as he set the roll of tape on the dresser. Something that almost looked like hope.

Tamping down my excitement that I'd still be able to be around them, I pulled my lips between my teeth and acted like I was considering the idea. It made me a glutton for punishment to be so close to him when he was being so closed-off and grouchy, but I was a desperate addict.

Being able to lay my eyes on him first thing in the morning and see him when I got off work had become a routine. One I'd enjoyed too much. Well, except for those few nights, but I didn't want to think about them.

Add Presley's spunky little ass to the mix, and I was a hopeless junkie for them.

"I mean, I guess I could. If it will help. Maybe I could find a place to rent close by after you're better." My finger trailed the stitch line of the comforter. "I need to find a vehicle I can afford though. Since we won't be here for the guys to give me rides."

"I can drop you off on my way to the shop. I'm starting up next week. Until then, you can either take my truck or I'll take you." Through his spiel, he stood with his hands stuffed in his pockets and staring at his black boots.

"Oh. Um, sure." My mind was in turmoil, because with the way he'd been acting, I'd been getting the idea he didn't particularly like me anymore. Then he made plans for me to move in with him. It didn't make sense, and I wanted to tell him to fuck off because he'd been such a jerk, but like a gluttonous idiot, I'd take it.

Even though I shouldn't.

TWENTY

Lock

"WAKING UP THE DEVIL"—HINDER

"**Y**ou can have this room. The furniture should be delivered by about five." I opened the door to a smaller but nice room next door to the master bedroom. The house was old, but it had character. Hardwood floors gleamed in the sun shining through the windows.

"Okay, um, thanks. I feel bad that you bought furniture for me when I won't be here long." Raiven's words set my teeth on edge. Fuck, I didn't even want her in a separate room, let alone leaving at any point in the future.

Except instead of telling her that, I'd been an asshole. My head was so fucked-up, but I selfishly wanted her, so I'd impulsively told her she was moving in with me.

Hell, all the brothers knew she was mine. I'd practically pissed on her leg when Slice had given her a ride home on his bike yesterday. Not like they didn't know before that, but fuck, it had pissed me off to see the woman I considered mine on the back of another's dude's bike. Whether he was a brother or not didn't matter.

Smoke had given me shit about being such a dick to her when he knew I wanted to claim her. The problem was, he didn't understand the war that I fought in my head. Hell, I knew I wasn't good for her, but I couldn't cut her loose. They mistakenly thought that me bringing her to the house was me finally opening my damn mouth and telling her how things were.

"It's okay. I'll need the furniture for this room to be a guest room anyway." *After you move into my room.*

The disappointment that flashed across her face vanished as quickly as it appeared, and she shot me a bright grin. "Well, that's good then."

"Yeah." Awkwardly we stood there staring at each other before I cleared my throat. "I'm going to go pick Presley up from Smoke's, if you want to hang up your clothes. There are hangers in the closet."

"Do you want me to ride with you?" Was that hope I heard in her tone?

Fuck, yes. In fact, I want you to ride me.

My palm slapped my forehead before sliding up into my hair. Truthfully, I didn't need to pick Presley up until three, but I was trying to separate myself from Raiven because the scent of her perfume was driving me insane. Seeing those fucking nipple piercings through her sweat-soaked neon-green tank top all day wasn't helping either.

"Sure." Anguish tinged the single word answer at the continued torment I'd be experiencing. Fuck my life. I could not win.

Her smile was brilliant as she slipped past me and grabbed her purse off the kitchen counter. "Ready!"

Moving of their own accord, my feet carried me in her direction. Everything about her had been getting under my skin. The two times I'd been inside her seemed like an eternity ago. As if maybe they never happened but were part of the escape my mind dreamed up during the dark moments in my pitch-black cage.

The closer I got, the more my body zinged. The more irresistible her pull became. If her deep, heaving breaths were any indication, she was experiencing something similar. For the last few weeks, I'd done my damnedest to stay away from her.

I'd worked to recover my body, I'd tried to get my head straight, and I'd tried to talk myself out of the need to claim her as mine. I'd made every excuse I could think of to talk myself into letting her go as I regained my strength day by day. Hell no, I wasn't back to where I was, that would probably take months, but I certainly wasn't the same weakened and unstable person I'd been almost a month ago. Not physically and not mentally.

The only people who knew I'd been seeing a shrink were Smoke and Styx. Was I still fucked-up in the head from the shit I'd seen and experienced both during deployment and during my captivity? Probably, okay, yes, but I had a better handle on it and I was sick to death of waiting.

There. I'd admitted it.

I was sick of watching her walk around braless when I couldn't touch those beautiful jiggling tits. Hell, I could barely look without drooling. It was literally killing me.

I was sick of walking around with a goddamn erection all day.

I was sick of keeping my hands to myself.

I was sick of denying the attraction that had existed between us from the first day.

Hell, even my daughter loved her.

Not that I loved her. No way. Lust was a far cry from love.

"Lock, what are you doing?" Her eyes shone with uncertainty as she took a step back from me. When I simply continued to move in her direction, she took another step away. The closer I got, the further she scampered backward, until the counter was against her ass.

Knowing I had her captive, I stopped when I was toe to toe with her and rested a hand on each side of her on the edge of the counter. "First of all, tell me why you stopped calling me Matlock and now it's Lock. I don't like it."

"Huh?" Confusion spread over her face as her soft breath tickled across my mouth.

Instead of acknowledging her confusion, I decided to cut straight to the chase. Movements slow and calculating, I leaned in to speak in her ear. I was so close, her perfume teased me again, and my lips feathered along her ear as I spoke. "Raiven, I didn't ask you to stay here because I need you to babysit me. I never did. I want you in my house, in my bed, and around my cock."

When she didn't protest or push me away, my lips curled up at the corners. I'd lived my life for my daughter for over a year. I'd had no interest in a woman or a relationship. I'd tried to stay away from her, too.

For Christ's sake, I'd slept on a fucking cot at the clubhouse to remove myself from the temptation that was Raiven. Also, my daughter had been in the same room and I refused to only be able to fuck her in the goddamn bathroom.

Maybe I didn't want anything long-term, but I needed to feel her, taste her. I needed to know if she was as sweet and tight as I remembered. Her lack of fight told me I was going to get what I wanted.

And I didn't want to wait another second.

"What about Presley?" she gasped as I blindly took her purse and set it to the side.

"I don't need to pick her up until three." My teeth sank into the silky flesh of her neck, then a swipe of my tongue soothed it before it was pulled into my mouth for a gentle suck. Teasing her, I took my time trailing the tip of my tongue along her skin until I dipped between her luscious, full tits.

Every inch of her salty skin I could reach was savored.

At my slow, sensuous movements, a raspy moan escaped her plush lips.

Before she could change her mind, my fingers deftly unbuttoned those cut-off shorts. The same ones that had been driving me crazy all damn day as we loaded and unloaded the few boxes from my truck and brought them in the house.

So short that the pockets hung down lower than the frayed edges, I'd wondered all day if she had any panties under them. Long, tanned legs went on for miles underneath them, with her thigh tats begging for my tongue to trace their lines.

Impatience my middle name, I wanted to rip those damn shorts open and throw them across the room to see what they hid. Instead, I fought tooth and nail for control. The zipper slid slowly down, leaving me almost disappointed to feel lace covering her pussy.

"Lock." My name was a breathless whisper as her head tipped back and I slid first one finger, then another under that damn lace. Frustrated with how it hindered my movements over her already soaking wet slit, I shoved down with the hand that was in her pants, forcing the shorts and underwear to drop as one to the kitchen floor.

"Matlock. Say it," I demanded as I hooked my hands around the backs of her thighs. The skimpy shorts fell with a soft thud when I lifted her to sit on the countertop. Her hiss as her bare ass hit the cold granite only drove me forward to grind my jean-clad dick against her sensitive flesh. "Say. It."

Defiantly, her eyes held mine, heavy-lidded and screaming sex. "If you want me saying your name, give me a reason to say it. Better yet, give me a reason to scream it."

"Game on." I grinned wickedly. She had no idea what kind of storm she'd unleashed with those words.

My fingers, rough from lifting weights, dug into her flesh at the backs of her knees as I raised them and pushed her legs open. The move had her falling back on the counter. Ever the defiant vixen, she didn't lie flat. No, not her. She made sure she was resting on her elbows so she could watch me.

In case she couldn't take what I was about to do to her, I gripped her knees to keep her from moving. My lips pressed to the tender skin inside those knees, sending chills up her thighs that I chased like a beacon leading me home. My beard grazed her skin as my lips moved up toward that glistening pink slice of heaven.

Paused at the most sensitive spot where her thigh joined with her mound, I nipped at the tendon just under her silken skin, then breathed in her tantalizing scent. If need had a scent, it would be her pussy. If it had a name, it would be Raiven.

"Yes," she sighed when my tongue swiped once through her leaking slit, and her fingers splayed on the cool granite. Dark as midnight, her hair spread across the surface as her head fell back. My palms slid up and pushed on her inner thighs when she attempted to tighten them on my head.

Inhaling deeply, I savored her.

Blowing on where I knew she wanted me to return, I reveled in her whimpers of desire.

"Do you know how many times I imagined my tongue slipping into your cunt? Do you know how that image kept me sane in the dark? It was so vivid, I could taste you on my tongue, yet it had nothing on the reality of you." I licked her again, then swirled around her clit.

A needy gasp preceded her head lifting until her chin touched the top of her chest. Dazed blue eyes met mine before squeezing closed when I flattened my tongue and ran it bottom to top, then pressed on her clit again.

A gust of air rushed from her lungs as she fell back to the counter and grabbed my hair with both hands. "Do you know how many times I dreamed of this? Feeling your hair threaded through my fingers? God, this is so much better than my imagination."

Smiling into her wet heat, I resumed tongue-fucking her until her pull on my hair became almost painful. Though it did send a momentary panic skittering through my heart, I told myself it was Raiven holding on to me.

It was Raiven.

Pulling me deeper into her wet core, she tugged.

And moaned.

And ground her plump pussy against my face, seeking the release I was teasing her with. Her actions spurred me to hurry, because I wanted my dick buried deep in there but I wanted her to come across my tongue first. Then I wanted her to come on my cock.

One, two, three fingers entered her tight-as-fuck sheath to prepare her for me. Once she shattered, I didn't want to have to work my way in; I wanted to be buried deep immediately.

Sucking her clit into my mouth, I alternated between curling my fingers in her, flicking that little nub with my tongue, and biting it until she screamed, "Oh fuck. Oh fuck. Oh fuuuuuck! Matlock! Yes! Jesus, Matlock."

Jesus fucking tits.

When she came, it was like biting into one of those fucking candies that the stuff came out of. Her come was on my tongue, down my beard, coating my fingers, my hand, and possibly on my damn shirt. Not that I was complaining, because it was the perfect combination of tangy and sweet. So good that I licked her clean like a fucking kid with a melting ice-cream cone.

Her hooded blue eyes watched as I sucked my last finger. The tip of her pink tongue ran along her bottom lip.

Reaction time was my forte, and I was on her mouth in half a second, running my tongue along hers so she could taste herself. When she deepened the kiss with a groan, I fisted her hair in one hand. The other one went down to release my cock, which had been straining at the zipper of my jeans all fucking day.

That motherfucker flopped out and landed on her clit with a smack as soon as my pants were out of the way. Her hands broke free from my hair and moved to clutch at my hips. Her pelvis tipped and wiggled in an attempt to get me lined up.

Chests heaving, we broke apart long enough to gasp for air.

Success didn't take long. As soon as the leaking tip of my cock was against her soaking opening, I thrust hard inside.

My three fingers weren't enough, because she screamed my name as I slammed in down to the base. It took every distracting thought I could think of not to start pounding into her. I struggled to suck in air, my eyes rolling in my head as my cock gave a little jump when she began to move, and I came a little.

"Fucking hell, stop," I rasped out. My hand that was tangled in her inky locks jerked, and her head tipped back, exposing the column of her throat. Licking and sucking the entire length of it, I didn't care if I left a mark. I wanted everyone who saw her to know she was mine.

Working my way back down, I bit the slope of her shoulder. Hard enough to leave a mark but not break the skin. Her core tightened into a stranglehold around my length, locking me inside her. I wasn't sure I could pull out if I wanted.

"If you don't stop that, I'm going to come, and I'm not ready for that." My grumble was met by a laugh that shook her body against mine.

Knowing I was well and truly fucked, I slowly slid out before plunging back inside.

She'd officially awakened the slumbering beast within me that needed more than I thought I was ready for. Likely more than she was ready for.

Knowing I was fighting a losing battle when she got even tighter around me, I began to pump in and out. Between the throbbing pulse of her hot cunt around the girth of my cock, her nails scoring my hips and back, those perfect tits bouncing with each thrust, and her screaming my name, I lost every thread of control I'd been desperately grasping.

I painted the inside of her pussy with a roar that rivaled a grizzly's. Every muscle in my body locked up, and the best feeling in the damn world coursed through my veins. Focusing on the absolute ecstasy that held me in its clutches, I panted through clenched teeth.

Sweat dripped from my hair, down my neck and soaked my shirt. Our eyes locked on each other, clashing and in shock.

She didn't know it yet, but she and her perfect pussy were mine.

I didn't share, and I was a needy bastard.

TWENTY ONE

Raiven

"COME UNDONE"—MY DARKEST DAYS

"**W**e didn't use a condom again." I had no idea where the rationale behind my announcement came from. It's not like I could get any more pregnant, and I knew after my doctor's appointment that I was clean. The dangerous thing was, I didn't know if he was.

Over the last week, I'd caught the skanky-dressed slut touching him. The same bitch that always seemed to be at the clubhouse. She'd been touching him in an extremely familiar manner.

I'd hated it, but I had no claim on him. He'd left the bed and slept on that fucking cot. In fact, there were a couple of nights he didn't come back to the room at all. Where he'd spent the night was never discussed.

"I don't give a fuck."

"Umm, excuse me?"

"Are you still clean?"

I tried to shove him off me, my temper flaring.

"Easy, baby. It was a simple question. I didn't know if you and Slice—" He trailed off. His acting like it was no big deal that he'd asked me that after his less-than-puritanical behavior pissed me off further. Especially since Slice and I may have become friendly, but there was nothing improper about our relationship.

"Get off! I should be asking you the same thing. You're the one who spent the night with that tramp at the clubhouse." Ineffectively, I shoved at him.

Clasping my wrists in his surprisingly strong hands, he looked at me like I'd lost my mind. "When the fuck did I sleep with Bertha?"

I froze. Blinking up at him, I deadpanned, "Her name is Bertha? Really? You fucked someone named Bertha?"

"Who the hell told you I fucked Bertha?" He had the nerve to sound affronted, his voice rising.

"You didn't come back to the room several times, and I saw how she simpered and groped at you every chance she got. 'Oh Looooock, you're getting soooo strong again.' It was disgusting," I snarled.

He laughed. The stupid, sexy, orgasm machine had the gall to laugh at me. What really sucked was that his laughing caused his softening dick to fall out of me. Our combined stuff leaked out of me and likely all over the counter, if not down the cupboards.

"Oh my God. You're cleaning that up," I threatened.

Still laughing, the hot-as-fuck asshole yanked his T-shirt off with one hand, grasping the back of it and tugging it over his head. That move was the sexiest damn thing I'd ever seen. I hated him a little in that moment for making me want to climb him again while I was still mad at him.

"It's got your pussy juice on it anyway." He chuckled as he used it to clean me, then whatever the mess had gotten on. My face flamed.

Watching him move, the tattoos that painted him had my mouth watering. To myself, I'd admit I was jealous of whoever had done them, because they'd had their hands all over that sexy landscape.

"Can you get another shirt? Please?" Exasperation bled from my request though I'd tried my best not to let it happen. I'd wanted to sound disgusted or angry, anything but desperate for him to cover all that smoking-hot temptation.

Embarrassed that I'd sounded like a jealous shrew about *Bertha*, I jumped off the counter and grabbed my panties and shorts. Before I could pull them on, he stilled my hands, then gently tipped my head up to meet his eyes.

The juvenile side of me wanted to jerk my chin free and avoid looking at him. The part of me that ached for his touch relished in that small contact. It wanted to lean into him, to feel his body heat.

"Raiven. I'd like to ask if that was a little green-eyed monster sneaking out, but I think I already know the answer to that. While I'd really like to revel in that for a little bit, I want you to know I've never touched her. You've been the only one for about a year or more. The nights I didn't come to bed were because I couldn't sleep. I was lying outside on one of the hammocks staring at the stars all night. Alone." His fierce cornflower eyes held mine. One corner of his mouth tipped up before he leaned forward and his warm lips tenderly brushed over my gaping mouth.

"Oh." It was all I could squeak out.

Well, don't I feel like an asshole?

A brief kiss led to his beard tickling down my neck to my cleavage, where his tongue dipped in and sent shivers across my skin. Without my realizing it, he'd let go of my wrists and his palms skimmed up under my tank top to cup my breasts.

Between kisses to my exposed skin, he spoke. "From what the guys said, she came home with Truth the night he was patched. She's been hanging out there ever since. She doesn't live there, she's not a 'club whore' or some shit like that. We don't have those. Our kids are there too much."

Thinking back on it, I knew she never stayed there overnight unless she was in bed with Truth or Slice. Which I thought was gross, that they'd willingly share her. That was my last thought on the subject because his hands and mouth were working their magic.

In no time at all, his arms shrugged the hem up and he crouched to pull a nipple in his mouth. The clink of metal against his teeth sent shivers down my spine as my nipples puckered.

Hands exploring and mouths kissing, biting, and tasting, we worked ourselves up until he was flipping me over and shoving my exposed chest to the cool granite. Where earlier it had startled me, as worked up as we were by then, it was amazing.

Again, he shoved that thick cock in me bare. Though I was already pregnant, he didn't know that. Did he not care? It was on the tip of my tongue to ask.

"One of these days, I'm going to fuck you in a goddamn bed," he growled low, then thrust hard. That's when my mind slipped back into a sex-induced haze.

As a final explosive orgasm washed over me, nearly drowning me like a tidal wave, a small voice snuck in on my euphoria. On repeat, it asked if I really thought he'd still want me if it turned out the baby wasn't his.

I'd had to reschedule an appointment to go to the ultrasound. Lock had dropped me off, and I nervously peeked out the windows about twenty times after he pulled away. I needed to make sure he'd actually left and not come back. It would've been tough to explain where I was going if he saw me walking down the road right away.

I cursed the furniture store for sending the wrong dresser for the master bedroom and him offering to get it. If he hadn't done that, I could've driven his truck and I wouldn't have had to worry about explaining where I was going.

The entirety of the short walk was spent with my heart pounding and my ears feeling like they heard his truck barreling down the road. Relief slammed into me when I safely made it into the clinic without getting caught.

I'd puked that morning, but I'd hid it from Lock because thankfully another round of animal sex last night left him zonked when I woke.

Thankfully, he'd also slept through the night with only a couple of bouts of restlessness that had woken me.

I'd been nervous of sleeping in his bed in case Presley woke and went looking for either of us. Not knowing where things were going to end up, I didn't want her getting confused. We'd agreed that I would return to my room early in the morning. Okay, he had begrudgingly agreed. I had insisted.

The day he'd awakened with his hands around my throat played into it a bit too.

Waiting on the exam table, I nervously chewed on my lip. The ultrasound tech was chatty but nice.

"Okay, we're going to try the least invasive option first."

"Ohhh-kay?"

She slopped some goopy gel on me, smeared it around, pushed here and there, clicked this and that. All the whole she yammered and made little humming sounds that I didn't understand.

The next thing she'd said was something about not getting great images. Then she told me she was sticking this fucking wand with a giant condom on it up my hooha to do the ultrasound that way since I seemed "on the cusp," whatever that fucking meant.

"Well, that's it!" She grinned as she printed out a couple of black-and-white images for me.

"So how far along am I?" I'd done a little research, but I had no idea if they could pinpoint how many weeks I was from the ultrasound. It wasn't an exact science, I'd found.

"Well, that's just an estimate." She pointed at the tiny numbers on the page. "Because of when you said your last menstrual cycle was, I thought you'd be around nine weeks, but it was hard to see, so that's why I did the transvaginal. Your raspberry-cherry is somewhere in between the eight and nine weeks, if I had to guess from my measurements. The little one wasn't super cooperative and was very active, as you saw."

Actually, all I saw was a white blob wiggling around. What she'd pointed out as limbs simply looked like parts of the blob. It made me feel like an idiot and not much of a mom.

"My raspberry-cherry?" I had no idea what she was taking about.

"Is this your first?"

I nodded.

"Have you done much reading up on pregnancy?" She gave me a look that clearly said I was the least prepared person she'd ever encountered. It kind of made me take offense to it.

So I lied.

"Of course I have." I laughed.

"Well, they've leaned toward comparing the size of your baby to the sizes of foods that people are familiar with. Maybe you didn't come across any of those sites." I could tell she was trying to make me feel better.

It wasn't working.

"Oh, right." Disappointment weighed heavy that I hadn't gotten the answers I'd been hoping for that morning. The whole in-between thing had me certain it was Stefano's baby, and I wanted to cry. I'd been praying it was Lock's.

Which was probably foolish, because I didn't know if he'd want a baby with me. Yes, he loved Presley, but she was his. What if he didn't want any more kids? What if he refused to raise a baby who belonged to the man who'd held him captive?

Taking a deep breath and letting it go slowly, I barely heard her directions before she left the room. The doctor came in briefly.

"Okay, so we're going to err on the side of caution and call it an eight-week embryo. At your next visit we'll do another ultrasound to see if we can get a better reading." She smiled kindly and I retuned it, but I knew it didn't reach my eyes.

We set my next appointment, and I slipped the images in my purse and headed into work. Telling myself I'd figure things out later, that I had time, didn't help much either.

Everyone noticed I was off, but they left me to my clients and didn't call me out on it. The guys and I weren't that close, and Nikki wasn't in that morning. She'd be in after lunch. By then, I'd have gone home.

Not having much of an appetite, I took a walk-in right before lunch who wanted a small music note. By the time lunch was over and I was done, Lock was waiting out front. I was happy to see Presley was in the truck too.

"Sorry, I'm a little late, I dropped the dresser off first because it looked like it might rain." His blue-gray eyes showed his regret.

"It's fine. Really. I had a walk-in, so it worked out perfect. Hey, pretty girl." I turned around in the seat to squeeze Presley's toes in her cute little sandals. When I twisted, my stomach pulled and I winced with a gasp.

"You okay?" Concern laced his question, and sweat beaded on my brow as I debated what to say.

"Yeah, think I may have pulled something last night." My face flushed bright red at the lie, but he took it for embarrassment and chuckled.

"Pwincess Waiven, you dunna stay at ow house a-den?" Her innocent smile and the excitement that lit her eyes added to my guilt. Again, I worried how the outcome of my situation could affect the sweet little girl I'd fallen in love with.

"I sure am, is that okay?"

"Yay! We habben a sweep ober! You dunna sweep in my woom?" She strained against her straps of her car seat to eagerly await my answer.

Thankfully, Lock stepped in.

"Probably not tonight, little Elvis. Princess Raiven has a sore back. She needs to sleep in the big bed so it gets better." Checking his mirrors, he pulled out into traffic, and we drove toward home.

"Den can I sweep wiff huh?" That eagerness was back.

"No, because you wiggle around too much and we don't want you to bump her and hurt her back." His eyes met hers in the rearview mirror. I glanced over my shoulder to see her pouting. He was trying not to laugh, and I rolled my eyes as I shook my head at him.

It didn't take long to make it back to the house and get Presley unloaded. Without putting much thought to what I was doing, I started lunch once we were all inside. Brain lost in clouds of worry, I was pretty much going through the motions.

Presley ran off to her room to play, and Lock disappeared.

Standing at the stove making grilled cheese and tomato soup, I listened to music as I cooked. The domestic quality of everything suddenly hit me, and my emotions exploded. For no logical reason, I started crying.

Standing in front of the stove, I sobbed with my face buried in my hands. Everything hit me at once.

Like it wasn't bad enough seeing Stefano kill someone in cold blood, then his doing what he did to me, then telling me he'd killed my dad? Top that off with being on the run, Lock being taken, taking care of Presley while hoping he'd make it home to us, a new place, new job, new faces and friends, watching Gabriel kill Stefano, finding out I was pregnant. It was too much.

The not knowing was killing me too. I wanted the baby to be Lock's so bad. But on the flip side, how he would take that kind of news after I'd confidently told him we were safe that first time? The fear that he may think I trapped him or was deceptive ate me up inside. The fear that I'd be a shitty mom was there too.

My mom had been a lot younger than my dad. She'd decided drugs and partying were more fun than being a mom and hauled ass. Dad never remarried, since my mother had been his fourth marriage and he'd said he wasn't trying again.

That left me being raised by a Vietnam veteran old enough to theoretically be my grandfather. Oh, and occasionally my biker uncle and his wife, Aunt Jean, who'd never had children of their own. There was no one to show me what a good mom was like.

I had an older brother and an older sister from my dad's first marriage who I'd never met, so I didn't consider them my siblings. Besides, they were old enough to be my parents and had in no uncertain terms said they weren't interested in meeting their father's midlife crisis child.

They were assholes.

Of course, Aunt Jean did her best to be a female influence in my life, but it wasn't the same. Having the "womanly changes" taught to you over the phone by a woman you knew from infrequent visits was mortifying and confusing. After I'd gotten older, we talked on the phone at least a couple of times a week, but it still wasn't the same as having a mom.

"Hey." Strong arms wrapped around me, and my back nestled to his chest. "Raiven, talk to me. What's wrong?"

"I-I-I don't know. Everything. It's just catching up with me," I stuttered and sobbed. My frame shook, and he held me tight. Every so often he pressed a kiss to the side of my neck, but he stayed silent and was simply there for me.

Finally, I either cried myself out or got my shit together. He'd removed the pan from the stove while I'd cried, so at least the sandwiches weren't burnt. Almost messing up lunch had me on the verge of crying again.

Jesus Lord, I'm a fucking mess.

"Raiven, do you want to go back to Chicago?" His chest quit moving behind me, so I knew he was holding his breath awaiting my answer.

The last thing I wanted was for him to think I wanted to run back there, so I spun in his arms. He tried to keep me facing away from him, and I knew it was because he didn't want me to see the expression on his face. There was no way I was not looking him in the eye when I told him my thoughts on what he'd asked, so I firmly turned and met his gaze.

Tormented was the only way I could describe it.

My palms cradled his face; his beard coarse against my skin. "Lock." Hurt flashed in his eyes so I started again. "Matlock. There is nothing for me in Chicago. I'm not leaving Texas. Thanks to your club, I have a great job, I'm making new friends…, and I'm close to you and that little girl in there." Through my response, I hiccupped and my breaths shuddered from my crying.

What I didn't say was that he may not want me around if he found out that I may have a baby growing in me conceived by a monster. The same monster responsible for fucking with Lock's body and mind after he'd been fucked up by his deployments. The stories Gunny had broken down and told me about while he was gone broke my heart.

Gunny had been trying to show me how strong Matlock was, to show me he was a survivor, but it had made me feel awful for him. No human should witness what he'd witnessed, experience what he'd experienced, both as a soldier and at Stefano's hands.

"I'm here for you, baby. We're here for each other. Stronger together."

His words ripped me apart and he didn't know it.

If I stayed and it turned out the baby was Stefano's, he'd have to look at the baby every day. He'd look at it knowing he or she was the product of the man who'd tortured him.

TWENTY TWO

Lock

"BRING ME DOWN"—PUDDLE OF MUD

Seeing Raiven break down last week made me realize I needed to get her in counseling. I'd been so wrapped up in my own shit that I hadn't stopped to think about everything she'd experienced. I was such a schmuck.

"Lock, Truth. Smoke's calling emergency church. Five minutes." I looked over my shoulder from where I was up to my elbows in grease rebuilding an old '68 shovelhead for a guy who found it rusting away in his grandfather's barn. Slice was spinning on his heel as soon as he'd made the announcement.

"Fuck, I'm never going to get this shit done," I grumbled as I wiped my hands on a rag.

Truth laughed as he did the same. "Get used to it."

Truth was a newly patched member who worked at the bike shop along with Clay, who was a retired member. He had less than eight months as a patch but he seemed like a pretty good guy. They'd desperately needed my help at the shop, and I was happy as fuck to be useful. It was a perfect opportunity to get me the hell out of Iowa, and I'd jumped on it.

Of course, I could've done without the detour I took on the way down.

Our chapter was pretty small. We were working on that issue, but shit like that took time. If we went handing patches out, they wouldn't mean much. Like everything in life, the things you worked for were more precious.

Right now the club consisted of Smoke, who was prez; Straight, the VP; Check, the road captain and computer genius; Slice and Truth, who'd been patched within weeks of each other; Styx, the enforcer; and now me. We had a few prospects, but it would be a while before they were patched. The other chapters called us the SSC—single syllable chapter. They thought they were really damn funny, but Smoke said they'd decided to embrace it and run with it.

Clay had been the sec/tres, but when he got T-boned on his bike, it messed up his back and he lost his left leg at the knee. He'd retired when he knew he wouldn't be able to ride anymore. I didn't know how he still worked on bikes with a rod in his spine, but he sure as fuck did. Straight was pulling the weight of VP and sec/tres until one of the patches had enough time in. I didn't want it. I was happy where I was.

I liked order. I hated surprises.

"Let's get this over with," Truth said, grabbing his cut from the office. I followed and grabbed mine as well.

"I'll hold shit down here. You boys get movin' 'fore y'all get your asses hemmed up," Clay said as he steadily worked on installing an after-market exhaust.

"Thanks, bro. See you in a bit," Truth replied.

Slice was waiting on us as I threw a leg over my bike. Standing it up, my muscles briefly protested, but I'd never admit it. Hell, I'd been beating the shit out of my body trying to get back to where I was before. Everything was sore but in a good way this time.

As the highest-ranking member, despite recently making the jump to their chapter, they both waited for me to mount up before they did. Once we were all ready, we pulled out and made the short trip to the clubhouse.

It looked like we were the last to arrive. Backing our bikes in at the end of the short row, I shook my head to see Gunny's bike still there. He'd been like a grouchy mother hen since my ordeal, and I couldn't convince him I was okay so he'd go home. If I had to guess, I'd say it had more to do with not knowing what Viper's end game was.

"Hey bro, what's doin'?"

Speak of the devil. The grin that hit my face at seeing him was shit-eating as hell. "Not much. Getting into the swing of things at the shop. If you could spare a minute from the AC and that cold beer, we could use your hands down there."

"Jesus, that heat out there reminds me too much of the desert. Are you sure this is where you wanna be? Damn, bro, that shit sucks." True to form, he grumbled as he tipped back the beer he was holding. "Besides, I'm on vacation."

"Vacation? You've been here, what? Over two months." A chuckle slipped out.

"Yeah, well, the first month was no vacation." His somber answer killed my grin.

"I know. I'm sorry."

"It's not your fault, Lock. Knock it off." His scowl was so much like Dad's, I almost laughed again.

"I gotta get into church. You gonna be here when I get out?"

"Well, I won't be out there until the sun starts to go down." His lip curled before he took another drink.

Turning on my heel, I saw Smoke standing in the doorway of the conference room. He didn't look happy either. "Gunny. I want you in here."

Without waiting for an answer, Smoke turned on his heel and went back in the room. Gunny, Truth, Slice, Styx, and I looked at each other. Shrugging, I tipped my head. "You heard the prez, let's go."

One by one, we shut off our phones, then dropped them in the basket on the table outside the room. Once we were all inside, Styx closed the door. Everyone took their seat.

Cutting right to the chase, Smoke met each of our gazes one by one.

"Viper was seen up in Waco yesterday." I could tell Smoke hadn't wanted to pass the news on to me. My jaw clenched as I processed the news. They all knew he'd been a part of my abduction and torture. They also knew about Letty.

Fuck, had that been hard to admit.

I looked Smoke dead in the eye, an angry chill racing down my body.

"You know that if he comes after me or what's mine again, I'm going to kill him, so you better be prepared. We'll need cleanup." I was dead fucking serious.

"Lock, come on, bro. We're not that kind of club," Straight, the VP, piped in. He looked frustrated but resigned. Like he knew that was exactly what I'd say.

"Well, if we're not that kind of club, maybe we should've called the cops and let them handle shit after I was captured and motherfucking *tortured* for damn near a month." I was pissed as fuck. That piece of shit, stupid motherfucker had been responsible for too much.

"We don't call the fucking cops," Smoke growled out.

"Exactly. So like I said. You better dig through your contacts for a cleaning crew or whatever we need, because he is a dead man. If you don't want the club to be part of this, I'll turn in my cut and I'll deal with it on my own." There was no changing my mind. The hatred I had for Viper was bone deep.

Smoke's jaw clenched, and they all exchanged looks. My eyes never left my president as I waited for the decision he'd make.

Regret flashed across his face, and I knew he was going to tell me I'd have to do what I had to do. The last thing I really wanted was to leave the Demented Sons, but I wouldn't take Viper's shit standing down. I'd been pushed beyond my limits as a human and a man by him.

Color me shocked as hell when Smoke put it to the vote.

"All in favor of dealing with Viper by whatever means are necessary, say aye." There was an immediate chorus of "ayes."

"All against, say nay." Dead silence. My heart stuttered.

Though he said it under his breath, his whispered, "Fuck," might as well have been shouted. I wasn't sure what he was expecting. Every single one of us was prior service. Combat veterans at that. We were fighters, not ones to lie down and take shit.

Every one of them would have my back. If it came down to me reporting it was in self-defense because we couldn't keep it hushed up and covered up, they'd have my back. I hated to pull them into my fight, but I had a feeling he wouldn't stop with only me. He wanted my entire club gone.

Not happening.

Now that I was back to work, Raiven was working full days. Presley stayed at the clubhouse with Mattie because it was safer there than in a daycare. At least, that was my opinion and the opinion of my brothers.

Since I had my bike now, I told Raiven to drive my truck. She would drop Presley off on her way to the shop and pick her up on her way home. She wanted to get her own vehicle, but I had to admit I really liked the way she looked driving my truck.

The truck was parked in the driveway when I rode up after work. Despite being fine on my own for the past year, I loved having my two girls to come home to. It was impossible to keep the grin off my face as I got off my bike and walked into the chaos that was our life.

"Hurry! Hurry!" Raiven tossed her purse with the pile of mail across the table and was running down the hall after Presley.

"Everything okay?" I called. I was hoping Presley wasn't sick.

"I go pee-pee, Daddy!" The shout echoed down the hall from the bathroom.

"Good girl!" Grin returning to its place, I picked up the mail to sort through it.

Nothing but junk. Good. No bills.

The toilet flushed, water ran, then Presley's feet slapped on the hardwood floor. She barreled into me, and I hugged her. "Hey, beautiful girl. No accidents today?"

"Nope! Look! I gots big gewl panties on!" She whipped up her shirt and reached down to pull the waistband of the padded underwear out.

Chuckling, I looked up as I caught Raiven come around the corner. A pained expression on her face had my happiness fading.

"Oh thank God. Can you watch her? I have to pis-pee so bad!" Before I'd had chance to say of course, she was gone.

Deciding I would grill, I took the steaks out of the freezer and put them in the microwave on defrost. When I turned around, Presley was digging in Raiven's purse.

"Hey! Get out of there!" I chastised my daughter, making her jump, which in turn caused Raiven's bag to tumble to the floor. The contents scattered.

"Dammit."

"Daddy! You said a bad wood!" The little shit had the nerve to scowl at me with her little fists propped on her hips.

Crouching down, I started gathering up Raiven's belongings. "Don't you get mouthy. You know better than to mess with other people's things." I pointed an accusing finger at her sassiness.

"Her said I cood put on some wiptick!" She pouted like a pro as I rolled my eyes and stuffed things back in the massive bag the woman called a purse.

Reaching for the few things that had fallen under the table, I saw a black-and-white printed-out piece of paper that looked eerily like an ultrasound image. Brow furrowed, I picked it up and studied it.

What the hell does she have this for?

Then I read all the info on it. Her name at the top, Raiven Knight, might as well have been in bright, flashing neon. Noting the dates, my stomach bottomed out.

No. No way.

Counting back, I knew it was possible.

Like a sucker punch, the image damn near bowled me over. Shock, disbelief, and a little splash of betrayal hit me. Unsure what to do about it, I set it on the table, finished grabbing the last of her things, and put her purse back where it was.

Once I was capable, I stood. Slowly, methodically, I walked to the refrigerator. Grabbing a magnet from the pizza place down the road, I stuck the images right to the middle of the door.

Unable to process everything in that moment without losing my shit, I grabbed the steaks from the microwave. My jaw wouldn't un-clench, and my heart was flip-flopping so hard it was rattling my rib cage.

"Daddy! Wisten, Daddy!" Blinking down at my little termagant, I cleared my head enough to acknowledge her.

"What, Presley?"

"I wanna wear some wiptick!" She gave me an exasperated look.

"Go talk to Raiven." I wasn't digging in that purse for diddly shit. God knew what else was in there that I hadn't paid attention to. I wasn't sure I wanted to know.

In a huff, she stomped off to find Raiven, who still hadn't come out of the bathroom.

Had she seen me find the ultrasound and I hadn't noticed her? Was she hiding from me now?

Snatching the new grilling utensils I'd bought, I stormed outside. A million things were roiling in my guts and mind. Facing Raiven at that second wasn't a good idea.

For one, I wasn't sure I wanted to be a dad again. Then again, I hadn't hesitated to fuck her raw every single time since we'd moved into the house. I wasn't stupid. I knew how babies were made. So that told me, deep down I did want her to be pregnant with my kid.

That clear realization rocked my world.

It meant that not only did I want to claim her as mine by putting my patch on her back, it meant I wanted her permanently. Except if I was honest with myself, I'd had those thoughts in my head for a while. Despite the brief period of time we'd known each other, she made me feel whole. In fact, visions of her swollen with my kid for all the world to see set off some serious caveman reactions in me.

Jesus. One raven-haired vixen I hadn't seen coming had fucked up every priority and plan I'd had for my life. Upon further self-examination, that didn't upset me either.

The only thing that upset me was the fact that she hadn't even mentioned a word to me about thinking she might be pregnant. Yet she'd obviously had a doctor's appointment and an ultrasound. None of which I'd known anything about.

Then another thought hit me like a Mack truck.

What if it wasn't mine?

TWENTY THREE

Raiven

"NO MORE TEARS"—OZZY OSBOURNE

"Pwincess Waiven?" The little voice carried through the door as I brushed my teeth.

Spitting the foam from my mouth, I rinsed.

Fuck. Puking in the afternoon was a first. Usually, it was only first thing in the morning. Except today, Presley had brought Play-Doh home with her, courtesy of her "uncle" Smoke. I wanted to beat his smirking ass when I picked her up and saw what he'd bought her.

Well, true to Presley's lovable but turd-ish self, she didn't listen when I told her not to open it in the truck. The smell hit me, and my stomach revolted. I'd held it as long as I could, but as soon as she'd gone to the bathroom and Lock had her, I beelined for the toilet.

I'd actually peed myself as I puked. It was mortifying. Thankfully, I had a pair of leggings in the bathroom that I'd been drip-drying on the shower curtain rod. After a baby wipe clean-up, I tugged the leggings on.

They were actually so much more comfortable than my jean shorts were.

"Yeah, Presley?"

"I wanna wear wiptick. Daddy say I no get in you puss wiffout you." Juvenile though it may have been, I giggled a little at how her words came out. My mind quickly snapped to the dirty thoughts that brought to my head. *Well, your dad doesn't have a problem with getting in my puss.*

"I'm coming." Trying not to laugh at my twisted humor, I rinsed my shorts and underwear out, then opened the door to find the pint-sized princess looking like a storm cloud. Exactly like her father did when he was angry.

"Come on, I'll help you," I chuckled as I made a pit-stop at the washer in the hall closet, setting it on a quick load with the few things that were already in there.

She followed me out to the kitchen where I'd left my purse.

Opening it, I saw everything was all jumbled up and knew she'd already been in it and likely couldn't find them because I kept them in the zippered pocket. Smirking at her stubborn ability to disobey, I dug around in the pocket until I found the pink one. "Okay, come on, let's make you look fabulous."

Crouching down, I carefully lined her lips in her favorite color. Once I was done, I held up my compact mirror for her to see the results. "Good?"

"Fab-you-us!" she announced with a huge smile. "I put my pwin-cess dress on!" Then with slapping feet, she ran off to her room.

My heart fluttered at the happiness her little smile brought me. Knowing I'd likely have to leave after I started showing was a knife to my stomach.

There was no way Lock would want me around not knowing if this was his baby. Even if he initially thought he'd be okay with it, I doubted it would be true for long. How could it be? I imagined him stewing over it, the uncertainty eating at him. It would be poison to anything we might've been building.

I'd have to enjoy what we had for as long as I could. Because heaven knew I wasn't ready to walk away from him yet. He was absolutely, positively my greatest and worst addiction.

The window in the back door framed him as he stood at the grill. His face was pensive, but God, he was beautiful. His beard had grown, but better yet, he had given in to Presley and my badgering and was growing out the top again. Lordy, and those arms. His muscles were rebuilding, and it showed.

All in all, he was hot as Hades.

The white T-shirt he wore like a second skin had grease smudges, as did his jeans, but it didn't detract from his overall sex appeal. In fact, it only increased it. I could only imagine him working hard on a bike, sweat soaking his tight shirt. Better yet, shirtless.

Get a grip, girl.

As if he sensed my gaze on him, his head swiveled to stare back at me. The storm raging in his eyes made me wonder what had him so keyed up. It seemed forever before he looked away.

Not once did he smile at me. Something was seriously bothering him.

The loss of visual contact left me cold and disconnected. It was disturbing how merely holding his gaze warmed me and made me all squishy inside. My feelings were beginning to develop into something that likely wouldn't end well, and I was more afraid of the damage to my heart than I had been of Stefano.

Since he was grilling, I figured I might as well make myself useful and prepare the sides. With a sigh, I turned to the bin and pulled out a few potatoes. Deciding to make them into garlic mashed, I prepared a pan, then peeled and chopped them before I dumped them in the water to boil. Once that was done, I went to the refrigerator to get some veggies out of the freezer.

My movement caused a paper on the fridge to flutter, catching my attention.

Heart caught in my throat and choking for air, I stared at the ultrasound images stuck on the refrigerator door at eye level. It was as if I'd imploded and was caving in at my chest. Instinctually, my hand slapped to my chest to contain the damage, but it was impossible.

Any hopes of having more time with him and Presley shriveled as the images mocked me from the shining black door.

He knew.

TWENTY FOUR

Lock

"SEX TYPE THING"—STONE TEMPLE PILOTS

L ooking up, I met her blue eyes through the glass. Captivated, I couldn't look away. No matter the turmoil spinning in my head, she owned me.

The thought was terrifying.

For so long it had only been me and Presley. I didn't have to worry about anyone but the two of us. Now there was a woman and another kid.

The thought of it being someone else's made me angrier than I would've thought possible. Because if it was, that meant some other asshole put his shit in what belonged to me.

A little voice whispered, "You were gone, possibly dead. She may have been upset."

Knowing her, and thinking back to that day, she'd definitely been upset. What if she'd sought solace in one of my brothers' arms? They all were good guys. Hell, I was man enough to admit that and that they were all good-*looking* guys.

Could I really find fault if she had?

Yeah, I could. Because I was a possessive motherfucker. Which made me irrational when it came to her. It was a fault that I was also man enough to admit.

Angry at the visions of her with one of my brothers, I forced my gaze back to the grill and the steaks. My teeth made cracking sounds, I was clenching them so hard. It forced me to work on the breathing exercises my shrink always made me do.

Removing the steaks from the grill, I told myself we were going to talk as soon as Presley was in bed.

Schooling my features, I entered the house. Presley was sitting on Raiven's lap at the table, coloring. The rest of the table was set for us to eat, with two covered dishes I hadn't even known I had. The day I'd furnished the house, I'd grabbed shit and threw it in the cart because I'd been in a hurry to meet Raiven and bring her to see the house.

She'd been fucking stuck in my head every single day since I'd met her.

"Hey, steaks are done. You ready to eat?"

Raiven quietly nodded. Presley clapped her hands and shouted, "Yes! I stahving!"

Dinner was unusually silent. The sound of silverware scrapping the plates filled the room.

When we'd all finished, Raiven hopped up and started clearing the table before I could. For a few seconds I was mesmerized by the perfect curve of her ass in the leggings she wore. As she walked around, it flexed and rippled beautifully. It made me have really dirty thoughts about violating the kitchen again.

Instead, I shook that shit out of my head, because it had my jeans uncomfortably tight in the crotch.

Though she'd gotten most of it while I sat transfixed, I got up, wordlessly helped her, then went in search of my wild child to give her a bath. I needed some space from her.

I'd had to fight grabbing her and kissing her each time I'd gotten close to her. If I had, though, we would've found ourselves doing things we shouldn't do with Presley still awake.

"Daddy, wook what Unco Smoke gives me!" She had freaking Play-Doh smashed all over the floor, and I'd never been so thankful not to have carpet in my life. Making a mental note to beat his fucking ass, I forced myself to smile for my daughter.

"Wow. That's, uh, pretty cool. You ready for a bath?"

She pondered the Play-Doh, then me before narrowing her eyes at me. "I hab duh bafftub cwayons?"

Chuckling, I looked upward for divine intervention with the spawn of myself I'd created. My parents had warned me after every incident where I'd tested their patience that I was going to end up with a child just like me. Their dire warnings had come to fruition. I could only hope she didn't grow up to be as wild as I'd been. Heaven help me if she was.

That had me thinking of the baby Raiven was carrying. If it was mine, would it be like me or like her? I really didn't even want to think about if it wasn't mine.

"Sure. Bathtub crayons it is." Her smug grin had me wanting to pull my hair out. Little shit was lucky I loved her.

"And bubbos," demanded the pint-sized negotiator.

The desire to roll my eyes but laugh at the same time was overwhelming. All I could do was shake my head.

"Fine. And bubbles. Now let's go. Grab your pajamas and clean undies," I firmly told her, then I sighed when she ran to get her clothes.

Bath time was an aquatic circus, as always. I was pretty sure more water ended up on the floor than in the tub. By the time we were done and the rest of the water was draining, I was damn near as wet as my daughter. Exasperated with her ability to rain bath water everywhere, I dried her, lotioned her up, and helped her with her pajamas.

I was surprised that she allowed me to help. She was extremely independent.

"Daddy?" she asked as she was stepping her second foot into her bottoms while holding my shoulders.

"Yes, sweetheart?"

"Is Pwincess Waiven dunna be my momma?"

Holy shit.

Talk about being knocked for a loop. Did the kid have ESP? Because I'd have sworn she always seemed to know things she shouldn't.

There was no way I had an answer for my daughter's question. Without knowing what was going on in Raiven's head, I couldn't make promises that I wouldn't be able to keep.

"Um, well, I don't know."

Presley appeared to ponder my answer before bluntly telling me, "You needa ask."

"We'll see." Cop-out answer. Her narrowed eyes were unnerving as she studied me. It was almost as if she saw through my non-answer. "Let's go tell her goodnight and get you to bed."

Presley raised her arms for me to pick her up. It was probably wrong, but after not having the strength to even think about carrying her for the first week, I'd take every opportunity to hold her. She leaped into my arms as I opened them.

My next shock was walking out of the bathroom door to find Raiven leaning against the wall. Her arms were wrapped tightly around herself with her bottom lip held tight in her teeth. The expression on her beautiful face told me she'd heard what Presley and I'd been discussing.

Shit. Motherfucking shit.

Well, one more thing for us to talk about.

"Hey. You want to tuck her in with me?" Softly and suddenly unsure, I asked her.

"Uh, sure." The hesitation in her answer didn't sit right with me. She'd tucked Presley in with me all week. Maybe that was part of the problem; we'd been doing too many domestic things in front of Presley and it was giving her the wrong idea.

Except I didn't care. I'd wanted those moments with Raiven and Presley. Every second with Raiven was simply right. I didn't know how else to explain the feelings I had. She'd become part of our little family, and that was big.

Really big.

I didn't let people in like that.

We went through our little routine, and before I knew it, we were closing the door to Presley's room.

"We need to talk." I didn't waste a second.

"Shit." It was a mere breath of a word, but I heard. Staring her straight in the eyes, I inhaled deeply and let it out in a rush. Then I walked to the kitchen and sat at the table. For the moment, I ignored the ultrasound.

Tentatively, she took the chair across from me and sat on the edge as if she was poised for flight.

Patiently, I waited to see if she would say anything. My eyes studied her every move. Each breath, the way the tip of her pink tongue licked her lips before she pulled the bottom one into her teeth. By then, I was surprised it wasn't bruised.

"What did you want to talk about?" Nervousness emanated from her.

Okay, we're going to play it like she doesn't know what I want to talk to her about.

Unsure of how to proceed, I stood up, ripped the ultrasound off the refrigerator door, and slapped it on the table. "How about we start with this."

My heart was pounding so hard I heard the rushing of blood in my ears as I awaited her response.

First, she swallowed hard, still looking me in the eye. Then her lashes fluttered as she lowered her gaze to the paper held down by the tips of my fingers. Her lids slammed shut tight, and I could see her pulse racing on her throat.

"Raiven?" The warning in my voice came out as a decided growl.

A visible shudder shook her head to toe. When those big, blue eyes reopened, the shimmer of tears almost had me caving. Instead, I steeled myself against them because I wanted answers.

"I'm pregnant?" It came out as a question. Her brow wrinkled.

"I can see that. You know what I want to know?" It was a battle to keep my voice steady.

"What?" It was a whisper.

"Why didn't you tell me?" I ticked off with one finger. "How long have you known?" Another finger raised. "Is it mine?" Last finger.

When her head tipped down to avoid my gaze, I used those fingers to gently tip her head back up. She closed her eyes, and I sighed.

"Look at me."

At least she listened, and her eyes opened again. This time the shimmer of tears had increased until they pooled on her lower lids. One slipped free and started a cascade of them down her cheeks.

"I was afraid. About a week." A shuddering inhale followed, then, "I don't know."

"Fuck." It was my turn to close my eyes. It was impossible to look at her without seeing another man's hands gliding over her colorful skin. When I saw it behind my closed lids, I opened them. Afraid to hear which brother it might be, I clenched my jaw, then forced it to relax. "Who?"

I thought I could handle a lot. I'd been through hell and back. My counseling sessions had been rough, even though they were sanitized to prevent my therapist from having to report everything that had happened. I'd led the therapist to believe I'd been captured in combat without actually saying the lie outright.

Falsely, my therapy let me think I'd gained some extreme fortitude.

I was wrong. So fucking wrong. Because her tearfully whispered answer was a sledgehammer to my knees.

"Stefano."

TWENTY FIVE

Raiven

"CAST IT OUT"—10 YEARS

T he torment in his eyes when I said whose baby it might be. Holy shit. Talk about ripping my damn heart out, because I understood his pain. The thought of the baby belonging to Stefano made me want to drop to my knees and sob.

It was the exact reason I'd tried my damnedest not to think about it over the past week.

"I need to ask you something else," he choked out. With his elbows resting on the table, his hands tugged at the hair of his lowered head. Realizing he couldn't look at me as he asked worried me. And damn, did it hurt. It gave credibility to my worries that he wouldn't be able to see me day in, day out with the baby of the one person he was sure to hate growing inside me.

"Look, I can leave now. When the baby is born, we can do a paternity test, and if…." I swallowed with difficulty. Then cleared my throat. "If it's not yours, I'll never bother you again. I'll look for another job, leave here, then there will be no worries of you running into us."

Saying "us" in reference to me and a baby was so alien. I wasn't certain if I was awake or dreaming. The thought of leaving the only other place I'd called home also flipped my world on end. Truthfully, I didn't want to go.

"Raiven, would you let me say what I have to say?" Weariness heavy in his words, he lifted his eyes to mine.

To keep myself from blurting out something stupid, I held my lips tight between my teeth. Tears threatened, but I rapidly blinked them away. Finally, I nodded.

The defeated breath he released didn't help my insecurities.

"After I found the ultrasound, I didn't know what to think. Which, by the way, was because Presley spilled your purse on the floor, not because I went through your purse. So many things, so many feelings, spun in my head. I was angry, hurt, upset, disappointed." Each of those words was a dagger to my heart. "Hell, I even thought you might be just like Letty, filling me full of lies."

"Lock—" He'd never really talked about Letty, and I'd been hesitant to ask since she seemed such a taboo subject. What I did know was it had to be difficult for him to talk about her death.

"No, Raiven. Where I'm going with this is… well, the more I thought, the more I had to accept that there was the possibility that the baby wasn't mine. Granted, my thoughts had leaned more toward worry that it was one of my brothers. Hearing you say it could be that fucker was quite a blow. It took me aback because I wasn't prepared for that part, and I should've been. You dated him. It is what it is. You didn't know me, and I didn't know you. Anyway, what I'm trying to say is that it doesn't matter." He sighed.

"One of your brothers! What?" I exclaimed. Then the rest of what he said sunk in. "What do you mean, it doesn't matter?" Breath caught in my throat, I waited for his response. Hope started to bubble in me regardless of how foolish I knew that was.

He stood quickly, and the chair fell backwards with a clatter. Hands splayed on the table, he leaned in toward me. "Raiven, you are mine, regardless of who you were with before or what happened between then and now. There was a reason we were brought together. There's a reason for my inability to remember what my life was like before you—other than lonely. Despite my love for my daughter and my brothers, I was lonely. Except I didn't want to let anyone in. Until you. So whether you like it or not…, you. Are. Mine."

By the end of his declaration, my heart was erratically thumping, and heat crept up my chest and to my face. Blinking owlishly, I was speechless. "What if I don't want to be with you?" Not a chance.

"Then I guess I'll have to convince you that we belong together." The corner of his lips kicked up, and my chest heaved with rapid breaths.

Without conscious thought, I sprang out of my seat. Much like his, my chair fell over with a clatter on the wood floor. My fingers threaded through his wayward, messy beard. Holding it like a lifeline, I leaned over, meeting him in the middle of the table where our lips crashed together.

My tears ran unchecked down my cheeks until they hit our connected lips. When his tongue teased the crease of my mouth, I knew he tasted them too.

A whimper escaped me as he kissed me with a volatile storm of emotion. It was so strong, I sensed it with everything in my being. His hands remained planted firmly to the table, allowing me to control our connection.

I wanted to climb over the table into his arms.

Trying to breathe through the kiss wasn't enough for how worked up I was, and I eventually had to break away with a gasp. Sucking oxygen in like it was going out of style, I rested my forehead to his. Every so often I pressed a gentle kiss to his lips because their absence from mine was painful to my heart. Every other one lingered, and he would pull my upper or lower lip into his mouth where he'd catch it with his teeth.

"Bed," he snuck out between kisses. My hands glided down until my palms curved around his neck.

"Yes."

Still hesitant to be separated after what seemed like finding heaven on earth, we didn't move.

Unable to bear the loss of his touch for the time it would take to walk around the table, I gave in to my crazy thoughts. Gripping his shoulders, I raised a knee to the table top, then the other. As I walked across the space on my knees, I leaned over, and he reached up to keep kissing me.

Once my body was in his space, he wrapped his arms around the backs of my thighs and pulled me flush to him. Holding tight, his hands gripped and squeezed.

My hair fell around us as I continued to kneel on the table. With each foray into his mouth, I tasted his lust.

His need.

His desperation.

Breaking away from my lips, he tipped his head to the side to slowly trail his lips along my cheek to my jaw. Stopping only to nip the tender skin or give a featherlight kiss, he took his time moving on to my shoulder. His lips followed one tank strap as his fingers seductively slid it down.

Moving across my chest, he dipped the tip of his tongue in my cleavage as he passed by. Reaching the other shoulder, he did the same with that strap. Only then did his gaze flicker up to mine and hold.

Eyes locked on mine, he used a single finger to hook the tank between my breasts. So goddamn slowly that I wanted to scream, he moved it down, down, down until it was caught on my peaked nipples.

I noticed his Adam's apple bob as he broke my gaze and looked to where his finger continued to pull until the edge popped over the tips, exposing me to his lustful stare.

"Have I told you your tits are absolutely perfect?" The raspy quality of his whisper told me the level of his need and how tight he was holding on to his control. A large, rough, grease-stained hand cupped each one. "So fucking beautiful."

First one nipple disappeared into his mouth where he suckled, licked, and teased it before releasing it with a drawn-out tug ending with a pop and a clink of the ring against his teeth. The other one was next, and I watched my chest rise and fall as the rosy-hued nipple disappeared into his talented mouth.

I was barely aware of my fingers digging into his shoulders over the stretched fabric of his tee. Everything he did was so good, so exquisite.

"I think they've already gotten bigger," he said as his hands hefted each boob, with a wicked gleam in his eyes and a small tip of his lips that had released my aching nipple to speak.

"Everything's already getting bigger. I'm already getting fat enough that my clothes are tight," I gasped.

His answer was a surprisingly swift and hard smack to my ass. A startled squeak escaped me, but he quickly returned his mouth to the first nipple, giving the ring a gentle tug. As he worshipped my boobs, his hands soothed and kneaded the stinging area until it was a tingly memory.

"I don't want to hear you call yourself fat again. You're fucking perfect, and you're only going to get better." He leaned down and settled a kiss on my lower belly.

Holy shit. I didn't know what to do with that.

We'd been living together pretty much as a couple without Presley knowing. He'd gotten sweeter, even though he could still be his assholish self at times. Though he was an attentive lover and man, something had definitely shifted, and I wasn't prepared for it.

"I heard what she said, you know," I whispered.

"I figured you did. So how do you feel about that?" Steadily, he watched me as I processed and thought about how to say what I was thinking.

"Well, it's one thing to sleep together in secret and for me to help out with her. I'm not sure if it's fair for me to step into the role of her mother. I'm not her mom, and I don't want to take her mom's place." The last thing I wanted was to have him or anyone else think I was swooping in and playing mommy. Though in my heart, I wanted that more than anything.

"You already have. Haven't you noticed? Her mother is gone. I've come to grips with that, and she doesn't really remember anything different. But I'll tell you what, how about if we are open about our relationship and we leave it up to her as to what she calls you? I'm going to tell you something for nothing, however. I'm twenty-nine years old. I'm not some high school kid. I joined the army at eighteen, was in combat the first time by age nineteen, the second time when I was twenty-one, third time at twenty-three. I got out, had a kid, and I've been busting my ass ever since. I've lost the mother of my child, who I thought was the love of my life. I've since reevaluated that after learning a few things, but that's for another conversation. I'm not interested in 'dating' and 'seeing where this goes.' I know how I feel about you. You're having my baby."

I started to protest, and he placed a finger over my lips. "You. Are. Having. My. Baby. Regardless of its conception, this baby is growing in my woman. The 'possible' father isn't in the picture, I am. It's my baby. So the only thing that will stop me from making you my wife is if you say it's not what you want."

"Uhh...." His speech had knocked my damn socks off. Hell, for a while after he'd returned, I'd honestly wondered if he hated me, then I realized he was frustrated with his physical condition and what had happened. It wasn't directed at me.

Seeing the ultrasound image on the fridge had me expecting our conversation to go so differently. He was so adamant and assured about his feelings and what he wanted, I was envious. To be that sure of things must be amazing.

But then again, he really was amazing.

"This is where you tell me to fuck off or take you to bed. But if I take you to bed, that means I'm fucking keeping you there. We clear?" One eyebrow rose as he waited to see what I would say.

"Take me to bed or lose me forever?" I tried to be my usual saucy self and steal a quote from a movie, but it came out more of a question because I was a little in shock.

"That's what I'm talking about." Before I could blink, he had swooped me off the table and carried me down the hall. Legs wrapped around his waist, I held on as he kissed me the entire way.

Once we reached the room, he spun, using my ass to close the door before pressing me against the old wooden panels. The thickness of his erection lined right up where it belonged, and I moaned into his mouth.

When we came up for air, I laughed nervously before whispering, "This is crazy, you know that, right?"

"No," he said matter-of-factly. "This is what it feels like when everything is the way it's supposed to be."

My heart melted, and I knew he was right. Even though we'd known each other a short period of time, we were good together. Not only in bed, but as a team, with Presley, and hopefully as parents.

"Bed," I gasped as he reached between us to slide my pants down.

I'd never been much of a praying person, but the last couple of months had made me question faith and a higher being more than any other time in my life, so I prayed with everything in me that my baby was Lock's.

And if it wasn't, I prayed it wouldn't tear us apart.

Because when he slid into me, thick, hot, and perfect, I knew in my heart of hearts that I loved him with every fiber of my being.

Each stroke was slow, deliberate, tortuous, as his eyes locked with mine. Our fingers were twined as he held my hands up on either side of my head. My hips rose up to meet his as I tried to grind against him. I was chasing my release, but he was intentionally holding me off.

"Fucking hell, you feel so damn good. Don't rush it. I want to savor this moment." His voice was strained and growly.

"I need you" was my whimpered reply.

"You have me. Forever. Now let me enjoy making love to my woman, dammit."

Eyes wide, I sucked in a shocked breath. I wasn't sure why; the man had all but told me I was the woman for him. It would make sense that he loved me too. Except actually hearing him say he was making love to me was so much more.

"Did you doubt how I felt about you?" He thrust hard and deep. I mewled.

He did it again, hips snapping with the force of his words. "Well, did you?"

"I wasn't sure." I barely got it out as he went in deeper and harder, sending my eyes rolling.

Suddenly I was flying through the air as we switched positions and then I was straddling him with my hands braced over his pierced nipples. "Jesus, are you trying to give me a heart attack?"

"No, I want to be able to watch you fall apart at your own pace. Now, you better get started or I'm taking over again." His rough palms slid up and down my torso before his fingers dug into my hips.

Doing exactly as he instructed, I began to rock against him, creating the friction I needed. Each stroke brought me closer to the explosive climax I'd had building since he first slid in. When I came, I knew I soaked him as I screamed, "Oh my God, oh my God, Oh my God! I fucking love you!"

Not how I planned on saying it the first time.

TWENTY SIX

Lock

"MY SACRIFICE"—CREED

"I do," I said with absolute conviction.

Raiven might have thought I was kidding, but I wasn't waiting. Which was why two weeks later we were standing in front of the Justice of the Peace saying, "I do."

Standing witness was my big brother, my brothers from both chapters, their families, my parents, and my daughter. My family, each and every one of them.

There were more from other chapters waiting outside because there wasn't enough room in there for everyone.

Presley was dressed in the frilliest, poofiest pink dress I'd ever seen. I had no idea where Raiven and she had found it, but my sassy princess was over the moon. She even had her own sparkling tiara. All topped off with her pink Chucks.

My girl.

Mom and Dad had told me they were coming down for Presley's birthday, and I figured it was perfect timing. I knew if I got married without them being there my mom would never forgive me. To say they were shocked would've been an understatement.

They were happy though. Especially finding out they were going to be grandparents again. I'd decided there was no need to say the child may not biologically be mine yet. I didn't plan on lying to my parents, but it was my child regardless. I'd tell them the details later, after they fell in love with Raiven as much as I had.

"Raiven, you look so beautiful. Thank you for making me the happiest man in the world," I whispered to her right before I did what the man had instructed me to do, and that was kiss my wife.

My wife.

Goddamn, I loved the sound of that.

Mom cried. She'd been hoping I'd find someone and dropped hints all the time. She was ecstatic that it'd finally happened.

"I love you," Raiven whispered when I finally pulled back.

"Ladies and gentlemen, I present Mr. and Mrs. Matlock Augustus Archer," the JP said.

Raiven whispered, "You never told me your middle name was Augustus!"

I laughed.

My grin was huge as my family hooted and hollered at the announcement of our new status. Raiven glowed as she looked around at the smiling faces surrounding us. My mom pulling her into a huge hug didn't hurt either. In fact, Raiven looked like she might burst into tears at my mother's show of affection.

"Congratulations, son," my dad said as he placed a firm hand on my shoulder and gave me a squeeze.

Amidst laughter, smiles, and congratulations, we left the courthouse. Nearly every chapter was there, and we were pelted by birdseed as soon as our shoes hit the sunlight. Presley was jumping up and down in my brother's arms beside us. "I wanna hug my pwincess mommy!"

A hush fell over everyone. Both my mom and Raiven, hell, probably every female in there, covered their mouths and held in their tears.

Presley didn't wait and threw herself forward into Raiven's waiting arms. For a second, I worried about Raiven holding her weight and how it might affect the baby, but she was so fucking happy, and there was no discomfort on her face. Still, I stood by ready to grab my daughter at the slightest sign of trouble.

Each day that went by had my worry for her increasing. By the time she delivered, I'd be a fucking basket case.

"I wub you! Fank you for being my mommy." Their cheeks were mashed together as a tear escaped one of Raiven's eyes. I quietly wiped it away with my thumb. Then I kissed both of my girls.

"Okay, pretty princess, let's get you buckled up so we can go have your birthday party!" My dad plucked her out of Raiven's arms with a smile.

Presley clapped her hands and with the biggest grin, yelled, "Time foh cake!"

All of the brothers who had ridden their bikes prepared to mount up.

Raiven fiddled with the waist of the full tulle skirt on her gown. I chuckled when it came undone and she handed it to my mom. She was left standing in a jewel-encrusted white corset-style tank top and white skinny jeans. On her feet were black biker boots.

Proud as punch, she stood there with her fists propped on her hips. "Well? What do you think?"

Laughing my ass off at how she'd pulled off her outfit, I hugged her. "Sexy as ever."

"Well, you were pissed that I wanted to ride on your bike in a dress and pregnant, so I fixed one of the issues you had." She grinned and shrugged.

She'd told me she was going to wad up the dress and hold it. I'd been pissed and argued about her riding on the bike to begin with. Riding with some big poofy-ass thing that could get hung up in something on the bike if she lost hold of it terrified me. We'd come to an agreement that it would be just this once until after the baby was born, and the guys had all agreed we'd take it slow.

I'd had a bit of an anxiety attack at the thought of something happening to her and the baby. Cue irrational worry.

The thing was, I hadn't had a passenger with me since the accident that claimed Letty's life. Though I'd wanted to pick Raiven up from work the day I bought my new bike, I hadn't known she was pregnant then.

That P word changed every-damn-thing.

"Well, you ready to ride?" Reminiscent of Presley, she clapped her hands and jumped up and down. The tops of her growing tits jiggled over the tight corset, and I almost swallowed my tongue.

"Christ, you're gonna have me riding with a chub the whole fucking way," I muttered.

Her bright grin took on a decidedly wicked cast, and those red lips pursed to the side.

Once Smoke, Snow, and the other chapter presidents were on their bikes, we all got on. They'd tried to say as the bride and groom we could mount up first and ride up front, but I'd refused. We'd be riding in the very middle of the pack because I didn't want her out front, and it was bad enough she'd be sailing her veil in the air as we went. She'd found a way to stick the damn thing to the top of her helmet.

That was something I wouldn't budge on.

She was wearing a fucking helmet.

Dad rolled down the window of the truck for Presley as we all racked our pipes, rattling the downtown street's windows. Presley giggled and waved. The bikes were so raucous, we could barely hear her yell, "Wub you, Daddy and Mommy!"

Raiven waved at her and blew her a kiss out of the raised face shield. "Love you, baby girl!" she shouted back to her.

That shit did weird things to my chest cavity.

As we pulled out, something caught my eye. If I was a betting man, I would've bet I saw Viper in the shadows of a tree across the road. But when I looked again, there was no one there. Shaking my head, I chalked it up to paranoia.

It was a long procession, and because we rode slower than normal, it took a while to get back to the clubhouse. The whole way there, people were passing us, taking pictures and video. Raiven would wave and blow kisses to them.

I couldn't quit smiling. I hadn't smiled that big since losing Letty.

I'd made peace with what she'd done, because looking back on it, regardless of why she'd come up there to me, in the end she'd loved me. I knew she did.

And she'd given me Presley. There could be no greater gift.

There was a crazy number of bikes once we'd all parked. It was a spectacular sight.

"Wait." I held Raiven back when she made to follow the crowd inside.

Gunny paused by the door with Mom, Dad, and Presley.

"This happened fast, but I love you. So fucking much it may not be healthy. Thank you for being my wife, and thank you for loving both me and my daughter. I'm so honored I barely have words." My hand tucked the stray hairs that had pulled loose putting her helmet on and off.

A soft tip of her lips preceded her framing my face with both hands. "You two were a package deal, and I love a bargain. Thank you for trusting me with your precious baby girl. It's me that should be honored."

"Let's go celebrate our daughter's birthday and our wedding." I'd been given strict instructions to be careful not to smear her lipstick when we'd met up at the courthouse. So I kissed her neck and snuck a little nibble in, causing her to giggle.

Gunny handed my daughter over to me when we reached them. "Thanks, bro," I said, cuddling Presley close and kissing her cheek.

"Anytime, little brother. Anytime." He looked happy for me, but I could tell something was bothering him.

We walked into the dim clubhouse, and everyone started to sing "Happy Birthday" to Presley. There were hot pink streamers and balloons everywhere. My little girl was nearly hyperventilating, she was so excited.

My parents quickly stole my daughter from me. I was no fool; I knew it was both to spoil her and to give me and Raiven some time.

Reaper and Steph approached us first, and I gave Reaper a big hug. "Good to see you again, bro," he said before stepping back. I made introductions, since I knew Raiven hadn't met his ol' lady yet. While Steph stepped up to me, he went to give Raiven a hug and started talking to her.

When Steph opened her mouth, I knew they'd arranged it that way.

"Lock, I wanted to tell you that I'm so happy for you, and I know Letty would want this for you. At first I was worried and thought maybe you were jumping into something because of all the shit that's happened. But I can see how happy you are and how much you love her. That's everything." She sniffled a little, then gave me a big hug. I wrapped my arms around her.

"Thanks, babe. That means the world to me, especially knowing that Letty was one of your best friends growing up." I spoke into her ear before I released her with a chaste kiss to her cheek.

Then I hooked an arm around my wife's waist, pulling her close.

Hollywood and Becca were next.

"Damn, I'm so glad you left our chapter!" Hollywood smirked, and Becca gasped in shock as she backhanded his abs.

"That's a shitty thing to say!" She looked embarrassed as hell, and her face matched her auburn hair.

"What? I was tired of competing with his pretty face. Now I'm the prettiest again." White teeth flashed in a wolfish smile, and I laughed.

"Shit, you keep telling yourself that," I teased, and it was his turn to laugh. Becca started to lose the deep red on her face when she caught on that we were fucking with each other.

Hacker and Kassi moved in next, followed by Joker and Sera.

"Oh my God, girl. I loved your dress and how you were able to take the skirt off!" Kassi said.

"Yeah, that was freaking badass, but the veil on the helmet was the best," piped in Sera.

Hacker and Joker rolled their eyes at the women with their giggling and shit. We shook hands and hugged.

"We sure miss you, Lock." Hacker was fairly somber, and Joker poked him.

"Aww don't cry, *cariño!*" Joker teased.

"Fuck you. You're such an asshole," Hacker grumbled, but I could see the grin he suppressed.

"Nah, I'm kidding. Yeah, we do fucking miss you. And Gunny, since he's still chilling down here with you." Joker grinned good-naturedly in typical Joker fashion. He was a far cry from the guy I'd prospected with. Well, our prospect time overlapped and he was patched first, but we were low-man-on-totem-pole together for a while.

"Yeah, funny thing is, he hasn't been to the house for breakfast for the last week. He wouldn't move to the house with us either. He's been staying here. Something's up with him, but I don't know what. I've had so much going on, it keeps slipping my mind to talk to him. Makes me feel like a pretty shitty brother." I scratched my beard, then smoothed it.

"Want me to try to feel him out?" Hacker spoke up.

"Nah, leave it be. I don't want him to think we've been gossiping about him like old women." I laughed.

"Oh, you mean like you are?" Reaper leaned in, and his ice-blue eyes crinkled at the corners in humor.

"Ahh, fuck off," Joker told Reaper as he gave him a teasing shove.

The women finally came and stole their men and went to get food. Raiven looped an arm through mine and leaned her head on my shoulder. "I like your friends."

I snorted. "Friends? Those assholes are family." My grin told her I loved each and every one of them.

Styx ran up to me and gave me a bear hug as he lifted me in the air. He gave a warrior's roar as everyone laughed. Even me. He was a crazy motherfucker, but he'd become not only a trustworthy brother, but a close friend.

"Congratulations, bro. I'm so fucking happy for you guys." He wrapped a big meaty paw around Raiven's head and pulled her close to kiss the top.

"Thanks Styx. That means a lot." Raiven beamed up at the man who rivaled my brother when it came to his Viking-like looks. A lesser man might be jealous, but I'd accepted that Raiven loved me and was loyal to me. I was one lucky bastard.

"Lock." The gruff voice that came from over my shoulder had me standing tall. Next to my dad, Pops had my respect more than any man.

"Hey, Pops, thanks for coming back up." He and Mama Jean had gone down along the coast and to the border with their RV for a while. They'd come back up when we'd told them what our plans were.

"You know you're like a son to me, boy," he grumbled, and I smirked at him calling me a boy. "But you better treat her right. That girl there is all the family Mama and I have left, and she's been like a daughter to us her whole life."

"Yes, sir. I can promise you, I'll keep her happy," I promised.

"You fucking better," he threatened before he wrapped his bear-like arms around me and squeezed. "I love you, son."

"Thanks, Pops. I love you too." We didn't say it loud enough for everyone to hear, because a man has his pride. But every word was the truth.

After Mama said her piece to me as well, they moved on to visit with everyone.

Raiven leaned in to whisper in my ear, "How happy will you keep me?"

Her twinkling eyes were full of mischief, and I had half a mind to take her to one of the rooms and show her.

Instead, I pulled her close, pressing my hard-as-fuck dick against her soft middle. "How happy do you think I can keep you?"

At her seductive chuckle, I nipped her ear and her neck. "You keep that shit up and I'm going to fuck up that lipstick of yours."

"As long as it's around your cock, I'm okay with that." She covertly slipped a hand between us and wrapped it around my shaft. I groaned at her boldness.

"Jesus fucking Martha, are you trying to kill me? Or are you trying to get me to take you to the back?"

"Maybe both?" The sexy-ass grin that she shot me had me growling as I grabbed her ass and hiked her legs up around my waist. The fact that my parents were there, Pops, Mama Jean, and all the brothers didn't matter shit.

"Daddy? Why you kewwying my mommy?" I heard my daughter say from behind me.

"You just got very lucky," I growled into her ear as she laughed.

"No, I'm hoping to get lucky later."

Not long after that, we were in Smoke's office with my back up against the door. She was on her knees in front of me, and I was quickly losing my shit as she sucked my cock deep down her throat. It was like a motherfucking vacuum, and my knees were on the verge of buckling.

"Goddamn, do you even have a gag reflex?" I asked in astonishment as I recovered from shooting my load down her beautiful, slender throat.

She chuckled softly. "Funny enough, I gag when I brush my back teeth with my toothbrush, but I can suck a dick like nobody's business."

"My," I said, knowing my eyes were flashing angrily.

"Your what?"

"My cock. The thought of those lips around any cock but mine makes me want to hurt someone. These lips don't go near another cock ever again. You feel me?"

Wide-eyed, she nodded. Then I got a good look at her face and my cock. Unable to help it, I laughed.

I'd fucked up her lipstick after all.

TWENTY SEVEN

Raiven

"SAVIOR"—RISE AGAINST

Shutting off the machine, I set it aside and wiped the piece off until it was clean, snapped a pic, prepped it, and covered it. Once I was done, I peeled off my gloves, washed my hands, and smiled. "Done. What do you think?"

"I think I just found my new tattoo artist. Sorry, Joker." Lock was looking in the mirror at his thigh, where I'd finished a phoenix that he'd asked me to work up for him. It was the first of my pieces on him and it left a ridiculous satisfaction to know he wouldn't have someone else's hands on him. The thought of another person leaving their mark on him left me feeling very possessive.

"No you're not." I snorted.

He simply shrugged and grinned. "You're right, I'm not sorry. Besides, he'd completely understand. If Sera could do ink, he'd probably be an inked-up motherfucker."

"Speaking of which, that's so weird. I've met him several times and I still can't get over the fact that he's a tattoo artist with only a handful of tattoos. Most of which he did himself." As I cleaned my station, I shook my head at the mystery of it. For me, my ink was an expression of who I was. Each and every tattoo had meaning. Also, they were addicting as hell. Which was why I had several. Okay, maybe more than several.

"At the reception he said he'd let you put something on him." Lock chuckled.

"Uh, yeah. He was also shit-faced and promised Sera she could pick out what he got. I don't think he'll be sticking to that." I laughed as I wiped down my counter and then leaned against it to look at the sexy-as-fuck man who had been my husband for almost a month.

My husband. I still had a hard time with the reality I was living.

"Are you picking up Presley or am I?" he asked as he carefully pulled his jeans back on over the covered piece. I'd enjoyed him sitting there in his underwear while I'd been doing his leg. He'd probably disagree, but he looked pretty much like when I'd first met him. Maybe a little leaner, but gorgeous nonetheless.

"I can get her. You were my last appointment."

"Cool. I'm going to swing by HEB to pick up some milk and cereal for Presley. You need anything?"

"You're on the bike?"

"Yeah. But I can get my truck from the house. That's what I was going to do if I needed to get her. I don't mind." He walked to the front, and I followed after shutting off my lights and closing my door.

"No, it's okay. I don't really need it anyway."

"What did you want?" He gave me a quizzical smile.

"Cheesecake." I grinned, showing my teeth and batting my eyes. He laughed.

We'd stepped out into the late summer heat, and I nearly melted. "Holy shit, it's hot out here. What the hell were we thinking, moving here?"

"You have auto-start on your truck. Why don't you use it, and it would be cooled off by the time you get in?"

My cheeks flushed. "Maybe because I'm barely used to having a vehicle, let alone having damn auto-start on it." Shrugging as sweat ran down my butt crack, I ran into his back because he'd stopped in his tracks unexpectedly.

"Ooof! Oh shit! Sorry! What's wrong?" I stepped around him to see what he was looking at. There was a man walking away, but other than that, I didn't see anything of interest.

Tense, he clenched and unclenched his hands. "Nothing. Thought I saw someone I know. I think I'll follow you to the clubhouse. I need to talk to Smoke and Straight about something anyway. I'll swing by the store later." He seemed preoccupied as he pulled on his helmet. I tried not to be disappointed that he hadn't kissed me first.

"Okay." Confused, I climbed in my new badass truck and started it up. Wincing as the air blew hot initially, I rolled the windows down to disperse the heat. I'd loved Lock's truck so much, I bought myself a white one just like it.

Intense blue eyes watched me while he waited for me to pull out of the lot.

The whole way to the clubhouse, he was constantly checking his mirrors and looking around. He was trying to be subtle about it, but I noticed.

I made a mental note to ask him, but it slipped my mind when we pulled up and saw Presley on the wooden swing set. The guys had all built it under a huge oak tree when Mattie started babysitting Presley at the clubhouse.

My heart swelled at her obvious happiness.

It nearly exploded when I heard her yell, "Mommy!" as soon as she saw me getting closer.

Lock was on my heels, and she gave us both a big hug. Then she ran back to show us how she'd learned to jump out of the swing.

"Fuck, she's going to give me a damn heart attack." Watching her jump out of the moving swing sent my heart rate into overdrive.

He snorted. "You?"

I'd taken a single step toward Presley when he stopped me and spun me around. The fingers of both hands threaded through the hair on the sides of my head. Stars exploded when his lips touched mine, and my hands wrapped around his wrists.

"Mmm, that was nice. What was that for?" I gave him a contented smile because I'd finally gotten my kiss I'd been missing.

"I have to have a reason to kiss my wife?" He smirked.

"Absolutely not, but is everything okay? You're being very... intense." He kissed me again, and I completely forgot my question.

"I'll be out in a bit. Wait for me?" he asked.

"Sure, but you can meet us at home if you want. I can take Presley and get dinner started."

"No. Wait for me." His somber insistence was unusual.

"Okay, sure." A last brief brush of his lips, and he turned on his heel to enter the clubhouse.

Shaking my head at his weird behavior, I braced myself for the pint-sized whirlwind heading my way again. Though she plowed into my legs, she was careful of my growing baby bump.

Now that I was about fifteen weeks, give or take, we'd told Presley she was going to be a big sister. I'd been worried she may be jealous or wouldn't understand. I'd worried needlessly, because she'd been ecstatic.

"Hi, baby bruver!" She stood on her tiptoes and kissed my belly. We hadn't had another ultrasound to find out the sex yet, but she was insistent it was a boy.

It was cooler in the shade and there was breeze blowing, but it was still hot out. "You wanna go inside, Presley?"

"No, I pway on the swide wiff Mattie. Hers my fwiend." Mattie gave a shy smile at Presley's announcement of their friendship.

"Mattie, are you okay with that?"

The teenage girl shrugged. "It's fine, Ms. Raiven. We have water in the cooler, so we're staying hydrated." She tipped her head toward a cooler at the base of the tree.

"Alright, well, I'll be inside. I'm not built for these temps," I groaned. Once they resumed playing, I entered the cool clubhouse, breathing a sigh of relief.

My relief was short-lived when I heard raised voices coming from the conference room where they usually held church. The door was closed, but I was curious so I stepped closer when I noticed no one was in the common area.

Pressing my ear to the door, I bit my lip, and my eyes darted around checking for anyone who may have come in that I missed. I shouldn't be listening, but I wanted to know what was up. Because I knew something was bothering Lock when we left the shop.

"I'm not putting up with his shit!" I heard Lock yell.

"That's not what I said!" Straight shouted back. Then there was a muffled response that sounded like Smoke, but I couldn't make it out.

After that, everyone quit yelling, so I couldn't hear what was said through the thick wooden door. Deciding it wouldn't do to get caught eavesdropping, I tiptoed over to a booth and sat down.

Since my feet and legs were a little swollen, I slid until my back was against the wall and propped them up on the bench. I wasn't there two minutes when Lock stormed out of the conference room.

"Lock!" Smoke shouted to him.

He spun in a fury. "What?"

"Don't be going off half-cocked and do something stupid. He hasn't done anything yet, and he's had plenty of time. I think he's just fucking with you."

"Well, I'm tired of him fucking with me. If he comes near me or my family, he's a dead man," Lock ground out.

Smoke noticed me first, and his face became impassive as he nodded in my direction. Lock turned, and his gaze caught mine.

Both men walked toward me, followed by Straight. Once they all reached me, they had smiles on their faces, though Straight's looked strained.

"Hey little mama, look at you. Pregnancy agrees with you," Smoke observed.

My eyes narrowed. "Did you get your name because you blow smoke up people's asses?"

Despite the earlier tension, they all laughed. I wasn't kidding.

"Come on, babe, let's head to the house."

Smoke and Straight followed us outside. As I was buckling Presley in, I heard them talking by Lock's bike.

"I'm going to have Check find out if he's staying around here somewhere or if there's anything he can find out. Okay?" Smoke said.

"Sure" was Lock's impassive answer.

Presley had been worn out after her day. She'd nearly dozed off in her plate, then in the bathtub, and finally fell asleep as soon as her head hit the pillow. Without even having her story read.

Lock and I were snuggled up in bed after a round of really exhausting, savage, sweaty sex. It never got old. Each time was like the first time, with each orgasm better than the last.

My head rested on his shoulder as I traced the tattoo on his chest.

"Is everything okay? You seemed very stressed after we left the shop today. Then you guys were yelling. I'm worried about you."

He sighed.

"I don't know. I've tried to tell myself I was being paranoid, but today I saw Viper outside your shop and he looked right at me. Even grinned and waved. It proved to me that I really have been seeing him. It hasn't been my imagination. I don't like that he was outside the shop." He pulled away from me to sit on the edge of the bed. Fingers laced in his hair, he hunched over.

"Matlock. He's obviously just trying to mess with your head. He hasn't done anything, has he?" He'd told me who Viper was and some of what he'd done, though I wasn't an idiot and I could tell he didn't tell me everything. I was also trying to be positive and optimistic because it made me a little nervous to hear that the man was hanging around down in Texas when I'd learned his club was up in Omaha.

"Not this time." The torment in his quiet reply hurt my heart.

His shouted words at the clubhouse made sense, and I worried about him. If he lost his shit and killed this Viper person, he'd likely go to jail. That would kill me. It would devastate Presley, his brother, his parents, and his club.

"Still, if he was going to do something, don't you think he'd have done it be now?"

"If he fucks with you or Presley, he's dead." He spoke low, but I caught the dead tone of his voice. It scared me.

"You're not a killer, Matlock."

His spine stiffened at my words, and he slowly turned to look me in the eye.

"You have no idea."

TWENTY EIGHT

Lock

"BOW DOWN"—I PREVAIL

Her blue eyes widened at my admission, but not a peep left her lips.

"Did you forget I was a soldier? I had three combat deployments, and I sure as hell wasn't just camping in the sand." Three of the worst years of my life, the last one being the catalyst to me calling it quits.

"No, but I didn't know you… I mean, not everyone who's been in the military has killed someone." Her voice was small, and it made me feel like I was a foot tall.

"Not everyone in the military has had my deployments, I guess," I said. My head going places I'd tried to forget, I got up and went to the bathroom. Every muscle in my body was tense, and I hoped a hot shower might help me relax.

It didn't take long for the water to reach a singe-your-skin-off temperature. Letting the heat beat against my back, I steepled my hands over my face. Images of the shit I never wanted to see again bombarded me. The atrocities of war we don't like to talk about were there in front of me in living color all over again. Mixed with the shit Stefano and Viper did to me.

"Aaaaaarrrrrgggghhhhhh!" I shouted to the heavens. If I didn't get it out, I would explode. Afterwards, I worried I might have woken Presley, but her room was on the other side of the house.

Even though the water was hot, I trembled from head to toe.

With a deep, ragged breath, I looked up through the water cascading over my face. The shower curtain slid slowly open at the end. Nervous eyes stared at me. It was like looking at her through a waterfall, but I wasn't sure if it was from the shower or my eyes.

"Matlock?" My name came out of her beautiful mouth like a question.

Staring at her, I rebuilt my walls against the memories. Her face gave me solace. Her voice was a balm to my fucking soul.

When I didn't bite her head off, she climbed in and stepped under the spray with me. Palms resting flat on my chest, she stepped closer. Soon, her chest was pressed to mine and my arms were wrapped around her.

Tightly, I held her. Never wanting to let go, I crashed my lips to hers.

She thought Viper was only fucking with me. I knew he was simply biding his time.

He was coming for me, but I'd be ready.

Days went by with nothing. Then two weeks. Another. No sign of Viper or any of the Demon Runners.

Each day I traveled with no less than three pistols and two knives. I'd never be caught unaware again. I watched my six like I had eyes in the back of my head.

One of the prospects followed Raiven to work, waited throughout her shift, then followed her home. If I was off before her, I followed her. If it was my day off, I took her to work and dropped her off, then picked her up.

Everyone said I was being paranoid, but I knew better. Call it instinct, my gut, motherfucking psychic bullshit, whatever. I knew.

I was at the shop working on a simple oil change when my phone rang. Seeing my mom's number on the screen, I wiped my hands on a rag and slid my thumb across the screen.

"Hey, Mom, what's up?" I tucked the phone between my ear and my shoulder.

"What time is Raiven's appointment?" Excitement rang across the line in her question. I grinned.

"In about two and a half hours." We were going to find out if the baby was a boy or a girl.

"I have something to run by you." She sounded hesitant. Like she knew whatever she had to say, I wasn't going to like.

"What's that?" Warily, I awaited her response.

"We sold the farm," she finally said.

"You whaaaat?" There was no way I'd heard right.

"We want to be near our grandchildren."

I laughed. "Your grandchildren, huh? What about your son?"

My mother huffed. "You mean sons?" She stressed the second *s* when she said it. "Because it doesn't look like your brother is coming back here any time soon either."

"Mom, that farm has been in your family since your great-great-grandparents came over from Norway. And Gunny will be back." Shock didn't even begin to describe how her announcement had hit me.

The five-hundred-acre farm had raised some of the finest quarter horses in the country. Our parents had been so upset when Gunny and I both opted for the military after high school.

We knew they'd have rather us go to college and then take over the farm, but while we enjoyed riding, it wasn't in our blood. My dad had joked that we had too much Viking blood in us and it was in our nature to be warriors. There may've been some truth to that.

"Yes, but it doesn't mean much when there's no one who'll want it after our day, now is there? And what's the good of staying here if we miss out on time with our grandbabies? And I don't know what's going on with your brother, but I can assure you, he's not coming back." Her words were firm. My brother had evaded every attempt I'd made to talk with him about what was going on.

"What about the horses?" Granted, Gunny and I rarely rode anymore, but it might really upset Presley if she knew her favorite horses were gone.

"Well, you see…." She hesitated.

"I see what?"

"We already found a place there. It seems our property values here have gone up considerably since my family started the farm, and we did very well for ourselves. So we bought a smaller, more manageable acreage there. Still room enough for the few horses we'll keep." She said it like it was no big deal to leave her home of generations. Then again, I kind of got it.

"Wait. When the hell did you have a chance to look at something here?"

"When we were there for Presley's birthday and your wedding. Your dad and I said if it was still on the market when our place sold, then it was meant to be." I could practically hear the shrug in her voice. I was stunned.

But I'd be lying if I said I wasn't happy. We'd been a close family, and I missed them.

"So do you need us to come up there to help you pack?"

"Lord, no! I've already hired movers. I'm too old to pack, and I need to get rid of some stuff. But thank you, Matty." My face flushed at her use of my childhood nickname despite no one hearing it. She hadn't called me that in forever.

"Oh. Okay. Well, when are you guys looking at heading this way?"

She proceeded to tell me about their closing dates for both houses and their planned visit prior to the big move. It was surreal, and I half wondered if I was dreaming.

By the time I let her go, my head was spinning and I needed a stiff drink. Because I realized my parents were moving here. Really realized it. As in, my kids were going to be spoiled rotten.

My kids. Shit, my life had changed so much since the day I'd left Iowa.

After looking at the clock and deciding it wasn't too early to leave work, I scanned the area before packing up my tools. Once I was done, I prepared to leave.

There'd still been no sign of Viper.

Nothing.

Instead of making me feel better, it made me really damn nervous.

Raiven was obviously pregnant. Her little bump had grown at what seemed like an astronomical rate. She was barely shy of twenty weeks.

"I'll see you guys in the morning!" I called out as I left the bay.

"See ya! Make sure you let us know about that baby!" Clay shouted back.

"Later, bro!" Truth replied.

Excitement coursed through me at the thought of finding out what the baby was. I remembered the ultrasound of Presley and seeing her move, seeing her heart beating on the screen. Surreal.

I'd been to an appointment with her where I was able to hear the heartbeat, but that was it. This would be so much more.

The trip to the tattoo shop took me all of about ten minutes because I was flying. The bell rang as I walked in, and Nikki grinned up at me.

"Hey, big daddy. You excited to find out what y'all are havin'?" Nikki drawled.

"Hell yeah," I said, rubbing my hands together in anticipation.

Raiven poked her head out of her room. "Hey you, you're early! I'm cleaning up from my last appointment. You can wait out there or come back."

Never one to pass up an extra five minutes with my wife, I went to her room.

Quietly, I watched her beauty as she threw away trash and wiped everything down with disinfectant. Her hair was in a sexy pinup updo style, complete with black-and-red handkerchief. Today she had on a polka dot dress that had a higher waist to accommodate her growing belly.

The entire scene had me smiling.

Her ruby lips tipped up, she cocked her head. "What are you looking at like that? Do I have something on me?" She looked down at her hands, arms, dress, and legs. Seeing nothing out of place, her gaze met mine again.

"No, but I'd like to see you on me," I teased.

Laughing, she rolled her eyes. "I'm supposed to be the horny one in this duo."

Smirking, I shrugged. "Well, maybe I'm having sympathy horniness."

Her laughter included a choked sound that time. "I'm pretty sure that's not a thing."

"Well, it should be."

"Whatever Mr. Horndog, I'm ready. Are you?"

"Yep. We walking or driving?"

Her eyes bugged. "Are you serious right now? It's like five thousand degrees out there!"

There was likely a slight exaggeration in her comment, but it was hot as hell out there. Still, I snorted at her. "Raiven, it's not that hot, but we'll drive the block and a half to the clinic."

"Really?" she questioned in a dry tone, her expression deadpan. "Do you see this?" Her hands made wild circles around her belly. The one that was barely visible under the dress she wore. The one that for some freaky, weird as hell reason made her more beautiful than she was already.

Taking a few moments to close in on her, I cupped her cheek and skimmed the thumb along her full bottom lip. Often, I wondered if she had any idea how quickly she'd gotten under my skin.

"Yeah, babe. I see it. Every day, I see it," I said as I stared directly into those mesmerizing eyes. Unable to help myself, I placed a soft, sweet kiss to her sassy mouth.

Full lips parted, and her cheeks flushed the prettiest pink.

"Damn. That was… so freaking sweet."

A bark of laughter escaped me. "Yeah, that's me. Sweet as can be."

Shaking out of her temporary stupor, she snorted. "Well, you have your moments."

Knowing she'd balk at walking, I'd grabbed the extra keys to her truck. My bike would be safe there while we were at the appointment.

Raiven was strong and independent, but I loved helping her up in our trucks. It gave me an excuse to touch her, though I didn't really need it. I touched her as often as I could.

It took all of five minutes and we were in the waiting room I hated. It had to be the most uncomfortable place for a dude. Especially one my size. The chairs were small, there were all kinds of pregnant chicks in there eyeing me like I was their afternoon snack, and there was nothing to keep me busy except my phone. I wasn't reading any of the magazines they had in there. At least not and maintain my manhood and dignity.

"Ms. Knight?" the nurse said from the doorway that went into the exam rooms.

"Mrs. Archer," I corrected her. They'd done that shit the last time and said they'd get it fixed.

"Can you not look so scary? I think the poor girl may have peed her pants!" Raiven whisper-yelled in my ear as she rose from the seat.

"I don't care. They were supposed to fix that shit," I grumbled like a small kid, but it pissed me off. She was my woman. They should use my name when addressing her. I didn't feel like that was asking too much.

We followed the young nurse to the area where they weighed

Raiven, got her vital signs, then to the room where the ultrasound machine was. Then there was more waiting.

Finally the tech came in and we got down to business.

"Okay, so if the little one is cooperating, are we wanting to know the sex?" Damn, the chick had to be the peppiest person on earth. Raiven and I locked gazes, and I raised an eyebrow, causing her to mouth, "Stop!" then cover her laugh.

"Yes, ma'am," I answered for my wife, who was too busy trying not to giggle.

"Excellent!" She beamed as she clapped her hands. I had to pull my lips between my teeth to keep my humor contained too.

"I'll get all the boring stuff out of the way and then we'll see what we have in there," the woman said. Then she was all business as she set everything up and started with the goop on Raiven's belly. The fat little wand thingy slid back and forth through that shit a few times before she stopped. There was a bunch of clicks on the machine, more moving of the wand, more clicks.

It only took minutes, but with my impatience, it seemed like forever.

"Okay! Here we go, do you see this right here?" She pointed at something on the screen. We both nodded. "Well, that's your little one's penis!"

It didn't seem like I heard her right. Even though there was a chance I hadn't made this baby, my chest seemed to swell.

I was having a son.

She printed a few images for us, then we waited for the doc to come in.

"What are you thinking?" Raiven asked as soon as the chick walked out.

"I'm happy. I'm having a boy." I grinned.

"Do you—" She didn't get to finish her thought because the doc came in.

"Hello, Archers!" At least she got it right. "So it looks like we're having a boy! Congratulations. Now, did you make a decision as to whether you were going to do the noninvasive paternity test prior to delivery? It's a send-out lab, as we discussed, and it will take a bit, unless you're rich enough to pay for expedited results—" She chuckled. "—but not too long."

We did discuss it, but we hadn't made a decision. Because we couldn't agree on it.

"I don't want it," I firmly announced.

"What? Matlock!" Raiven wanted to do it, because she still had it in her head that if I found out the baby wasn't mine, I was going to shit-can her. She'd insisted that it wasn't fair to me to not know. I disagreed.

Even though a tiny voice whispered, "What if he comes out looking just like Stefano?"

TWENTY NINE

Raiven

"SYMPATHETIC"—SEETHER

Returning to work, I had mixed feelings swirling in my head.

"I'm pretty much done for the day, so I'm going to drop my bike off at the house, then pick up Little Elvis. Do you need me to do anything for you?" That infuriatingly wonderful husband of mine asked me.

"No, I'm good. I'll be home as soon as I finish this last client. It's going to take me a while because he has me doing a pretty big piece on his chest. But I shouldn't be too late. I'll call you before I leave." Pressing a kiss to his amazing lips, I wove my fingers up through the hair growing out. My ever-growing belly pressed into his hard abs, causing something else to get hard.

"Mmm, keep that up and you're gonna have to cancel."

"Despite that incredible offer and my immense desire to do so, I can't afford to cancel. I'm still building my clientele." Pouting, I trailed my nose up his neck as I inhaled his scent. It was his own special intoxicating blend that was a mixture of his cologne, engine oil, and exhaust.

With a smack to my ass, he gave me a sexy tip of his lips before he backed out of my room. "See you at home, beautiful."

The grin that spread across my face was glowing with my love for him. My earlier frustration was forgotten for the moment. "See you at home."

With one last kiss, he backed up and left my room. I followed him to the hallway entrance.

"I hate to see you go, but I love to watch you leave," I announced across the shop, grinning. Nikki snickered from her post at the front counter. My sexy man gave me a lustful glance over his shoulder before shaking his head with a smirk. Before exiting the building, he slid his sunglasses on, covering his gorgeous eyes.

Shame.

The roar of his bike was background music as I returned to my room to set up. A quick peek at the clock said I had time to pee. It seemed I was doing that all the time lately.

Which brought my thoughts back to my pregnancy and Lock's refusal to do the paternity test. He'd adamantly refused, saying it didn't matter. I'd disagreed. He'd said we had to agree to disagree.

"Well, hello again." The voice startled me, as no one had been in my room when I'd left for the bathroom.

I squealed in surprise, and my hand flew to my racing heart.

"Sorry, you scared me."

Dark, bottomless eyes stared at me, sending a shiver down my spine, but his smile was friendly. Smiling back at him, I washed my hands again.

"You ready to get started?" I cheerfully asked the man.

"You have no idea."

Leaning forward, he pulled his shirt off, then sat back in the chair. I'd seen his chest before when he came in for the consult almost a month ago, because I needed to see what I was working with. I'd forgotten all the scars he had and tried not to think about how they looked suspiciously like knife wounds.

Shaking off the weird vibes he put out, I prepped him and started the design we'd agreed on. It was a big gory demon ripping the head off of a zombie-looking thing. Not exactly my thing, but who was I to judge.

"Go ahead and take a break." I stood and stretched after shutting my machine off. "I'll be back in about five minutes."

I'd been working for a good two hours. Everyone had left except Nikki.

After I peed, I went out front to grab a water from the fridge behind the counter.

"Your guy is out front having a cigarette. He's hot as hell, but kinda scary. You okay in there?" Nikki looked at me before her gaze flicked to the front of the shop where said client was smoking as he talked on the phone.

"Yeah, I'm fine. He's creepy but harmless. He's not a talker, so I popped in an ear bud and I've been jamming out." We both laughed.

"You need me to stay until you're done? I have a dinner date, but I can cancel. I don't like you being here alone with that one. One of the guys should've stayed with you. Where's that prospect that was hanging out here?" Nikki looked uncomfortable.

"Girl, I'm good. I sent him for pizza right before Flint got here." I glanced at the clock. "He should've been back but maybe the guys needed him for something. I've got my phone, and we have the cameras. Besides, I know you've been waiting for this dinner forever." She rolled her eyes when I waggled my eyebrows at her. She was having dinner with a guy she'd met when he came in for a piercing the month before. They'd been flirting back and forth since, and he'd finally asked her out.

"Those won't do much good if something happens. And I don't think the guys will be too happy that the prospect left you." She bit her lip.

I rolled my eyes. "This isn't some movie. He's harmless, the prospect will be back soon and I'm going to finish then go home to my family. I'll see you tomorrow. Get out of here."

"Well, I'll wait until y'all are back in there and I won't make a big deal about my leaving," she said.

"Okay, no problem. I'll see you tomorrow then. Have fun tonight." I winked at her, and she blushed bright pink.

The bell on the door rang. We both looked over to see my customer, Flint, entering.

"Ready?"

"As I'll ever be." His smile didn't reach his eyes as they skated over Nikki from head to toe.

We went back to my room, and another hour and a half later, I was done. I'd finished cleaning and covering it and had turned to grab the care instructions when I heard the chair creak.

The cold blade against my throat startled me so much I jumped and it nicked me. The warm dribble down my neck told me it had cut me deep enough for blood to run.

"I'd stay still if I were you," he breathed into my ear, and I froze.

A million things were going through my head but none that I could grasp as a feasible idea to get out of this. Fear seeped from my pores, and it was as if he smelled it.

"We're going to go out the back door really quiet-like. If you scream, then I might accidentally slip again. That would be a real shame, because I'd like to keep you around longer than I had your old man." His chuckle was sinister and cold.

My stomach bottomed. I'd just tattooed the man who had been part of Lock's torture. Nausea churned, and sweat beaded on my forehead.

"I don't feel good," I whispered, hoping to minimize my movements and to prevent him from having a knee-jerk reaction.

"The trash is right there, let's go." He continued to hold the knife to my throat as we carefully walked to the trash.

Once I reached the trash and he moved away enough to let me lean over to puke, I caught him turning his head away as vomit spewed from me. My phone was on the counter close to where I held on for balance.

With my next heave, I kept my movements slow, but placed my hand over it. Right before I stood up, I slipped it into the pocket in my dress. I'd never been so glad for fucking pockets before in my life.

"Jesus, are you fucking done? That's so goddamn disgusting." His lip curled, and I wanted to throat punch him.

"I'm pregnant, I can't help it. My stomach is sensitive."

"Whatever, let's go." He waved the knife toward the door, motioning me to go ahead of him.

"I need my purse," I burst out.

He laughed cynically. "You think I'm stupid? Yeah, let me allow you to take your purse that probably has your phone in it? I don't think so. Move!" He gave me a shove from behind, and I stumbled toward the back door.

His next shove had me on my knees in the doorway to the back employee parking lot.

"I said move! We don't have that much time."

There was a gray truck I'd never seen before running outside the door. Another man I didn't recognize was in the driver seat.

"Get in the back," he ordered. Once I was there, he took my hands, zip-tied them together, then zip-tied them to the child seat anchor. It forced me to sit somewhat sideways in such a way that I had no access to my phone.

Great.

"Let's go," he told the other guy after he was in the passenger seat.

We drove out of town to the next small town over. Lock and I had talked about going there to eat at a restaurant that the guys had raved about. We'd never made it, and now I wasn't sure if I ever would.

There was a shitty old motel, and we turned in and parked at the end. This was getting worse and worse. My heart sank. All I could think was Lock was never going to find me.

The big knife was in his hand when he opened my door, and I shrank away from him.

"I'm just cutting the ties—for now." He leered.

243

It was impossible to swallow. A fricking boulder was caught in my throat, and my mouth was so dry my tongue stuck to the roof. The other guy had gotten out and opened the door to the room.

Once I was cut loose from the truck, he grabbed my arm and dragged me to the room. As inconspicuously as I could, I glanced around in hopes of cameras. Nothing.

"Get on the bed," the man I knew as Flint ordered.

"Look, I don't know what you want, but I'm sure there's another way to deal with this." The thought of what he might be planning was making me ill.

"Get on the fucking bed," he ground out as he held the knife in my face again.

"I need to go to the bathroom."

"You'll be fine," he insisted.

"No, I won't. Hello, I'm pregnant. I'll pee on the bed if I don't go now."

"Jesus fucking Christ," he bitched. "Go, but I'm not taking those off yet, so make do." He nodded toward my zip-tied hands.

"Fine."

When he followed me to the bathroom, I stopped and glared at him. "I'm not peeing in front of you."

"Then you're not pissin', are you?" His snide reply made me want to punch him in the eye.

My bound hands motioned around the bathroom from the doorway. "Do you see any windows? Where the hell am I going to go?" I asked him in exasperation.

"She's not going anywhere, for fuck sake," the other guy started to say, but Flint cut him off.

"Did I ask you?" he sneered.

Clenching his jaw, the other guy shook his head. It gave me a little bit of hope that maybe he might be an ally if he didn't agree with what Flint was doing.

"That's what I thought." He turned back to me and snapped, "Go, but make it quick."

"Fine."

Able to go in by myself, I wasted no time wadding my dress up then sitting down. I needed them to hear me actually peeing. Thankfully, since I'd gotten pregnant, I could go at the drop of a dime.

Seated on the toilet, I worked my phone out.

As fast as my thumbs would move, I tapped out a message to Gunny. I was afraid if I sent it to Lock he would lose his shit and come in half-cocked.

Me: I was taken. Video feed at shop. Motel in next town. Two

That was as far as I got before Flint yelled from the other side, "Two more seconds and I'm opening the door!"

Afraid he would burst in before I could finish, I hit Send. "I'm working on it! It's not that easy with this dress and my hands bound!" Asshole, I added silently.

That little bit was better than the nothing I'd be able to send if I got caught. I'd try again later.

It was harder to get the phone back in my pocket with my hands together that to get it out, for some reason. I was able to do a cursory wipe and was pulling up my panties when Flint barged in.

Before I could so much as blink, he'd grabbed them and ripped them off me. The force with which he pulled nearly made me fall over.

"You won't be needing those," he whispered in my ear, and my skin began to crawl. "Now get your sweet ass out on that bed unless you want me to bend you over right here."

Silently, I shook my head and returned to the bed with the threadbare comforter. There was no way in hell I was lying on that thing. I grasped it and jerked it to the bottom of the bed, uncaring if it fell to the floor.

Watching him out of the corner of my eye, I crawled on the bed, then curled up in the fetal position. I'd no sooner set my head on the pillow than he was jerking my legs down by the ankles.

"What are you doing?" I screeched.

"Hold her leg," Flint ordered. The other guy complied, but I saw distaste flicker in his eyes. I'd have thought I imagined it if he hadn't then given me a look filled with apology and regret.

Flint yanked the leg he held out and looped something around my ankle, then tied it off to the bed leg. The whole while, I tried to kick and pull free, but I was no match for his strength. He cinched it down tight.

"Tie that one," he instructed the other guy before tossing the strips of fabric or whatever he was using to him.

"I'm not tying her to the fucking bed. You do it."

I thought Flint was going to go ballistic, "You fucker. You're gonna find yourself in the ditch before you wear my patch if you don't learn to fucking listen."

The guy stubbornly held my leg but refused to tie it. Flint reacted like lightning striking. One second, he was holding my leg down. The next, he was up and punching the guy in the face. The other guy stumbled backward and crashed into the cheap dresser before falling into an unconscious heap.

It looked like it hurt like a motherfucker.

Flint didn't pay him any mind, as if he expected the guy to bow down and kiss his ass after that. Maybe he normally did. While I had a second, I was trying to get loose.

"Don't be stupid. You don't look stupid, but then again, you are married to one of those fucking Demented Sons." His voice was deadly calm, and the knife was pointed at the curve of my belly.

Oh God.

"I could carve that bastard right out of you while you lay there and bled out. You better learn real quick who's in charge, and it ain't you," he said with deadly calm.

Pulse racing at an unhealthy rate, I stilled.

With an ice-cold laugh, he gagged me, tied my other leg, then cut the zip ties and tied each wrist to the legs at the head of the bed. The cold blade of his knife trailed from my ankle up the inside of my leg. It reached where my dress had bunched up and pushed it further until I was exposed and unable to cross my legs or do anything to cover myself.

Utter helplessness washed over me, and I started to slip into a quiet place in my head.

THIRTY

Lock

"WHAT I'VE DONE"—LINKIN PARK

I 'd started dinner on the grill, Presley was playing, and I was watering Raiven's flowers on the front porch. She'd wanted them, but couldn't ever remember to water them, so I tried to do it for her. I wasn't even sure if she knew I did it or if she thought we had magic fucking flowers.

Five bikes pulled parallel to the curb and didn't even bother to back up. Smoke had Mattie on the back of his bike. Everyone jerked off their helmets. Mattie climbed off, rushed up the steps, gave me a shy smile and a quick wave, then went inside. She was a quiet kid, but a good kid. Presley adored her.

Gunny approached my front porch where I stood watering. Styx was hot on his heels.

"Hey, big brother, what's up?"

"Raiven here?" He'd stopped at the base of the steps.

"Well, hello to you too. No, she had a late appointment. She should be home any second though."

When his eyes closed and his head tipped slightly forward, I had a bad feeling.

"Gunny? What the hell is going on?" Dropping the hose on the porch with a thunk, I stormed to the sidewalk where he stood. "Gunny! Tell me. What is going on? Why are you all here?"

"I got this, Gunny." Smoke placed a hand on Gunny's shoulder. Gunny clenched his fists, ground his teeth, and turned away to push his fingers into his hair.

"Lock, I need you to keep a clear head. We were going to take care of this without you because I felt you'd be a loose cannon. Gunny insisted. Viper has Raiven. We've tracked them down to a shithole motel in Bertram. We're heading over there, but if you can't keep a level head, I'm ordering you to stay here." Rage turned my vision to red.

He ordered me?

"Lock!" Gunny had stepped up and was holding my wrist in a punishing grip. Looking down, I realized I'd pulled a pistol out of the holster on my belt.

"If you want to go, let's go. Mattie has Presley. She knows to lock the door. But you leave that here," Smoke demanded.

A reptilian smile was my answer. "Sure." I handed that one over to Truth. I still had two more on me.

I didn't waste another second before I was in the garage backing my bike out and closing the door with my remote. "Let's go."

They all rushed to their bikes, pulled on their helmets, and started them up. Flipping protocol the bird, I raced out of my driveway. The brothers caught up to me quickly, and Smoke pulled up beside me.

It took us mere minutes to get to Bertram. At the first gas station, Smoke signaled for us to pull off. When we stopped, I demanded, "Which hotel?"

That's when I noticed no one was wearing their cut. Not even me. Then again, I'd been doing stuff at the house; I'd had no reason to wear it and I wasn't in a frame of mind to grab it. That was precious time wasted. I only had my helmet on because it'd been hanging on my handlebar.

"We leave the bikes here or they'll hear us coming. Check is over there. We're getting in the SUV." He nodded to the black SUV to the side of the building.

Autopilot was driving me; I didn't wait, I simply moved. If not, I might crumble.

Everyone piled in the SUV, and we drove on down to probably the shittiest motel in town. There were three vehicles parked out front, and I had to wonder what desperation drove the owners of the other two vehicles to stay there. It looked termite-infested and like something you could rent by the hour.

"This is it. Pretty sure that's the truck we saw in the security footage," Check said as we pulled in at the opposite end of the long, single-story structure.

Smoke gave instructions as we quietly closed the doors and grouped in front of the vehicle. "Truth and Check, you go around back and come up from the other side. Lock and Slice, go from this side. That way none of us goes in front of their window to tip them off. Gunny and I are going to go into the office to see if I can, uh, persuade the desk clerk to give me another key to my room. No one goes in until I get there. Let's move."

Expecting us to all follow directions, he entered the office. The rest of us moved into place.

Except I wasn't waiting to see if he could get a key.

Fuck that.

As soon as we made it to the door, I waited until Truth and Check were at the left of the room's window and Slice and I were at the right. Lifting my pant leg, I withdrew the pistol I had clipped inside my boot.

"Lock!" Slice whispered frantically. Looking him dead in the eye, I shook my head, telling him I wasn't waiting and I wasn't backing down. Making sure my gun was good to go, I took a step over and listened at the door.

What I heard sent ice running through my veins. Muffled sobbing, and a man cursing.

"Go get Smoke," I told Slice.

Not caring if it was the right room, I stepped back and kicked. I'd ask forgiveness if it was the wrong one. The flimsy door burst open, and what I saw was worse than what I heard.

There was Viper jumping off the bed and wiping his face off. A pistol was in one hand and he pointed it at me. Undaunted by the barrel he looked down, I held steady aim at the motherfucker with his pants undone. "You are a fucking dead man."

In my peripheral vision, Raiven was strapped to the bed with her dress shoved up. She was gagged and crying but shaking her head no as she stared at me with wide eyes. The fury that swept through me nearly knocked me over.

"Lock, you're just in time for the party. And you brought friends to watch too. This gets better and better. I figured it was only fair that since you got to fuck my wife, I should be able to fuck yours. She's feisty. I like that."

"You piece of shit motherfucker!" I yelled as I closed in on him. He simply placed his finger on the trigger and laughed in my face. Then he had me stopping in my tracks because he turned the gun on Raiven.

"I'm a motherfucker? I'd say that title goes to your—oh wait, technically they were *my* shitty in-laws." He chuckled as if I didn't have my loaded 380 pointed at his chest. He was fucking crazy.

At my narrowed eyes, he laughed louder. "You do know we caught up to you thanks to the information Letty's scumbag parents gave us, right?"

"What?" Shock had me wavering. He shook his head, smirking.

"Oh yes, ol' granny and gramps were quick to sell Stefano the info they'd overheard. They were at the gas station the morning you left Grantsville. They heard you talking about going to Omaha and then on to Texas. All he had to do was start asking around for where his 'sister' was headed. They jumped to the front of the line when they heard he was offering a reward for her safe return." I wanted to shoot him in his sick, smug smile.

My finger touched the trigger.

"I wouldn't if I were you." The words were accompanied by the cold steel of a revolver being held to the back of my head. My gaze held steady on Viper, but a frisson of fear snuck down my spine at our situation. We were in public, which meant witnesses. If I shot him, it wouldn't be considered self-defense. It would be vigilante justice. Then again, if I shot him, his guy who'd snuck in behind me would kill me and Raiven would be at his mercy if my brothers didn't get him first.

"Neither would I," said Slice's voice from behind me, and I experienced some relief.

"Well, boys, it would appear we have a standoff on our hands." The smug grin on Viper's face set fire to my rage. My finger trembled on the trigger.

The guy behind me swore under his breath.

From outside the door, I heard feet pounding. The gun barrel at my head jumped slightly when they stopped outside the room.

"Jesus fucking Christ," Smoke muttered. I heard the rest of our guys poured into the room. I smirked when I glanced to the side and saw that the pistol Truth had in his hand was the one he took from me. He saw and shrugged.

"Grayson, long time no see. What's it been? Four years? Five?" Viper had a decidedly cynical look in his eyes as he looked at Smoke. My eyes and those of my brothers darted between Smoke and Viper.

"Eight."

"Ahh well, I'm getting forgetful and all." Completely unconcerned with all the firepower in the room, he pressed his pistol barrel into Raiven's stomach. "So where do we go from here? Because I'm thinking I'm going to take my prospect and leave."

"You're outnumbered, Viper. I don't think you or your boy are going anywhere," I said.

"That's where you're wrong." He gave us a half smile. "I may be outnumbered, but I believe I have the upper hand. Wouldn't you say? So either you let me leave, or your pretty pet goes bye-bye." He pulled out a knife and cut the ties that bound her to the bed.

251

Keeping the pistol pointed at her, he sat her up.

The only part of it I was thankful for was that when he pulled her upright, her dress fell back down. Her dignity in tatters, those eyes pleaded for something I didn't know how to give her. Without her words, I was at a loss.

The tears that tracked down her cheeks were fucking shredding me inside.

"You're not walking out of here alive," I growled.

"Oh, I think it's you that should be worried about that. I'll be sure to enjoy the wife swap. Sorry you lost out on your half."

He grabbed Raiven by the hair and began to jerk her off the bed.

There was no time to react. The gun was suddenly gone from the back of my head and two shots fired one after the other into Viper's chest.

"What the fuck?" Everyone was stunned as they watched Viper gasping for breath on the floor. His incredulous gaze locked on his prospect.

I'd jumped to pull Raiven out of the bed and away from the gruesome sight on the floor. Once I had her away from him, I pulled the gag out of her mouth. "Don't look at any of that, baby," I'd whispered in her ear as she clung to me.

"You all may want to get her out of here. Anyone not associated with this might want to leave. My suggestion is only Matlock and Raiven stay outside, but that's merely a suggestion. Oh, and I'm assuming all of those weapons are legal?" He didn't look at any of us, but it didn't matter. Everything was on the up and up. He ruffed a hand through his hair.

"Who the fuck are you?" Smoke demanded.

"Name's Fitzgerald. FBI, undercover—well, I was. I'd say my days of that are likely over now. I've got him and his club on a hundred petty charges, but now I finally got him on something big that may stick. Kidnapping and attempted murder. At that's what it looked like to me, don't you agree? The cops will be here soon. I'm assuming a shots fired call went in the minute I squeezed the trigger. Fuck, I only wish I'd found enough to nail every one of those assholes to the wall. They are all such pricks." By that time, he was kneeling by Viper, checking for a pulse.

There must have still been signs of life, because he cuffed Viper's hands and zip-tied his legs together.

"You wanna add sex trafficking to that?" Check questioned.

Fitzgerald's brow furrowed and he looked at us in confusion. "I've only been able to nail down vague traces and nothing concrete."

"Here." Check tossed him a thumb drive.

"What is this?" The agent looked at it like he'd never seen one before.

"All the proof you need to nail him and his club for sex trafficking. You're welcome, and I'll deny I gathered it." Check grinned as he shrugged.

"Jesus. Umm, thanks? Now you better go." We could hear sirens in the distance.

"No."

"What?" the agent shouted in surprise.

"We're not leaving Lock and Raiven here alone," Smoke insisted.

We did, however, hand all of our weapons over to Truth, who put them in a cinch bag and left. In the nick of time too, because he'd barely been gone a minute before flashing lights pulled up. Everything was a chaotic shit-storm after that.

It seemed to take forever to get through all the bullshit involved. The local cops were real heroes and initially refused to call the number Fitzgerald gave them to verify his identity. I'm not sure how the dude got there so fast, but a thick, gruff guy with salt-and-pepper hair showed up. He announced himself as Fitzgerald's acting SAC, Special Agent in Charge while he was in our area.

Then he did exactly that—took charge.

Once everyone had given their generic, vague statements, we were reluctantly released. Raiven had only given one- and two-syllable answers all night from what I could tell. They separated us for questioning, and I hated it.

A nurse had been called in to examine Raiven. It took forever for her to get there, so that added to my anxiousness. To top it off, I was worried she should've gone to the doctor to get checked, but she'd refused. She could say "no" really well. That was why the SANE (Sexual Assault Nurse Examiner) had come to the scene; they wanted an exam, and Raiven had said only if someone could come to the location.

She was buckled into the front passenger seat, and I stepped up to her. "Are you sure you don't want me to ride with you? I can come back for my bike tomorrow," I offered.

She shook her bowed head.

Styx stepped up to the vehicle. "Hey little mama. You need anything else?"

She kept her head bowed and she whispered a shaky, "No."

"If you're okay with it, I can ride your bike back and you can drive her," Check offered.

Raiven tried to say no, but I didn't give her a chance. I tossed the key fob to Check. He caught it midair with a nod.

The ride was silent as we traveled with the guys in formation behind us.

By the time we all made it back to our place, we were exhausted and it was late as hell. Once I'd helped Raiven up the stairs, I had her wait on the porch.

"Get her inside and cleaned up. We'll talk tomorrow." Smoke seemed highly disturbed, and I belatedly wondered if it wasn't connected to the odd exchange he and Viper had in the room. To me, it sure sounded like they'd known each other well at some point.

"See you at the clubhouse. I'll be driving because I'm bringing her with. I don't want her to be alone." I kept it quiet because I didn't want her to think I was coddling her.

He gave me a nod, then climbed the stairs after me to get his daughter.

My fingers wove through Raiven's as I led her inside. Presley was long since asleep, and I'd called Nikki to tell her Raiven wouldn't be in the next day.

Flipping on the water, I closed the curtain and turned to face my wife.

"Raiven, will you be okay with me helping you get undressed?" I was afraid to touch her too much. She still hadn't talked to anyone but the nurse about what that sick fuck had done to her. It was taking everything for me to hold my shit together, because I knew what he was capable of.

The thought of his sadistic hands on her, doing some of the awful things to her that he'd done to me, was testing my control. It was making me face things I'd suppressed, against the therapist's advice.

"Yes," she whispered.

Like handling a skittish colt, I moved slowly but with purpose.

It was killing me that we'd finally seemed to move past all the bullshit in our lives and then that shit had to happen.

When I raised her arms over her head to pull her dress off, her phone fell out of her pocket to the floor.

And she burst into tears.

Shit.

THIRTY ONE

Raiven

"THE SOUND OF SILENCE"—DISTURBED

❝I love you." He kissed me on the top of my head as he held me to his chest. Sobs wracked my body as we stood with the water running behind us.

There was no rational reason for my tears simply because my phone dropped to the ground. Other than it flashed me back to thinking sending that message was going to be a magic spell that ended it all. All in all, though the experience was terrifying, I had been relatively lucky.

I was alive.

"I love you too. So damn much." My arms wrapped tight around his ribs.

"Let's get in the shower." He spoke softly and had undressed me like I was fragile and I hated it. It made me empathize with how he'd felt when I'd coddled him after his rescue. It gave me a sense of inner strength when I thought about everything he'd endured, and yet there he was, standing strong and proud for me.

With a new determination, I wiped my tears and climbed in the warm water. With my eyes closed tight, I could hear him undressing. The thump of each boot as it dropped. The rustle of his clothes, the weight of his belt as it fell to the floor, still on his jeans.

Finally, the slide of the shower curtain open and closed. Opening my eyes, I blinked the water from my face as I stood in the cascade watching him. I was struck with his beauty and strength.

Sleek lines, contoured muscles, a massive array of tattoos that spoke volumes without words. Those piercing, uniquely beautiful eyes. I sought out the tiny brown spot and allowed it to ground me.

Licking my lips, I tasted the water.

Fine mist from the shower was bouncing off me and beading on his thick, dark lashes. When I couldn't stand his silent scrutiny any longer, I reached for him. His firm hand clasped mine and gave a slight tug. It was enough to bring me against him when he stepped forward.

Meeting me in the middle, his hands cradled my face. "I was terrified when I heard he had you. If I'd lost you, I don't know how I'd have gone on without you; how Presley would've gone on without you. We need you because we love you so fucking much."

His hard length jumped at his words, sliding against me where it was sandwiched between us.

"I'm so sorry. I can't help how that responds to your closeness. Please don't worry, I'm fine and we don't need to do... that, or, um, anything." His expression screamed regret and sadness. In an attempt to soothe him, my thumb traced the fullness of his bottom lip.

Swallowing hard in preparation of getting out what I needed him to know, I inhaled a shaky, swift breath. "Lock, he lied to you. He didn't actually, umm... not like that. I'm not saying he didn't uh...." I started crying.

Breaking down in sobs that shook my body, I buried my face in his chest as he wrapped his arms around me. He silently held me as the water washed over us.

"I love you, Raiven. No matter what, I love you."

Pulling back, I looked up at him through the haze of tears and water. "I was so afraid you'd lose it and kill him. The thought of you having that on your conscience because of me would have destroyed me more than anything he'd have done to me."

His eyes closed tight, and a rush of air left his lungs. Our foreheads met and our noses lay side by side. "Goddammit," he whispered, "I'd have gladly killed him for what he did to me and for what he did to you. With absolutely zero regrets." Though his words were spoken with great conviction, I truly believed they would've proved false had things played out differently.

Needing his closeness and the security I found in his embrace, I turned my head, slightly grazing my lips across his as our breaths mingled. I continued up his jaw to his ear.

He still smelled of the lingering remnants of his cologne, grease, and exhaust. Straight sex emanated from his pores, and I needed him. I needed him to help me forget what I'd experienced. I needed to be touched with love. I needed him to remind me that I was resilient. My teeth skimmed along the shell of his ear; his respiratory rate jumped, and his fingers slid further back to grip my wet, tangled hair.

"Fuck, Raiven, we shouldn't…." He was trying to be so valiant, but I didn't need a knight on a white horse. I needed the dragon.

I sank my teeth into the tendon of his neck. He groaned, and my tongue flattened as it ran the length of his corded neck. The salt of his skin was lapped up with each trail I made along his neck and shoulders. It was the best aphrodisiac in his arsenal, and it hit me full force.

Slowly, the tip of my tongue traveled to the center of his tattooed chest, circled each of his drawn-up pierced nipples. One circle, pull it between my lips, suckle, bite, and tug. On the second one, I could feel his racing pulse against my lips.

Steam rose to cloak us in a cocoon where we clung to each other.

Hands splayed, I memorized every inch of him as I lowered myself to my knees. His fingers remained tangled in my hair but he wasn't hurting me.

In the hazy air of the shower, I gazed up at him. The flats of my palms had stopped on his muscular thighs. My nails dug into the flesh to prevent me from jumping to where I wanted to be. I needed to savor this moment.

Eyes still trained on his, I flattened my tongue and licked up the underside of his cock to circle the thick head at the tip. Movements unhurried, I worshipped his length.

Up, down, curl, over and over. Watching the effects my actions were having had me wet, and it wasn't from the shower. It was returning my self-confidence. It left me feeling powerful.

It gave me control.

When I reached the crown, I tilted my head to swallow the tip but didn't stop there. His moans drove me forward, and my hands slipped around to grip his tight ass. His muttered curses made me lustful, and I hollowed out my cheeks to suck him hard and slid further down the shaft.

"Fuck! Fuck, fuck, fuck," he mumbled over and over.

When he tried to pull me off by my hair, I dug my nails into his ass, holding him in place. Over and over, I watched the ecstasy blossom on his face as I refused to let go. I needed his taste across my tongue and sliding down my throat. I wanted him to lose control and come so much it overflowed my mouth, running down my chin, throat, and to my breasts.

"Raiven," he choked out in desperation. A desperation I craved. "I'm going to come if you don't stop."

I didn't stop.

Once he finally understood I wasn't giving it up, he guided my head as he fucked my mouth. Each time he thrust in, I could feel him at the back of my throat.

Yes, I wanted to feel him stretching my pussy, but I needed this first. Desperately.

When his movements became erratic, I knew he was close.

The vibrations from my moan were the catalyst he needed to explode. Guttural, his groans echoed from the shower walls, punctuated by each spurt of his cock across my tongue.

I didn't let up until he was jerking and gently pulling my head back by my hair.

"Jesus fucking Christ, Raiven. You're going to kill me. I'm sorry if I got rough. You were so… fuck!" His eyes closed as a shudder ran down his spine.

Raising myself up higher, I rested my cheek against his hard abs, and we simply held each other. We stayed that way until the water ran cold and we had to rush through washing or freeze.

Lying in the bed after he'd flipped me over and fucked me with all the pent-up anger I'd needed, we were quiet. Completely and totally satiated, we hardly moved. His fingers absently trailed up and down my hip and side while mine traced the ink on his chest. Other than that, our limbs were a limp tangle in the sheets.

"My wife."

"My husband."

"I love you more than I ever thought I'd love a woman. You are the other half of my soul, and I had no idea I was floating through life incomplete until I found you. That sounds corny as fuck, doesn't it?" he murmured.

"No. That sounds absolutely perfect. You should show me again how we complete each other." I gave a small smile, as I attempted to joke with him.

He smacked my ass with a soft chuckle that echoed through his chest. "Insatiable wench."

He showed me again.

EPILOGUE

"Babe, I changed Memphis's diaper. When the hell is this kid going to potty train again? I don't remember the other ones being this bad." I loved him but the little asshole kept hiding under the fucking kitchen table to shit in his pull-up.

From behind me, Presley laughed. "Dad, he's only two. Oh, and the swear jar is getting full. When are we going for ice cream?"

Izzy, our raven-haired five-year-old, came running down the hall. "Ice creammmmm!"

Memphis squealed, "Eye cweeeeeam!"

I groaned. Great, I was going to have to deal with pissed-off kids because we had no ice cream in the house and I wasn't missing the game I'd been waiting for since the beginning of the season to go get fucking ice cream.

Rolling my eyes, I looked at her. "You know what? Come to think of it, you were worse. You used to strip naked when you peed in your pull-up, hide it, then run around naked. It wasn't until your mom came into the picture that you finally had an interest in using the toilet on a regular basis."

"Dad!" She shot a mortified glance to her friend who was spending the night.

The doorbell rang.

"Come in!" I was wrestling my two-year-old son into his jeans.

"Hey, Truth. Your brother could use a little help. I think he's in over his head with this one." Glancing up, I saw my gorgeous wife leaning against the hallway arch of our new home. Her smirk had me shooting her a glare with promise of retribution when we were in bed that night.

The woman had the nerve to grin and waggle her eyebrows at me before she grabbed her purse. She gave me a too-short kiss and prepared to head out to the store. "I'll be back shortly. Tell the girls I'll bring the wine back with me if they get here before I get back."

"You better get some fucking ice cream for these heathens of yours," I growled.

"What was that? You want me to get a pedicure before I come back?" She blinked her gorgeous eyes at me. All damn big, blue, and wide. Innocent, my ass. She was just as much a hellion as our spawn.

With a sexy sway of her full hips and a low, sultry laugh, she left.

I sighed once she was out the door. "This was supposed to be our day. How did we get wrangled into having it here and the women inviting themselves? And when are Mom and Dad supposed to be here to get these three?" I waved at my two youngest and toward the hall that led to the kids' bedrooms.

Gunny shrugged. Helpful as always.

Memphis ran and pounced on the loveseat with a giggle, followed by his older sister. He was damn near an exact replica of me. I wasn't sure if that was a good thing.

"Because you have the biggest, newest house. And a big-ass fucking TV," Gunny announced before taking a swig of his beer.

"Big ass!" Memphis shouted. Presley gasped. Like I hadn't heard her cussing like a sailor in her room when she was made to clean it before her friend could come over.

I slapped a hand to my forehead, then glared at my brother.

Styx came in from the kitchen with a big bowl of popcorn and walked by Truth, stealing his beer.

"Dammit, you were just in the kitchen! Why didn't you get your own beer?" Truth complained.

"I forgot," Styx said as he shrugged, then tipped up the bottle.

Truth shook his head and dropped to the couch next to Gunny and stole the beer from his hand.

"Dammit, you're such an asshole!" Gunny grumbled. "Not a fucking one of you knows how to get your own damn beer."

"Uncle Gunny!" Presley was trying like hell to seem all mature. I knew she and her friends had little crushes on most of my brothers. It was insane, and I wasn't ready for that shit. They ran off giggling to her bedroom at Presley's urging. The door slammed. God help me from the world of ten-year-olds going on twenty-five-year-olds.

"Dad, Presley made me drop my Play-Doh castle in the hallway!" Bryson, our almost seven-year-old son, pushed his mop of inky bangs off his face.

"Fuck, I just wanted to watch the game with the guys," I muttered.

His hair was exactly like his mother's. Thick, dark, and unruly. But he didn't want to cut it yet because he was in some independent phase, according to Raiven.

Though he was an old soul at times and very mature for his age, he was sensitive. His eyes were tearing up, and I knelt in front of him. Wiping an escaped tear with a thumb, I spoke quietly to him so he wouldn't get embarrassed. "Hey, little man, it's okay. We're gonna build a new one, and I'll help you get it safely to Uncle Smoke's."

A wicked grin spread over my face at the thought of payback for all the years of fucking Play-Doh.

Rapidly blinking his big blue eyes to clear them, my son sniffled, then grinned. Holding my hand up for a high five, I met his eyes, and my heart stopped. I couldn't push words out of my mouth.

"Dad? You okay?" My son stared at me like I'd lost my marbles.

Stared at me with inquisitive blue eyes.

With a small brown spot in the left one.

The End.

OTHER BOOKS BY
KRISTINE ALLEN

The Demented Sons Series

Iowa Chapter
Colton's Salvation
Mason's Resolution
Erik's Absolution
Kayde's Temptation

Texas Chapters
Lock and Load
Styx and Stones (Coming Soon in full length!)

The Straight Wicked Series

Make Music With Me (Levi)
Snare My Heart (Dominic)
No Treble Allowed (Logan)
String Me Up (Aiden)

Coming Soon Zane's Story!

ABOUT THE AUTHOR

Kristine Allen lives in beautiful Central Texas with her adoring husband. They have four brilliant, wacky and wonderful children. She is surrounded by twenty six acres, where her seven horses, four dogs and four cats run the place. Kristine realized her dream of becoming a contemporary romance author after years of reading books like they were going out of style and having her own stories running rampant through her head. She works as a night nurse, but in stolen moments, taps out ideas and storylines until they culminate in characters and plots that pull her readers in and keep them entranced for hours.

If you enjoyed this story, please consider leaving a review on the sales platform of your choice, www.goodreads.com, allauthor.com, bookbub.com, or your review platform of choice, to share your experience with other interested readers. Thank you! <3

Follow Kristine on:

Twitter @KAllenAuthor

Facebook www.facebook.com/kristineallenauthor

Instagram www.instagram.com/_jessica_is_kristine.allen_

All Author www.kristineallen.allauthor.com/

BookBub www.bookbub.com/authors/kristine-allen

Goodreads www.goodreads.com/kristineallenauthor

Webpage www.kristineallenauthor.com

Made in the USA
Middletown, DE
27 May 2022